The
Raven
Hunters

STEPHEN PHILLIPS

This story is a work of fiction. Any similarities to names, people, places are purely coincidental.

ISBN: 978-1-7368738-3-0

Table of Contents

Chapter One
The Story Teller

A young woman sat, reading from the book before her, the audience hanging on her every word. She looked up and the light above created shadows across her face.

"And the fairy flew close to the wall. As she turned the corner, her eyes widened; she could see that the sorcerer was gone. There was only a burning wand left in his place. As she returned to her friends, her light once again was shining brightly as she spoke."

She gave a dramatic pause and watched as some in her audience held their breath, waiting for her next words.

A woman asked, "Well, what happened?"

The young woman, smiling, took a breath and spoke in a high-pitched voice, "We are free, magic and all. The wizards flee, we beat them all!"

The young woman paused before returning to her normal voice. "The fairy flew around to her friends, stopping as she spun at each in a pirouette. Jim had lowered his magic shield as Rae held onto his arm, steadying herself from her injury. The silence was abated by a great cheer that rose from them all. They had defeated the evil sorcerer, releasing the magic creatures who had been captured. Magic was free once again."

The young woman laid the book down as she looked around. The faces of both young and old smiled. They were clapping, and even gasping in disbelief.

"And that, everyone, is the end of this story. But not the end of *the* story," the woman said as she closed the book.

Her audience again cheered although some grumbled, realizing the story was over. Behind them stood the shop owner, smiling as she watched Amanda tell the tale.

"Hey, Linda, sounds like the story's over. Guess I missed the ending," Ron said as he walked up beside her. She could barely hear over the cheers of the crowd surrounding their friend.

"Ron, perfect timing. Amanda just finished reading your latest story." Linda turned, giving him a loving kiss. "I think she put a great spin on this one."

Ron laughed, "Well, it's not like it's fiction or anything."

Linda glared at him. "Not so loud," Linda warned. "It's a good adventure. But it's not like we live this every day."

Her statement made them both laugh.

Linda enjoyed her joke, and no one but them knew the truth. Things like this *did* happen in real life. It had been part of their reality for the past seven years. Linda watched as some of the patrons turned, hearing the banter between them.

Little did they know the two were being serious; the fun and fantastic tale they had heard was something that happened only a few months earlier.

Amanda stood. "Thank you for coming to Paragon Rising bookshop, everyone. That is it for the latest Haunter Maples adventure. If you'd like to meet the author and purchase a signed copy, he is standing right behind you."

Ron waved, "Thank you, Amanda. I don't think I've ever heard that story told with such belief. You gave it a feeling like it actually happened."

The expression on Amanda's face turned to one of happiness muted by careful concern, her mind thinking, *I can't believe you just said that.*

Amanda knew the secret, as did they. The names were different, but the story was as real as the air they were breathing. If anyone knew the truth, the forest would be overrun with people looking for their friends.

She watched Ron's face light with a smile as a rush of people, young and old, surrounded him. He rushed to the counter as many grabbed books, waiting for him to sign. Linda gave him another kiss, telling him, "You're on your own, my love," before she left to speak with Amanda.

"That's probably the best I've heard that story told," Linda said as she took the book from Amanda. "The artwork you did came out wonderful."

She held the book and admired her friend's artwork. Amanda smiled, seeing her friend enjoy the pictures she had drawn. But Amanda could see the sadness in her friend's eyes.

Linda sighed, pushing back tears. "I'm going to miss you. Ron is too. We're so happy you were able to get into that school."

Amanda wiped away her own tears. "It's been so much fun, Linda; you've been such a good friend to me. I'm going to miss you too." Amanda hugged her. "Both of you."

Linda tapped the picture of the fairy on the cover. "I know she'll miss you as well."

Amanda stared at the picture of the fairy. The face was Roween's, though she did change the color of her hair from green to pink.

It had been over seven years since Ron had helped her, and just over ten since she had met Linda in the bookshop. Amanda had known Roween since her family bought the cabin, and her heart felt heavy as she realized that tonight and tomorrow were the last two days she would see them all for some time.

The school she had chosen was in another state, and at least a several hours' drive away. Her family and friends were going to be far away. But she had a chance to do something she had always wanted.

Unconsciously, her hand pulled on the silver chain that hung around her neck, making a small wooden ring peek from beneath her shirt. Amanda held the ring, grasping it tight. Its feeling of softness and the power it contained were comforting. Roween had given it to her for protection. Since Amanda had started sharing in adventures together with Ron and Linda, Roween figured Amanda could use all the help she could get. Her magical friend also wanted to make sure she was protected while she was away.

A fairy cannot leave her tree, but Amanda was moving far away. And because she worried about the girl, her fairy friend added a few additional enchantments telling her, "No magic or force, tragic or source. Foul attack or sling will be sent back to harm, for this ring is yours and no one's charm. Never hardship or forsaken. It can only be given, never taken."

Amanda sighed as the softness of the wood rolled between her fingers. She knew the power it held. Roween had told her that the magic would not allow the ring to be removed by anyone unless Amanda chose to let them do so, although she did so in a much more musical, rhyming way.

Amanda smiled and a tear rolled down her cheek. "I'm going to miss you guys so much."

Linda hugged her for a minute, but as Linda turned to look at Ron for support, she could see the crowd overwhelming him at the counter, making her laugh.

"What?" Amanda said, sounding almost hurt.

Linda pointed toward the counter. They could see him feverishly signing books and trying to run the register at the same time. His predicament caused the line to run around the shop. He juggled trying to take people's money and sign books before looking at the two women in his life staring back at him.

"Ah, a little help, please!" he pleaded, making their sadness turn to laughter.

"He can handle powerful sorcerers, evil magic creatures, and demons, but he can't handle the shop counter," Amanda said before they laughed at Ron's predicament.

For a moment, the feeling of adventure they shared was again with them and the sadness lifted from their hearts. Both stood tall and Linda took a breath, put her hand on her hip and declared, "Well, guess we have to save him."

* * *

Amanda arrived home, throwing off her coat as she headed to her room. Jinx heard her and ran across her feet as she headed up the stairs, making her stumble.

"Jinx, that wasn't nice," she scolded him.

The cat had been with her since they arrived in the forest, and he was in good shape for a seventeen-year-old feline. The vet was amazed at his longevity, although was at a loss as to the reason. Amanda, on the other hand, suspected Jinx had interacted with her fairy friend so many times, mostly trying to eat her, that the magic she used started to affect him. Jinx had been frozen so often that his aging had slowed; at least that was the theory Linda had. Of course, Roween did mention cats were part magic and that Jinx was probably absorbing what she used on him. Amanda had researched, finding that since cats were almost always depicted with witches, it made sense. Although, none of them knew for sure.

Amanda sat on her bed as she ran her hand gently along the top of the suitcase before closing it. Most of her other belongings were already packed into her car. Tomorrow she would leave on her trip to upstate New York. She felt a little sad having to leave; even Jinx sensed what she was feeling and he nuzzled up to her.

"I'm going to miss you too, you naughty cat," she said, holding him close.

Jinx purred, then licked her face before nuzzling further into her embrace. Amanda held him for a few minutes, then let him go when she saw a dim glow appear behind the curtains.

She rushed over and opened them to find Roween floating there gently in the light breeze.

"I'm going to miss you," Amanda said as she held out her arms.

Roween flew to her and held her cheek.

"Adventure makes you more to be, please, just don't forget this humble fairy," Roween said in her usual musical tone.

Amanda could hear sadness in Roween's voice as she spoke. But as Roween explained many times, fairies live for very long, and she has known many humans. Every one different from another, but they all felt the same when they moved on. It didn't matter whether they stopped believing or had left and forgotten her. It was always the same. Roween reminded her that as long as magic never disappeared, there would always be hope.

"This home you leave, there will always be. Friends and love, so never grieve," Roween said in a slightly saddened note.

Roween then pulled the chain Amanda wore and took hold of the wooden ring; it glowed brightly.

"Adventures you seek and bring this charm. In times so bleak, you'll be never harmed," Roween said, and her light grew so bright that Amanda had to shield her eyes.

When she asked what Roween had done, the fairy's response was, "A little extra, you never know. And you betcha, help will show"

Amanda rolled her eyes with a groan as Roween smiled back. Ron had been challenging their fairy friend to bad rhymes for the last several years. Roween knew she could beat him; besides, the worse they were, the funnier they seemed. It always made Amanda laugh when they were terrible, and this time was no exception.

They said their goodbyes, Roween making Amanda promise to return. A fairy cannot leave her tree, but the wooden ring Amanda wore would tell her if her friend was in danger. Her fairy friend reminding her, "Magic is always connected," and Roween would find a way to send help. Amanda was sure Ron and Linda would make the trip if needed.

Amanda again said goodbye and watched as Roween disappeared into the forest. There was a heaviness in her heart as Amanda turned to see the suitcase on her bed. Tomorrow she would have to leave for her new home, even if it was only for a short while.

Turning to her bedroom door, Amanda paused. It would be months before she saw the inside again, so she memorized each scratch and crack, burning it to memory. And as she held onto the wooden ring, the world didn't seem so lonely.

Amanda placed her case on the floor and set her alarm. Her father had reminded her that it would be best to leave in the early morning to avoid the city traffic and Amanda grumbled, knowing she had to be up at 2:00 a.m. at the latest. As she lay down, her mind filled with so many thoughts it seemed like it would be hours before she would get to sleep, but they all faded and the world disappeared as sleep crept up on her.

Chapter Two
The Journey Begins

Amanda was still thinking about the tears in her mother's eyes as her father put the last suitcase in the back of her car. She smiled, resisting looking back in the rearview mirror again as she had done many times over the previous few hours since she left. The full weight of her journey now starting to show, she wiped a tear from her face. Amanda had always wanted to be an artist, and now she was heading to school after all her hard work. She wasn't alone; Amanda had friends who were going to school there as well. And she knew her parents and friends were only a phone call away.

As the early light of the sun started to show, Amanda decided to make a stop. She needed to stretch her legs and get something to drink, so she stopped at a coffee shop. Warming her hands, she breathed in the familiar aroma of tea before taking a sip. The heat of it burned her tongue.

"That's gotta cool off a bit," she mumbled as she pulled out the directions to look at them again. She knew the way, having insisted on driving there when her parents went along with her to see the school previously. But knowing she was on the right path gave her some comfort. The school was several hours away with traffic, but leaving when she did, she was almost halfway there.

As she started the car, she turned to look at the horizon just above the trees. The sun hadn't risen over them yet, but its light filled the sky. She smiled seeing the trees swaying from the wind. Amanda chuckled; she knew a secret that most would never believe. The wind did indeed influence the leaves, but when there was no wind, it was sylphs.

Her heart again started feeling heavy as she turned the corner and resumed her journey. The only worries she hoped to have were her classes and everyday things. Money was not a problem as long as she was careful. Amanda was paying for school with what she was making from the book sales about their adventures.

She took a breath, but as Amanda turned her head to look forward, she saw something out of the corner of her eye. There on the light pole next to her car was a small shadow. It was of a small man about a foot tall wearing a pointed hat looking strangely toward her. Amanda smiled and waved as she drove. She chuckled looking in the rearview mirror and seeing the small man hesitantly wave back to her before turning to another and pointing to his eyes. She smiled, "Can't wait to tell Linda I saw a gnome."

Amanda pulled into the housing complex parking lot the school provided. She was a week early, but since this was her first year, her counselor recommended she arrive as soon as possible. It took time to process and move into the complex. She had her own room, thankful she didn't have to share with anyone. She was concerned it may have been awkward if she came across any unusual inhabitants. Erant and Josclyne had told her to ask for the spirit of the place she was staying in, as it was best to know if they were a welcoming one or not. Most were, but with so many people coming and going, you never knew. To make things better, they did give her a charm to leave for the spirit, saying it may smooth things over.

She parked and headed to the office; it was just after 8:00 a.m. As she was about to open the door, her eyes were drawn to movement in the shadows of the building, as if someone with a hood was jumping between them. She shook her head and focused as she opened the door to the office to see only one person inside, and he was engrossed in paperwork. She walked up behind him and after a few moments, asked if this was the housing check-in. Her words startled the young man and he stumbled as he turned.

Amanda backed away. "Sorry, I didn't mean to do that."

The young man hesitated as if unsure, "I didn't expect anyone to be in this early."

Amanda smiled, "Sorry, um, do you know if this is the housing office?"

The young man nodded. "Yeah, I'm getting my room done now. There's a lot of paperwork. I thought I had everything done already but they said they didn't have anything in my file."

Amanda felt her heart skip. She had spent hours filling out the paperwork, making sure every bit of information was given. Her parents also went over everything, hoping to make it easier when she arrived. She looked for anyone behind the counter so she could ask.

"They went to look for my file again. They should be back in a minute. Are you checking in today to?" the young man asked. "Oh, what's your name?"

Amanda looked at him before again looking to see if someone was behind the counter. "Uh, Amanda."

She said nothing else as she continued to search behind the tall row of file cabinets.

"Amanda, what? Maybe I can help."

Amanda looked at him with a forced smile. "Just Amanda for now."

"Oh, right, well, my name is Tyler, Tyler Fenris. I'm new here. I'm majoring in computer graphics. What about you?"

Amanda looked at him. "I'm studying classical and commercial drawing."

"Ah, old school. You'll eventually have to change over to computer graphics; that's what everyone's hiring for."

Amanda tilted her head, looking at him strangely. "I've done fine so far. Without using a computer. But you never know."

Her eyes brightened up as a figure came into the window from between the files. "Mister Fenris, we found the rest of your paperwork, but it seems you're missing form ED457D. You should have received it by email last month."

"Hold on a sec. Let me check," Tyler replied as he pulled out his phone and scrolled through emails. "Found it. I have a copy on my phone already filled out. I'll email it to you."

The woman behind the counter gave him the email address and told him to come back in a couple of hours. She then yelled, "Next!"

Amanda looked around, and seeing no one else, cautiously approached. "Hi, my name is Amanda Supp, I'm checking in today. I called a few days ago."

The woman looked at her before typing away on her computer. "Hold on a minute. Let me find your paperwork."

Amanda shifted her weight to one foot before looking back at Tyler. He only shrugged his shoulders. "I don't think they've updated their systems much here; that's why it's slow."

Amanda nodded.

She was relieved when the woman came back holding a file, and paused seeing what looked like a copy of *Adventures in the Haunted Maples*, *Dyden's tale* underneath it.

"Is everything all right?" Amanda asked.

The woman nodded. "Oh, yes, all your paperwork seems to be in order."

Amanda watched the woman grasp the book beneath a little too tightly, from what she could tell. She tilted her head to get a better look as she asked, "Is it all right if I check in?"

"Of course, here are the papers you need. Oh, and Dr. Brentwood asked you to meet her tomorrow at two p.m. It's all on the paperwork there," the woman said as she placed the pile on the counter. "Once they're signed, someone here will show you to your room for the semester."

Amanda thanked her and looked over the paperwork. She signed where she needed and handed them back to the woman, who was still gripping the other book tightly.

"Is there anything else I need to sign so I can get the room?" Amanda asked.

"Yes, could you sign this please?" the woman asked innocently, handing her the book. "The stories are so much fun. I love reading them when they come out."

Amanda started to blush; she now understood what Ron felt when everyone asked him to sign the books at the store. She had never been asked to sign her artwork before.

"I love the stories, they seem so real, and the pictures you draw, they're almost as if you've seen them in real life."

Amanda stumbled, trying to sign the book, and looked up at the woman. "What do you mean?"

The woman praised her, "They are so detailed and full of life. I mean, things like that don't exist."

Amanda felt her heart starting to beat again as she finished signing.

"Yeah, Ron can really describe the characters sometimes, even if it's not in the story. It's fun working with him." She forced a smile, handing the book back to the woman who pulled it quickly away from Amanda's grasp.

"Thank you; Colleen will show you to your room," the woman said. Amanda jumped as the woman yelled, "Colleen!" and watched as a young woman suddenly appeared as if almost by magic. Amanda looked at the tall, blonde woman. Something about her seemed odd; her face was thin, and her outline seemed fuzzy. It also seemed to shimmer a little in the light behind her.

"Colleen, this is Amanda Supp, the artist I told you about," the older woman said.

"It's nice to meet you. Diana here can't stop talking about the stories you've been involved with." Colleen's tone sounded almost accusing toward Amanda. Then when the young woman smiled, Amanda's fears abated. "C'mon, I'll meet you outside, we'll get you settled."

Amanda turned and exhaled, trying to remain calm. She jumped when she heard, "No way, you're the artist for *Haunted Maples*?"

Amanda stumbled back, seeing Tyler staring at her over his phone as she nodded nervously.

"Wow, I met someone famous, and it's only eight thirty. That's awesome!" Tyler yelled.

Amanda looked toward the door and saw Colleen suddenly appear in the shadowed light of the threshold. Amanda squinted her eyes, and it still looked as if the woman's image was shimmering. Amanda was brought back when she heard, "C'mon, let's go. Believe me. You'll want to get things done before it gets busy around here."

Amanda nodded and turned. "It was nice meeting you. See you," she said to the woman behind the desk as she walked toward the door muttering, "Great, things seem to be starting off just as normal as back home."

For those who search for glory and distinction, of all the actions one can take, the worthiest are those who go unseen.

-Aiden Hoff

Chapter Three
The New Place

Colleen showed Amanda the apartment. It was small, but to Amanda it didn't feel empty, it felt like she belonged there.

"I know it's on the third floor but the walk up isn't that bad. At least you'll keep in shape," Colleen joked.

Amanda laughed; Colleen seemed to be doing her best to make Amanda feel at ease. She somehow sensed this was Amanda's first time away from her loved ones. She turned to say something but stopped when the wavering edge around Colleen became more pronounced.

"Everything all right?" Colleen asked.

Amanda took a moment before nodding, even though she felt that the light-haired woman before her was hiding a secret. On her adventures, Amanda had come across several instances where creatures were mimicking something or someone else. Roween had told her to look at a reflection and see if it showed two faces, one inside another. She didn't see a shiny surface around, and noticed that the windows were very dusty.

"Are you sure you're all right?" Colleen asked.

Amanda nodded. "Yeah, I just realized that the windows are really dirty."

"Hey, that's just part of the charm!" Colleen laughed, and that made Amanda laugh as well.

"C'mon, let's get you moved in. It's not after eleven yet; maybe we could head out for some lunch afterward? Then you can get settled in."

Amanda accepted and they headed down to unpack her car.

It took a few hours to bring everything up to her apartment and as they were bringing the last of the boxes up the stairs when they stopped on the second floor. Another young woman came down the stairs and stopped before them, she turned as if going back up, barely glancing up from her phone. Amanda watched as she scrolled through her phone and tapped on a name. Moments later, Amanda's phone started to vibrate.

She wrestled the box she was holding and contorted her arm to grab her phone from her pocket.

"Hello?" Amanda answered. Moments later, the other woman started talking.

"Mandy, you here yet? Your last text said you were about an hour away."

Amanda pulled her phone from her ear, hearing the voice of the woman in one ear and on the phone in the other. She then smiled and spoke. "Gabs, I'm right behind you."

The other woman asked, "You're running behind? What happened?"

Colleen looked at Amanda as she pointed to the woman in front of them; she couldn't hold in her laugh.

"Gabs, I'm behind you," Amanda said before lightly tapping her friend's leg with her foot.

"Ugh, I'm having trouble hearing you, and I've got some nut kicking me while I'm standing in a stairwell."

Amanda hung up her phone. "Gabs, I'm right here!"

"Stupid phone, why do you all stop working on me?" her friend grumbled.

"Gabriella, it's me. Amanda," Amanda said, tapping her friend on the shoulder.

Gabriella turned around looking angry. "Listen, I'm worried about a friend. Will you stop—"

It took a few moments as Gabriella looked at her phone and then back to Amanda.

"Mandy! You made it!" she yelled, throwing her arms around Amanda, making her drop the box she held on her foot.

"Ow, Gabs, ow, you're crushing me! And my foot . . ." Amanda pulled back, hopping on her other foot as the pain subsided.

A few minutes later, they were in Amanda's apartment. Gabs started looking around.

"You didn't bring that much stuff," Gabriella said.

Amanda looked at her. "This is pretty much everything I own; I don't have a lot of things. Can't fit them in my room back home."

"Weren't you going to rent that cabin? The one from the stories?" Gabriella asked.

She was referring to Ron's house. Since he had moved in with Linda, the cabin was used as a second home. Amanda did stay the summer, and a few times when she wanted to go and see Roween. Amanda's father had taken a global sales job and her mother returned to work as an attorney, so she was mostly on her own. And since her parents sold the house in the woods a couple years ago, it was the only way she could see her fairy friend. Amanda figured it would be a great place to live. It was quiet, and she knew everyone who lived there.

"Probably not till after I'm finished with school," Amanda replied.

Gabriella laughed, "You're gonna like it here. The teachers are great, and the town . . . we can get into so much trouble. Know what I'm saying?"

Amanda smiled, then turned to see Colleen looking at her with a suspicious raised brow. Amanda reached out to Gabriella but missed as her friend moved away.

Looking at Colleen she remarked, "She's joking. She's kind of hyper."

Colleen laughed, "I get it, believe me I do. Just don't try to get into any bars unless you're old enough to drink. You'll really get in trouble."

Amanda watched as her friend started moving boxes. "This should go here, and this here. Uh, I have no idea what this is, so that can go here."

"Gabs," Amanda said loudly, but her friend continued to arrange things where she thought they should go.

"Gabs!" Amanda yelled, making the girl spin around.

"What?"

"My stuff, no touch. I'll put things where I want . . . okay?" Amanda told her friend.

Gabriella looked at her sheepishly as she placed the box she held gently on the floor. "Sorry, got carried away."

Amanda told her it was all right. Colleen could tell they'd know each other for quite a while. In fact, Amanda told her that she'd known Gabs since she moved to the cabin after they lost the house in the city. Gabriella had been her best friend since they met. Amanda felt lucky; Gabriella had been in school for a semester already and knew about things all around.

"It's good to know someone when you move to a new place. It makes life a bit easier," Colleen said.

Amanda asked them to help put things around the apartment and she would unpack later.

"I can't believe it's four o'clock already," Amanda said as they finished. "I don't know about you, but I'm hungry."

Colleen agreed, and Gabriella looked over a pile of boxes. "I know a great place for pizza."

Amanda motioned to Colleen. "Pizza?" Then to her friend.

Colleen nodded and Gabriella grabbed her purse. "Great, my tr . . ."

Amanda looked at her friend when she stopped talking. "What's wrong?"

"I don't think I have enough on my card," Gabriella said looking disappointed. "I was going to treat."

Colleen offered to pay, but Amanda disagreed. "Nope, you both helped me get my stuff up here, the least I can do is pay for the food. C'mon." Amanda headed for the door, motioning for them to follow.

"Okay, Gabs, where to?" Amanda asked as they headed outside.

"Bella Napale, it's down on Front Street," was her reply.

Colleen remarked, "Oh, their pizza's good. They make the best crust."

"Is it far?" Amanda asked.

"Um, we should probably drive, it's getting dark. You never know what weird things come out at night around here. You think those Haunted Maple stories are something, you should hear what they have around here," Gabriella mentioned.

"I'm sure she's joking," Colleen interjected.

Her response piqued Amanda's curiosity. She had a feeling this woman was hiding something earlier, but now she was becoming certain. But, as Gabriella grabbed her arm, Amanda realized that her suspicions could wait.

They headed into town. The food was good, and they spent a few hours telling stories and getting to know each other. When Amanda stretched and yawned, it became contagious.

"It's been a long day, girls, and I'm beat; I still have unpacking to do," Amanda said.

Gabriella yawned. "That was a lot of work, and a lot of pizza," she agreed, making them all laugh.

"We should head back; remember, you have a meeting with Doctor Brentwood tomorrow afternoon."

Amanda nodded. She was tired and still had some things to do, so they headed out.

As they were walking out of the restaurant, Colleen saw someone she knew.

"Hey, Shrive! You back already?" Colleen squealed as she ran up to her friend.

"Yeah, came back two nights ago. We were busy hunting some—" Amanda couldn't help but notice the woman stop talking as she walked up.

"Hi." She greeted Amanda with a slight head nod before she looked to Colleen.

"Amanda, this is Shrive. She works with me, sometimes." Colleen introduced her friend.

"You work in the office too?" Amanda asked, and reached out to shake her hand.

Shrive hesitated. "Yeah . . . in the office. That's where I work."

Amanda winced in pain as if something scratched her hand as Shrive pulled hers back.

"Oh, sorry, I haven't had a manicure in a while," Shrive apologized.

Amanda looked at her hand and made sure she wasn't bleeding. "No harm done, been there a few times myself. I have to admit, you've got some claws."

Amanda watched as the smile and color drained from Shrive's face, almost as if she was afraid of something, and was startled when Colleen took control.

"Hey, it's late; we should all probably get back. I just have to ask my friend something," Colleen told her. "I'll meet you in the car."

Amanda waved as she turned to walk to the car, but her eyes caught the same shimmer around Shrive as Colleen in the light of the restaurant. Amanda now knew there was something definitely going on around here, and it brought a smile that lit her face. "Oh, this place just got interesting."

They arrived back at campus. Colleen got out of the car and turned to see a figure jump from the shadows from across the courtyard. She could see movement near the art building and squinted. She used her eyes to focus in on the person, and recognized her. "Selese, what are you doing here so late?" she mumbled.

"What?" Gabriella asked.

Colleen looked at her purse. "Uh, I think I forgot something back in the office. It'll only take me a sec; I'll catch up with you two tomorrow," Colleen said as she rushed away.

Amanda noticed that she seemed to run fast for her size, something else she decided to add to the list of growing questions.

"I hope she finds what she forgot," Gabriella said.

Amanda nodded. "Yeah, me too."

* * *

Amanda said good night, and Colleen headed toward the art building. Coleen turned to see if her new friends were watching and seeing them laughing at something, she smiled and tugged on her collar. Within seconds a hood appeared and she drew it over her head. As she walked into the shadows, she disappeared.

Colleen reappeared across the courtyard near where she had seen Selese. She covered one eye and spoke words not heard by many humans, then removed her hand and around her eye a subtle, green ring floated. She then scanned the ground.

Wavering images of Selese's footsteps appeared. She followed them to the shadow of the wall, only to find them stop before seemingly turning around. Some were deeper, as if she jumped to get a better look at something. Colleen jumped, her hood falling backward, but saw nothing in the window, and since her target was no longer around, she decided to head home. There was nothing she could do for the moment. But, as Colleen pulled the hood over her head, she paused to ask out loud, "What are you looking for, Selese?"

Chapter Four
Trouble Finds Her Fast

Amanda heard the alarm from her phone and knocked it off the table as she clumsily tried to grab it. Giving a heavy sigh, she reached from under the covers to pick it up off the floor and yelped as she slumped lazily onto the floor. She pulled the warm covers down and it took a minute for her to move herself from the spot. She had gone to sleep sometime around 2:00 a.m., wanting to get some things done last night and before she met with Dr. Brentwood.

She didn't know why, but ever since she applied, Doctor Brentwood had been someone interested in Amanda's work.

"There are too many coincidences here; something's going on," Amanda muttered as she touched the wooden ring. She raised her eyes to look around the small kitchen. She hadn't gone shopping, and realized she had much more to do today. She shook her head before muttering, "I should probably get settled in first before I start looking into things." And, as her stomach growled, "And get some breakfast, too. I wonder what the food's like here?"

Amanda hurriedly took a shower, got dressed, and headed out for some breakfast.

She adjusted her purse as she walked out of the student center. The food was okay, nothing like what she'd had back home. She took sip of tea as she walked back toward her apartment. She stopped, seeing Shrive seemingly searching around. Amanda was about to wave but noticed someone running nearby, and that person was being chased by two others in the accessway between buildings. She flinched at seeing what looked like a bolt of lightning come from one of those pursuing.

Amanda ran toward the action to find out what was going on. She had seen too many things that normally don't happen, and she wanted some answers. She followed them down the alley. That decision turned out to be a mistake as she collided head-on with someone, the impact knocking them both to the ground. Stunned, Amanda opened her eyes to see a sharply pointed ear next to her rolling over to stand, Amanda followed suit before grabbing the woman's arm.

"Why are they chasing you?" Amanda asked as the woman pulled the dark hood over her head and tried to run away.

Moments later, Amanda felt a sharp pain in her back and the world lit brightly around her. Stunned, she swayed as a powdery fog encased her, the cloud choking her as she breathed. She turned to see the two pursuers now standing a short distance away.

"Get out of here. Go, I'll be fine!" Amanda yelled as she stumbled. The world around her became fuzzy and she felt someone grab her; the strength of the grip was almost painful as they wrenched down on her arm.

As the world blurred, Amanda watched as the hooded woman looked toward the two men pursuing her, yelling, "You people are going to kill someone one of these days!"

Before she lost consciousness, Amanda could swear she heard Elvish curse words.

Amanda opened her eyes to see a room with gold ornamentation all around and a very soft bed, almost like she was sleeping on air. As she moved to sit up, she realized that she was sleeping on a bed of wind. She smiled. "You've got to be kidding. That is so cool."

Amanda carefully hopped off the cushion of air and toward the door. Silently as she could, she opened it and surveyed the area; she needed to know where she was.

Stealthily, she walked down the hall. As her hand was about to touch the wall, she noticed a symbol lit on the stone. Amanda smiled. "That's Sylph writing for 'light.' Guess asking Roween to show me stuff did pay off."

She pressed the symbol and the whole room was illuminated. Amanda marveled at the grand decoration all around her, but as she looked toward the window, she could only see the reflection of the small building in the windows across the street. "No way. This is a magic room."

"How are you not freaked out by this?" Amanda heard a voice beside her.

"I am freaked out by someone sneaking up on me," Amanda warned, taking a stance to fight.

Amanda watched as the woman put her hands up. In the light, she again noticed a shimmer before seeing the face of who was speaking.

"Who are you, and where am I?" Amanda demanded.

The young woman sighed, turning her hood down, "It's me, Shrive, and you're in a magic safe house."

Amanda looked around, relaxing for a moment. "Wow, don't usually hear the truth that quickly."

Shrive looked puzzled. "What? I don't get it; how are you not freaking out right now?"

Amanda looked around the room. "Is this an illusion, or is it really this big in here?"

Shrive leaned her shoulder on the frame of the door. "Seriously, how, are you not freaked?"

Amanda turned, about to say she's seen something like this before, when she noticed something else in the shadows. The outline of another hooded figure was barely visible in the hollow ink dark shadows. Amanda's eyes could just make out the dim light of what looked like tunnels as she scanned the darkness.

"Whoever you are, come out so I can see you," Amanda demanded.

Moments later, another hooded figure emerged from the darkness. "You can see me?"

Amanda was again on her guard but answered, "I think I saw you at the college center."

The woman shook her head. "Wasn't me. I haven't been out there today."

Amanda thought for a moment before saying, "Probably have to watch myself around here then. How close to the school are we?"

Shrive stepped forward. "About three blocks; we're close by."

Amanda walked over and touched the window. "How long was I out?"

Shrive shrugged, "Only about an hour. Usually, sleeping bolts last for a day. I don't know how you're walking around."

"Sleeping bolt?" Amanda asked before saying, "Never encountered those before."

The hooded woman looked at Shrive. "How is she so calm?" she asked, making Shrive shrug her shoulders.

Amanda stared at the other woman. "You look thin, sort of like . . ." Amanda's eyes widened and she smiled, saying, "Dia duit?" Amanda's words made the young, hooded woman step back.

But as Amanda waited for a response, there was a sudden breeze. Amanda felt a wall of wind separating her from the others before she heard a familiar-sounding language. It was the whistling language of the sylphs. Amanda whistled back, and the wall of air left as quickly as it arrived. She again heard the words of the sylphs but answered back in English, "Sorry, I only know a few words. I usually wasn't listening to them when they were trying to teach me."

"You know some Sylph; that's impressive," a light-haired woman said as she walked from the shadows. "What are you doing here? How do you know Sylph?"

Amanda stood tall as she looked around. "That depends on who's asking."

The woman laughed, "Sorry, I'm Arianna. And you are?"

"Amanda."

"How do you know Sylph? And how did you know she was an elf?" Arianna asked.

Amanda looked at the woman. "You're an elf; that's why you look familiar. Do you know a Dyden in West Falls?"

The hooded woman became angered. "Who the hell is she? How the hell does she know these things? She doesn't even have any magic. She's not one of us!"

Arianna motioned for the hooded woman to calm. "You brought her here, Selese."

"Selese, cool name. I'm Amanda, Amanda Supp." She offered her hand in greeting to Selese, who reluctantly shook it.

"And I thought seeing a gnome coming here this morning was cool. Instead, I wound up in a magic house," Amanda said.

"Safe house," Shrive corrected her.

"What do you mean you've seen elves before?" Selese asked.

"Well, that is a story in itself. Have any of you read *Haunted Maples*?"

It only took a short time for Amanda to explain. Shrive seemed really interested in some of the tales Amanda told. Arianna was enjoying the stories. However, Selese remained skeptical.

Amanda enjoyed telling her stories, but then looked at her phone. "Damn, I have a meeting in an hour."

She looked around. "Thank you for bringing me here, but I have to meet with Dr. Brentwood."

Shrive pushed from the door, "You just got here. Why are you meeting with her?"

Amanda shrugged her shoulders. "She just asked to meet."

Amanda then walked toward Shrive and passed her hand along the edge of the shimmer. "I keep seeing this shimmer around you. What do you really look like?"

Shrive's eyes widened.

Arianna looked toward Shrive. "She already knows you're not human."

Shrive growled, "I'm human, just not *all* human," before she pulled out a pendant she wore. As she removed it, Shrive's cat-like features suddenly came into focus.

"Wow, a real live cat-girl!" Amanda said.

"Don't get any ideas, I'm only part cat. The rest would easily kick your butt."

Amanda laughed as she asked to see the pendant. Amanda pulled out the wooden ring she wore, showing it to Shrive. "I've got one too."

As Amanda held the wooden ring up, Selese grabbed onto the silver chain. Knowing Roween had given the ring some extra magic, the hooded woman's actions making Amanda yell, "Don't!"

As the ring was about to pass over Amanda's head it gave Selese a shock powerful enough to send her flying before it slowly floated back down around Amanda's neck.

"Are you all right?" Amanda asked as Selese waved for her to get back.

"What the hell was that?" Selese yelled, pushing at the air to keep Amanda away.

From the darkness, they heard a man's voice. "That was the protection of a fairy ring, young lady. You would be wise to not touch something like that very often."

Amanda again readied herself for a fight as the man helped Selese from the floor. He turned to Amanda, saying, "My name's Raymond Cranston, I run this place. All seeking refuge are welcome, but we have rules." He turned to glare at Selese.

The woman was saying, "I wasn't going to steal it, I wanted to see what she looked like. She can see us but we can't see her."

Raymond smiled, "There's a simple reason for that."

"Raymond, if I wanted out of here, how do I?" Amanda asked.

The man pointed to the second tunnel. "Take that tunnel to the end, open the door, and walk out. It's that simple."

Amanda turned back after looking to the tunnel. "Nothing's that simple."

"A shame; someone so young, but already so cynical," he commented.

"So what?" Selese yelled. "How is she able to see us. And us not see her?"

Raymond looked at Selese. "Please be calm, Selese. You cannot see her because you are already seeing her. She neither had nor has need to hide any magic of her own."

"You mean she's a full human?" Arianna said in disbelief.

Raymond nodded. "As to why she sees you; that, I think, is a gift she was given by her friend. I'm guessing to keep her out of trouble."

Amanda relaxed for a moment and thought, *Roween put something extra into my ring before she left; was it the ability to see through magic?*

She was about to ask Raymond when the alarm on her phone went off.

"Shoot, I'm gonna be late. That way's out, right?" she asked, pointing down the tunnel.

Raymond nodded.

"Thank you, I've gotta go. It was nice meeting you all. Maybe we can get some tea or something later. But I really have to get going." Amanda put her phone away as she yelled from the tunnel, "Bye!"

Arianna motioned to Raymond. "If she's just human, why does Brentwood want to speak with her?"

Raymond replied, "She'll find out shortly."

Arianna turned to Selese. "You were out earlier, you lied to her. You're the one who brought her here. Who was chasing you?"

Selese groaned, "All right, I was out. So what?"

Arianna rolled her eyes. "Who was chasing you?"

Selese sighed, "A couple of Raven Hunters."

Shrive stepped forward. "You didn't tell me that; you said someone hit her!"

"I didn't want to leave her, all right? Those two hunters were playing too rough," Selese defended herself.

Shrive rolled her eyes. "But why were they chasing you?"

Selese looked to the floor. "I may have taken something they wanted."

We are the guardians of the world and all who walk it. It is our duty to protect, to cherish and to uphold the natural order for all beings, magic or otherwise

-Alex Pertu

Chapter Five
The Hunters Appear

Amanda Stopped by her apartment to pick up her portfolio, and ran as fast as she could, hoping she wasn't too late. *Wouldn't be a good first impression,* she thought. When she reached the building, she allowed herself some time to catch her breath before entering. With her portfolio in hand, she headed in, only to be stopped by a woman at the front desk.

"This is the administrative building, young lady; do you have an appointment?" the silver-haired woman confronted her.

Amanda took a moment before answering, and she had an uneasy feeling that she was being watched.

"Yes, I'm here to see Dr. Brentwood. She's expecting me."

Amanda waited as the woman flipped through her low-tech planner. She still felt as though someone was watching her.

"I don't see you listed as having an appointment. Are you sure you're in the right place?"

She was about to reply but was startled when she heard, "Amanda, you're right on time."

Amanda's head snapped in the direction of the words to see Colleen standing beside her. As she placed her hand over her heart, she replied, "Don't sneak up on me like that! I didn't even hear you come in."

Colleen gave a quiet laugh and a small nod to the receptionist, who pointed to Colleen. "It seems you are expected. Please enjoy your day."

Amanda followed Colleen into the elevator and they headed up. As they did, Amanda noticed the shimmer around Colleen in the metal wall of the elevator and decided to make some small talk.

"I wonder why she didn't have my appointment listed?"

Colleen shifted on her feet. "Dr. Brentwood doesn't always list her visitors."

Amanda became curious. "Hmm, why not?"

Colleen didn't answer; she just looked ahead as the doors of the elevator opened.

"Come on, the office is this way." Colleen guided her to Dr. Brentwood's office.

Along the way, Amanda was in awe of the furnishings: Neoclassical Hepplewhite, Victorian, old and newer styles. She couldn't help but wonder why there were so many different types. It kept her occupied, and she almost walked into Colleen when she stopped before the office.

"She's waiting for you. Good luck," Colleen said as she opened the door.

"Ah, Ms. Supp, good to see you. Most of the time, I have to drag students in here because they are sleeping or lose track of time. You're punctual; that's good. Please have a seat."

Dr. Claire Brentwood motioned for Amanda to sit as she took her portfolio. She seemed to show a concerned expression as she glanced at the computer screen before she took the portfolio

Amanda handed her. Opening it, the doctor walked around to her chair.

"Now, I have a few questions. We can look over your work while we chat."

Amanda agreed.

Several minutes passed; the questions were what Amanda had expected. Mostly about her style, where she took her influence from, how was her trip here. The usual time-wasting banter that we all endure. Then Dr. Brentwood asked about one picture in particular, the one she had done of a fantasy creature, a basilisk.

"You know, according to legend, this is supposed to turn you to stone," Dr. Claire told her.

Amanda thought, *unless you're wearing mirrored sunglasses,* before smiling and saying, "I read so much about them, I just had a feeling that's what they'd look like."

Dr. Brentwood smiled and continued to examine Amanda's portfolio, stopping every so often to ask something. Amanda became comfortable and answered her questions reasonably easily and quickly. Then the doctor asked, "Everything all right? No ill effects from the sleeping bolt?"

Amanda replied without thinking, "That didn't last long, but . . ." before she wished she hadn't.

The doctor looked over her glasses at Amanda as she placed her portfolio caringly down on the desk. The doctor remained emotionless as she turned her monitor around. Amanda recognized the entrance of the safe house and saw herself being carried in, and video of her leaving followed by two others. "You've been on campus less than a day, and you're already in trouble."

"They were chasing someone and firing lighting. Am I supposed to just stand by?"

The doctor gave a simple answer. "Yes."

Amanda suddenly felt very uneasy and her adrenalin started to kick in. She would fight this woman if she had to.

Dr. Claire could see and feel the tension in the young woman before her, so she backed off, asking if she wanted something to drink before standing and moving toward the small refrigerator in the office.

Amanda's eyes followed her every move as she pulled out two bottles of cold water.

"Are you really Dr. Brentwood?" Amanda asked.

The doctor nodded, then took a deep breath before responding. "Sorry, we were worried you'd been injured after being hit at such close range."

Amanda sat forward. "Who hit me?"

The doctor paused, deciding to choose her words carefully, remembering that they've had to adjust memories before. But, she also knew of Amanda's adventures and her involvement with other magical entities. All the council agreed, "Things may be difficult to adjust with her."

"You got in the way; that's all," Dr. Claire responded.

Amanda stood. "Who shot me with the sleeping bolt?"

The doctor placed the water on the desk in front of Amanda before leaning back in her chair. "His name is Dennon Fierst. He's one of our best."

Amanda continued to ask questions. "Why was he attacking her?"

The doctor stood to match the fiery young woman before her. "He was hunting her, not attacking."

"Hunting, attacking, He was still trying to harm her," Amanda protested.

"He's one of our best, but not the most subtle," Dr. Claire said with some annoyance.

"One of your best, what?" Amanda demanded an answer.

"They are called Raven Hunters. They subdue those who, shall we say, misuse their abilities."

"You're like Terrell, aren't you?" Amanda said with accusation, making the woman raise her voice.

"Terrell was a disgrace to all of us; he craved power. We're trying to protect you and them!" Her yelling brought the attention of Colleen, who rushed in the door as if looking for a fight.

Dr. Claire held her hand up. "It's all right, Colleen, we just have a misunderstanding."

Amanda looked over at Colleen. "Are you an elf?"

Colleen stepped back. "Y-Yes, partly."

Amanda turned to the doctor. "And you're a Raven Hunter?"

Dr. Claire looked at Amanda and again took a calming breath before answering. "Yes, I am. But you misunderstand. We're not trying to harm anyone. It's just that you got in the way. You need to be careful."

"That still doesn't explain why he was hunting her," Amanda shot back.

Colleen moved next to Amanda. "She used her abilities to steal something, Dennon can sometimes be a little heavy-handed. Especially with repeat offenders."

"Who, Selese? She seems a little standoffish, but she seems okay to me," Amanda said.

"You know where she is?" Dr. Claire asked with a less harsh, almost caring tone in her voice, making Amanda reply, "That depends on who's asking, you or the hunter?"

Dr. Claire sat down. "Both. She stole a statue from one of the archives. It's not hers, but we've had some people interested in purchasing it. Unfortunately, it's not for sale; it contains some disruptive spells. We don't want it getting out. I'm sure you are familiar with a situation like that."

Amanda sat down. "It feels relieving, telling the truth, doesn't it?"

Her statement made Dr. Brentwood laugh.

"You know, I asked you here to get to know more about you and your adventures. It seems you are in every way, capable." The doctor paused. "We wanted to make sure there were no issues following you."

"You mean magic creatures and the like?" Amanda asked. The doctor nodded.

"Come, let me show you something." Dr. Claire stood and motioned for Amanda to follow as she walked toward the bookcase before tilting a book out from the shelf; it made an audible clicking sound.

"Oh, all this secrecy, and you have a simple bookshelf entrance to your lair," Amanda chided.

Dr. Brentwood remained unfazed. "Not exactly."

Then, with a wave of her hand several books tilted in and out, making several sounds before the whole wall moved backward and split apart, revealing a glowing entryway.

"Wow, combination book lock to a secret lair! Haven't seen that before," Amanda said in awe as she followed the doctor through the doorway.

The world dimmed and gave way to a stone hallway. Amanda turned to see the office in the glowing portal only a few feet behind. Their footsteps were the only sound as they approached a much larger room. As the dim light was lost, a very large, well-lit cavern dwarfed the three.

"Now *this* is a secret lair," Amanda said with pride, making Colleen look at her with confusion.

"Wait, how many secret lairs have you seen?" Colleen asked.

Amanda looked at her, about to speak, but paused as if counting. "Um, five," she answered nonchalantly before following Dr. Brentwood.

Colleen stood in astonishment, saying, "Five?" before rushing to join them.

Amanda followed the doctor as they entered a large meeting room just off the cavern. There was a long heavily built wooden table that spanned over thirty feet. Amanda noticed a man standing with a younger man about Amanda's age standing near it.

"Ah, I see you've brought a visitor," he said with a muddied English accent.

"Good to see you, Cale. Amanda, this is my husband Lord Callum Cunningham. He's been with us in the US for some time. And this is Luke, his apprentice." Dr. Brentwood introduced her.

"Charmed, my dear. Please call me Cale. As for my apprentice, hopefully, you won't be seeing him around much. We try to keep a low profile here," Cale said as he leaned on the sturdy-built table.

"Luke Harrison, at your service." The young man reached over to shake her hand and seemed to hold on a little longer than his teacher. Amanda swore she felt herself blushing. She was about to ask him something when she heard the loud noise of a door being kicked open.

She watched as the same man she had seen chasing Selese scuttled angrily through the door.

"Ah, I see Dennon has graced us with his presence," Cale mocked him.

Now Amanda had a better look at the man who shot her with the sleeping bolt, and put a face to the person known as Dennon Fierst.

"You brought the FOF in. Good riddance; she should be locked up. All her kind should be locked up," Dennon argued.

Amanda put up her hand and with an annoyed tone asked, "Excuse me, what's an FOF?"

Cale answered, "Don't worry, young lady, it's not a derogatory term; at least not for most of us." He then looked toward Dennon. "It means Friend of Fairy. They usually have some leeway with our organization."

Dennon slammed his fist down on the table. "She should not be here! Expel her, erase her memory; she does not belong in this hall."

"Dennon, you were using magic in plain sight, during daylight. Not to mention we have students arriving. You were careless," Dr Brentwood argued.

"This is outrageous; we are here to protect them, to make sure that everyone follows the rules!" Dennon replied.

Amanda rolled her eyes as she listened to all three of them arguing. Then Cale sent Luke off to gather the rest of the council, since it seemed as per Dennon's argument they now had to make a decision.

Amanda looked at Colleen. "Is it usually this heated around here?"

Colleen shook her head. "Nah, it's usually pretty dull."

Amanda sighed, "Well, while they hash things out, think you could show me around? I've never been in a good, secret society lair before. I'm usually fighting for my life."

Colleen smiled, "C'mon, I'll show you around."

As they were walking away, Dr. Brentwood yelled, "Bring her back in about an hour; they should be finished by then!"

Colleen nodded and laughed as she led Amanda away. "You know, since we don't have much time, maybe I'll show you the grove," Colleen told her.

Amanda asked, "What's the grove."

Colleen pointed to the ring around Amanda's neck. "You'll find out."

The two talked and laughed as they walked. Amanda was telling her about Dyden's fortress when the roof above them suddenly became the sky.

"Whoa, where are we?" Amanda asked.

"This is the Grove; it's what I wanted to show you. As for *where* it is, I know it's outside. I thought about placing a locator spell once but from what I heard about what happened to the last person who did that, I changed my mind."

Amanda looked around; she could smell the sweet air and the forest all around her; it felt like home.

Colleen pulled her along to a large group of trees. "These are the trees for all of the fairies that have lost their homes to a human building. They stay here until they find a new place to reside."

Amanda felt sad. She knew how Roween felt about her forest, and these other fairies were probably no exception.

Then, from the between the trees, they could see a light; in fact, many lights appeared, and they greeted the two standing before the trees.

And from a magical chorus they heard, "We wish you health and welcome to the Grove. Introduce yourself, and friend or foe."

Colleen spoke. "I am Colleen, you know me all. This is Amanda. She's a friend of all."

"You speak in rhyme when you talk to them?" Amanda asked.

"Yes, don't you?" Colleen replied.

"Nope, don't have to. Roween knows no matter how I say it."

Colleen looked at her strangely. "Are you sure you don't have any magic?"

Amanda shrugged her shoulders. "You're the ones telling me that I don't." Before she took a breath, she said, "Hello, everyone."

One fairy flew close to Amanda and circled before using her power to lift the ring from beneath Amanda's shirt.

"Wait, don't take it off; I don't want you getting hurt," Amanda warned.

The fairy smiled, "You care and warn, your heart is fair and warm."

She asked to touch the ring that Amanda wore. Amanda nodded. When she did, a vision of Roween appeared. It was like a message, but all Amanda and Colleen heard were words of whistle and wind. Neither could make any sense of it. However, all the fairies gasped and cheered before looking at Amanda.

They told her, "Adventures you've seen, and battles you've found. Saved our kind, and others around. And friends you find, that's good for you. You save the day, and a friend so true!"

Amanda looked around as another fairy flew before her.

"When trouble abounds and there's endless fight. Call without sound, we'll bring endless light."

Amanda looked at Colleen. "What's that mean?"

Colleen looked at her. "You're the fairy expert, you tell me."

The fairies drifted away, but one stayed behind. She hovered before Amanda, then sat on her shoulder with a smile. Amanda smiled back, then remembered something.

"Wait, I have something you might like. Roween gave it to me before I left. If I wanted, I could give it to the local fairy as a gift."

The fairy floated before Amanda as she searched her purse and pulled out a small package, then handed it to the fairy.

"Hope you know what you're doing," Colleen whispered.

The fairy opened the package to find a small cake. The fairy before her glowed brightly.

"This is a cake of honeybee, all for this fairy? You make things sunny, my name Alicee."

Amanda laughed. "Guess I found her, and her name is Ah-lee-see?"

The fairy nodded and happily ate the honey cake Amanda had brought before floating off into the trees.

Amanda smiled, "I guess I am a FOF."

"It would seem so," Colleen said. "We should probably head back; I'll have to tell everyone about what just happened."

Amanda laughed as they headed back to the meeting hall. Colleen looked at her. "You know, I may have a faster way to get back to the Great Hall."

When Amanda asked how, all Colleen did was pull her hood over her head and say, "Let me show you."

The world is a wonderous place, filled with Life, hope and magic. To deny any being this, is a crime against ourselves.

-Alon Tarnus

Chapter Six
What the FOF?

Out of the shadows, a hooded woman appeared, a backpack slung over her shoulder. It hung heavy from something substantial inside. Within moments, another figure appeared from behind a column nearby.

"You're late, thief. I was beginning to wonder if you had decided to find another buyer." The man's voice echoed around the stone room.

"Relax, old man. I had some errands to run before coming here. Besides, I wanted to make sure I wasn't followed," Selese replied.

"Smart girl; you'd serve us well. If it wasn't for your mixed blood," the man retorted.

"Of all the blasted things to say, you, you . . . argh! Just give me the money you promised and I'm out of here," Selese growled. "Don't know why I bothered to take this job. Your buyer better have the cash for me now."

"To answer your question, it's simple. You're greedy."

Selese pulled the statue from her pack. "Here it is, the *Effigy of Tarnus.*"

The man moved close to inspect the twisted sculpture. It was an image of a man wrestling a snake of mud and stone as it tried to devour him. He looked closely at the writing around the base; with a few magic words, more became visible.

"This isn't a copy, I'm surprised. Some of our fellow members believed that you would have crossed us, thief." The man smiled. "You just won me some good money."

"Glad to hear. Now, speaking of money," she said before speaking some magic words of her own, causing the figure to become intangible, her spell allowing only her to hold the item.

"Not a smart move, thief," the man cautioned.

"No statue until I get paid." Selese smiled.

The hooded man handed her a small box and she placed the statue on the ground next to her before she opened it. She examined the little wooden box and thought, *Pretty small for a stack of cash.* She opened it, revealing a broken raven feather.

"The Broken Feather! Y-You said nothing about giving this to them," Selese said, the fear evident in her stutter.

"What does it matter, thief? You brought the statue, and I'm taking it to the one who wants it." The man's words echoed as a brilliant flash of light came from his hand. Selese watched as a ring expanded above them, blocking out all other light from the surrounding area.

"Shadow wall? No! I won't . . ." Selese's voice trailed off.

"That's right, thief; your kind cannot port if surrounded by nothing but shadows," the man said with a tone of victory. "Oh, and I have a special gift for you. Courtesy of my benefactor."

The man produced a wooden tube. He poured its contents onto the floor, making Selese cringe in horror, seeing the golden-red glow in its eyes.

"Pyramites?" Selese placed her hand over her heart.

"That's right, thief, and they're hungry for gold," the man gleefully sneered.

Selese's heart raced. Pyramites were small, rodent creatures programmed for only one thing, and they would do anything to reach their goal at any cost. She had encountered them only once in her life, and the small creature nearly destroyed her chest plate to get its prize. If it weren't for Cale, the beast would have dug through her body to retrieve the golden heart made to replace the one taken by the wraith mage.

Selese ran, but within the shadow, she again found herself facing the same small pack of pyramites she was escaping. She tried porting away but couldn't; the shadow wall was too powerful. She searched for a way out when one of the creatures jumped on her. It scratched at the front of her jacket, its sharp claws shredding it instantly. But as it tore through, it broke off something shiny. The creature paused as its claw caught on a small plate of gold. It became mesmerized by it. Seeing the glint of its prize the others suddenly jumped to continue what the first had started. Within seconds the scurry of activity ceased and the small creatures cooed and swayed in satisfaction as they brought their treasure back to their master.

"This is armor scales, you idiots!" the man yelled at the small creatures bearing their prizes.

Selese panted heavily but sat up with a show of anger that she rarely displayed. She rushed to grab the statue.

"Tell your friend that this is not for sale. I'm taking it back!" Selese yelled.

"To where, thief? You cannot escape," the man said victoriously.

"There's always a way out," Selese said as she took a deep breath. Holding the statue and her hand to the now damaged gold chest plate, she spoke the same words as before, making her *and* the figure intangible.

"You still have nowhere to go, girl!" the man yelled.

Selese smiled and waved to him as she slowly sank through the floor below her. The pyramites clawed at nothing but her ghost as she vanished from their sight.

Beneath the floor, Selese gave the command to make herself stable again. She then ran for the nearest shadow created by the open balcony. She didn't care where it took her, she needed to be out of there. To her surprise, she found herself reappearing in the museum she had taken the statue from.

"Shouldn't have taken this job. I didn't know the Broken Feather was part of the deal. Of all the stupid things you've done, Selese," she muttered to herself as she opened the enclosure to replace the statue.

She closed the lid and pulled out a small wooden flower, placing it on the pedestal of the statue. She pulled out a piece of paper and spoke to it. Her words wrote themselves on the page. It read, "The Broken Feather wants this; keep it safe."

She then spoke to the wooden flower and her words made it unfold into a straight piece of wood. "That should give me some delay to get out of here, like last time."

She pulled her hood over her head and with a sullen look of regret, she disappeared into the shadows before the small flower set off the alarm, encasing the whole area in a shadow wall.

Selese reappeared within the Shadowed Hall, a corridor of light and shadow used by all elf who cared to visit the great meeting place. Of course, there were guards at the end to prevent unwanted visitors. All elves who used the portals had to register when they arrived. When Selese appeared, she was noticed. They stopped her and asked her to state her business. She thought about lying, but remembered the Broken Feather had set pyramites on her.

"I need to speak with Lord Cale; it's something urgent," Selese pleaded.

Behind her, two others arrived in the shadows. Amanda stumbled as Colleen pulled her through the portal.

"Okay, that's a weird way to travel. But pretty cool," Amanda said, making Colleen laugh.

Selese turned around to see Amanda and Colleen as the guard stopped them.

"Hi, Talon. You know who I am. And this is Amanda. We're both trying to get back to the meeting hall. We have business there."

"Wait your turn, elf. We're processing this thief first," Talon growled trying to maintain a commanding presence. But could see the look of disbelief Colleen gave, having known him since she came to the Sanctuary.

"You don't understand. I have to talk to Lord Cale, it's urgent. Let me in!" Selese protested, trying to push her way past the guards, only to be repelled back by them and the security spell.

"Selese, you're under arr—" Colleen's words stopped when she saw the gold chest plate exposed, several of its small scales missing, and her clothes ripped to shreds. "These are pyramite marks. What happened?"

Amanda touched the plate. "Is this gold? What happened to you?"

Selese didn't know if she could trust the guards; she only knew Cale would help her if she asked. Then, looking at Amanda, she leaned in to Colleen and whispered to the blonde elf.

"The Broken Feather wanted the statue," she whispered.

Colleen's eyes widened. "Talon, move out of the way. You need to let us in, now. The Circle has to be told."

Talon held them at arm's length. "We'll be the judge of that."

Colleen looked at Selese, who said, "Don't trust 'em. I have to talk to Lord Cale."

"I'll vouch for her, Talon. Let us in," Colleen pleaded.

The large guard could see the concern in the elf's eyes and Selese straining to keep herself composed.

"It must be serious," Talon said as he waved the shield away.

As they walked by, he heard a meek, "Thank you," from Selese, making his heart heavy.

He mumbled, "Something serious indeed."

Within moments they were in the meeting hall, and Colleen explained to the guard at the door the situation. He immediately allowed them entry as the others were debating, causing the room to go silent. Selese ran toward Cale, who stopped her, seeing the damage to her chest plate.

"You were attacked by pyramites," he said out loud, causing a murmur around the room.

Selese leaned in, telling him that it was the Broken Feather that wanted the statue. She then pulled back and stated for all to hear, "I took the figure to sell. I know you all knew about it. I was only trying to get some money. I didn't know who was asking for the statue, and I returned it. It's back in the museum."

"Who was it for, Selese?" Dr. Brentwood asked.

Lord Cale looked at her and then mouthed what Selese had told him. Dr. Claire stood quickly before asking for a short recess. They then pulled Selese and Colleen away.

Amanda was left on her own in a room of magical creatures. Amanda asked questions about them and found many easy to get a response from. She learned that the Circle was created to help those who wanted to blend in, and that it mostly consisted of magical creatures and people who wanted to do the same. Most people were part Fae and preferred peace to any competition. They also protected those of mixed lineage from magic-users trying to rid the world of mixed, or mottled blood, as they were called. Those protectors were known as the Raven Hunters.

Within her conversation, one of the dryads told Amanda that she has no magic; the only spell she had was what has been given to her—the wooden ring bestowed by a fairy, as the Fae put it, "A special gift indeed." Among them, she again heard the term *FOF*.

She was about to ask about the ring when Shrive walked up behind her, startling her.

"Didn't mean to do that again," Shrive spologized, showing her cat-like teeth in her smile.

"You're worse than my cat, Jinx, you know that?" Amanda retorted.

Shrive looked angry. "What's that supposed to mean?"

Amanda looked repentant. "That's not what I meant. Jeez, have to watch what you say around here; it may not mean what you think."

Shrive smiled, "I know you didn't mean anything; I've read your file. Jinx is pretty lucky. I meant to catch up with you after the safe house. How're you feeling?"

Amanda sighed in relief. "Good, considering I saw the Grove, just took a trip through a shadow gate, and ran into Selese, who was attacked by something called pyramites."

"Oh, God, is she all right? I mean, she's bad news, but no one should be attacked by those things," Shrive said, concerned.

Amanda told her that she seemed a little shaken up but all right. Then Shrive asked her a question.

"Hey, did you get Collins for Art Theory this semester?"

Amanda told her she did, for the morning class.

"Good, I'm in the morning class too. We'll sit next to each other," Shrive told her.

"I didn't know you were an artist. I thought you were one of them," Amanda said.

Shrive nodded. "I'm good at art." And then produced a very sharp claw from the tip of her finger. "Especially fine carving." She laughed, and Amanda joined her. But Amanda was thinking in the back of her mind that maybe Shrive was there to watch her. She was probably ordered by the council, since they are curious why a fairy chose her.

After several minutes Dr. Brentwood returned. "I trust everyone is all right, getting to know everyone, Amanda?"

Lord Cale came in behind Dr. Brentwood. Amanda could hear Cale tell Claire, "She's in the infirmary, but fine. Just shaken up."

Amanda sighed with relief, hearing the news. Dr. Brentwood then said, "We were discussing your situation."

Amanda replied, "Hey, if you're asking me to join, I'm in. Been doing this for years anyway."

Dr. Brentwood looked at her. "Yes, but you have not been under our rules. You may find it difficult."

Dennon finally brought himself out of his brooding. Amanda noticed he seemed deep in thought when Selese showed up. "You're a FOF. That gives you no right to claim a place here, girl."

His statement caused a murmur in the creatures all around. "She's a FOF, not one of us . . . Human, no magic, useless to us, no magic, she cannot join us . . ."

Amanda looked around. "Some of you are calling me a FOF, not even trying to say my name. And FOF coming from some of you with such a disgusted tone. I don't know who you all think you are."

As Amanda paused, Brentwood moved to say something, but Amanda spoke again.

"I have seen amazing things. I still wonder at so many of the things that many of you can do—such incredible things, actions, and abilities, all worthy of fantastic delight. But I've seen terrible things as well. Horrid creatures and actions, many of which I had never wished to encounter."

Her words caused the room to go silent.

"I have protected people and creatures, fought, healed, and housed those who have had nothing left. You claim to protect the same beings, the same creatures, and humans, but you look at me in disgust?"

The silence was broken when Dennon spoke up. "You dare to judge us, girl?"

Amanda turned to him, poised and steady, and replied, "The same as you are judging me. But I am willing to see what you can do to change that. Prove me wrong."

Dennon stood suddenly and hastily fired lightning toward Amanda, the flash and sound stunning many in the chamber. To his disappointment, as the light subsided, Amanda was still standing before them, her wooden ring glowing brightly, its light bringing the fairy representing the Grove before her to inspect the ring, who then gave a nod before returning to her place beside Brentwood.

Dr. Brentwood spoke. "Such a charm cannot protect you every time, my dear."

Amanda stood tall. "It never did so in the past." Holding the ring up she wondered, "This is new; why would it do it now?"

Amanda watched as the fairy whispered to Dr. Brentwood, who smiled.

"You have, in under a day, become involved with the Raven Hunters, been struck by a sleeping bolt, and casually walked from a safe house back to your apartment. Is that not true?"

Amanda nodded.

"If we were to ask, you would have time to decide. This is something not to be taken lightly."

Amanda looked to the floor in thought, "I wanna finish school. My artwork, a career; do I want to do this?"

Dr. Brentwood approached her. "We have not made you an offer yet, but it is something to think about."

Amanda looked all around. "Yes, I'd have to think about it."

She could see Dr. Claire straining not to smile. "Then, for now, we only ask that you try and keep yourself out of the affairs of the Circle for the moment."

Dr. Claire turned, giving a gentle bow toward the others at the large table. "I nominate Lord Cale to be my substitute for this meeting. I trust you will allow him the same courtesies as such."

From deep within the darkness around they heard, "Agreed . . . we agree, that is satisfactory."

Cale sat in the chair where Claire had before tapping the mallet on the stone. "I accept. I'm sure the others understand the situation, and I'm sure Amanda would not want to be burdened with the affairs of this council—for now."

Dr. Claire smiled, gave a nod to Cale, and gently pulled Amanda away, whispering, "Come, we should get you out of here before some of them try and roast you."

"I'm not afraid of any of them!" Amanda shot back quietly as Colleen joined them.

"I know, dear, but I don't think any of them know that," Dr. Claire said as they entered the darkness of the hallway, heading back to her office.

When those who betray the trust of the innocent walk through the world. We are the ones who make their steps disappear from the sands.

-Shannon Delf (Raven Hunter)

Chapter Seven
Hunter's Mistake

After returning from the Great Hall, Amanda remained true to her word. She stayed too interested in school and her artwork to be concerned with what the Raven Hunters were doing—even covering for Shrive when she didn't show up for class. Altogether, the rest of the semester was quiet.

Things were normal, at least as normal as Amanda was used to. There was little to no activity around campus as it would pertain to magic. She and Shrive had become good friends; of course, Gabriella was always by her side. And as per usual, things would break or move while she was around, the happenings making even Colleen concerned, swearing she sensed magic, but it was subtle.

On one of their weekly visits to the Italian restaurant, Tyler noticed Amanda when he arrived. He tried getting her attention, but the place was so busy he never made it to her before she left. It took several minutes before he finally got his order and headed to his car, hoping to run into them again.

"What do you mean we're out of gas?" Amanda whined.

"I forgot to fill it up, all right?" Gabs shot back. "I didn't want to be late. We could have taken your car."

Shrive laughed, "No, we couldn't, remember?"

Her words making Gabs smile, "Oh yeah, that's right; someone put the washer fluid in the wrong tank," before looking at Amanda, who was not amused by her reminder.

Then Gabs started to laugh. "I'm messing with you! I hope your car gets fixed. It's much bigger inside."

Shrive shifted in the back seat as if trying to extricate herself from a trap. "Yeah, I'm with her on that."

Amanda faced forward. Gabs had always been good with mechanical things, and she brought up the one time Amanda messed up her car.

"Hey, everything's good. There's a station about a quarter-mile away. We'll see if we can get some gas and head there. Everything will be fine," Gabs said.

Shrive said, "I'm for that. I need to stretch my legs. It's cramped back here." But, as she then pulled the door handle and pushed, nothing happened.

Gabs looked back. "Yeah, been meaning to fix that. It only opens from the outside."

Shrive cursed as she rolled the window down, almost falling out of the back as she reached around and pulled the handle from the outside and the door opened. But Shrive never touched the ground. Instead, she balanced herself on the step of the door using only one hand. Amanda noticed Gabs looking back and took a sip of her tea.

"Wow, Shrive, good save; you're like a cat or something."

Amanda started to choke, spitting tea all over herself.

"And I think Mandy needs a bib," Gabriella added, laughing.

Amanda grumbled, but joined her friend's laughing as she pulled herself out of the car.

While they were walking, Shrive noticed two people running toward them. Squinting her eyes she said, "It's Luke and Cayden," before yelling, "Hey, you guys out for a run?"

Amanda watched as the two jogged toward them and she unconsciously made sure she didn't have tea still all over her.

Gabriella looked at Amanda, asking, "Who's Luke and Cayden?"

Amanda shrugged. She didn't know them personally, but she'd met Luke when she was in the meeting hall.

As the two handsome men got closer, she remembered Luke and turned to Shrive. "Oh, *that* Luke and Cayden," making Shrive give a broad grin.

They talked for a while. Luke and Cayden accompanied them to the gas station and were willing to carry the gas can back for them. Amanda commented at the tattoo of the flying raven on Luke's forearm. On the way back, Shrive noticed Amanda was taking a liking to Luke, but also noticed that Cayden seemed interested as well.

This girl doesn't have any magic, but she's got something, Shrive thought, a bit jealous.

Then Amanda asked Luke, "How do you two know each other?"

"Well, we're rav—I mean, we work in the same office."

Shrive glared toward him sternly, making Gabriella laugh and say, "I thought you were going to say rave. Oh, that'd be cool. Go dancing, hang out, loud music."

They all laughed and were generally having fun as they headed back to the car.

* * *

Tyler was heading back toward campus when he passed them. He slowed, seeing them coming back with the others.

Ha, guess they ran out of gas. Maybe they need some help. But who are the guys they're with?

Tyler had been chasing Amanda since they met; he had always wanted to be friends with someone famous.

Tyler slowed, turning his car around to see if they needed help. He found himself driving past them and had to turn around again. As Tyler pulled up behind their car, a sudden darkness blocked his view. In a panic, he slammed on his brakes. Rolling down his window, his sight became engulfed with a fog that coated everything. He got out of the car and started walking toward where he saw everyone last. As he moved, his footsteps sounded muffled, but then he froze, noticing several flashes in the distance before him. Fearing the others were in trouble, he decided to investigate.

"Whoa, where'd this fog come from? I can't even see the car anymore!" Gabriella stated.

Amanda looked around; she had never encountered anything like this. When she looked toward Shrive, she could see a stare of concern in her feline friend's eyes.

The mist continued to surround them and when she turned to see where Luke and Cayden were, she heard Cayden say, "Fade wall, keep your eyes open."

There was a bright flash that stung her eyes and several loud bangs. Amanda knew what the sound of a wand firing was like, and she readied herself for a fight. Within moments, streaks of light whizzed past her. Amanda could see each ribbon wrap around the others. Shrive was first, then Gabriella. The one aimed at her dissipated, with Amanda seeing the fairy ring glowing beneath her shirt.

Amanda was ready as a dark figure came rushing toward her, but felt the impact as whoever it was took them both to the ground. She rolled and stood quickly, before feeling the pain in her shoulder. Amanda turned to see the person who ran into her gasp and cough as if the wind were knocked out of her. A few moments passed before she watched the figure raise her hood and suddenly disappear, only to reappear next to Shrive, who was struggling to untangle herself. There were several louder bangs, and Shrive and the others were secured even further.

Amanda focused on the direction of the lightning and was finally able to make out a figure in the fog. Then the hooded woman yelled, "All right, I give up! You're gonna hurt someone, you moron!"

"Selese!" Shrive yelled angrily. "Is that you? What did you do? Who is attacking us?"

Amanda rushed over to where Selese stood. "Selese, do you know who's attacking us?"

Selese pulled away. "No, I've never met him before. I thought I knew all the hunters."

The figure chasing her faded from the fog, becoming visible. Amanda could see his face only in the shadow of his hood, and his eyes focused on her.

"Who the hell are you?" the man asked, not recognizing Amanda. He pulled out a wand and tried to secure her, only to have the spell bounce back toward him.

He aimed the wand again and Amanda said with a smile, "I've faced sorcerers before," and she rushed forward, snatching the wand from his hand. She reveled in the look of confusion as she broke the wand before him.

"You shouldn't be able to do that," he said and held up a small crystal, which did nothing.

"That should have nullified your power." The man looked at Amanda, confused. "Everyone here has magic, except you. You're human. You're not one of them."

Amanda stepped toward him. He scurried back as she said, "Leave them alone."

The man used another spell but again watched it disperse before her. Amanda stood unmoving.

He looked on in disbelief. "You have protection; nothing magic can harm you. You're a FOF."

Amanda looked at him. "Do you know what it means?"

The man replied, "You're a friend of Fairies. A human protected by magic."

While Amanda kept him busy, Luke and Cayden finally freed themselves and rushed to stand beside her. "Who are you, and why are you attacking us?" Luke demanded as he looked at the man's face.

"Ken, what the hell are you doing?" Cayden asked.

The man looked at them. "Luke, Cayden, what are you doing here?"

Luke removed the man's hood. "Ken, what the hell! Why'd you attack us?"

The man held up the small crystal. "Someone was using magic here; there's no magic allowed in this area, Circle's rules, remember?"

Amanda interrupted, "Who's Ken?"

Cayden replied, "He's one of us; a new guy, actually. Don't know why he's off on his own, though."

Selese heard them arguing and hurried to free herself from her bonds. She changed her size and slipped out of the restraints.

With a wave of his hand, Ken cleared the fog from around them and Luke looked over to see Colleen and Gabriella on the ground. Selese was caught pulling up her hood.

"Um, I was just trying to get home faster," she said, hoping someone would believe her.

Luke laughed, "I'm sure it's nothing, Ken. We're here, Selese is here, and, um . . ."

Amanda pulled Gabriella from the ground before pulling off the magic bands restraining her. She was focused on her friend before noticing everyone staring at them.

"You know, I've had some weird falls, but glowing bands of energy?" Gabriella said.

Amanda remained silent, looking frightened toward her best friend. "You all right?"

Gabriella nodded before looking around at the others, all staring. "Magic, huh? Didn't think it existed."

Amanda looked toward Shrive. "Look, I'm sure it was just special effects, right? From the theater group?"

Colleen thought to herself, *Good cover story. What are we going to do if she doesn't believe it?*

There was silence before Gabriella looked at her friend. "It's all real, isn't it?"

Amanda stepped back, and Colleen felt her heart sink.

"All the stories you've told me, the adventures in those books. How many of them are real?" Gabriella asked softly.

"Gabs, I don't know if it's a good idea . . ." Amanda warned.

Her friend looked at everyone, stopping on Ken. "You said everyone here had magic."

Ken held up the crystal. "Well, everyone except her."

Luke put his hand over the crystal. "Shut up, Ken."

Cayden pulled the crystal from his hand. Gabriella rushed over, grabbing the crystal from him, and it glowed brightly, making her ask in a terrified tone, "Then why is this glowing when *I'm* holding it?"

Gabriella rushed back to Amanda, handing her the crystal. Amanda reluctantly took it, and the gem was again dormant. When Gabriella took it back, it again glowed brightly.

"All my life I'd had bad luck, things always went wrong. That was until you became my friend." She then hugged Amanda.

"I'm your best friend, Gabs. You know that," Amanda said with a tear in her eye.

As Gabriella pushed away she said, "Then tell me why this is glowing, please."

Amanda took a breath, glancing toward Colleen. "Maybe you should tell her; I'm new to all this secrecy," she said, then looked to Luke, and could see Colleen shaking her head.

The air remained silent, only broken when Selese spoke up. "For Pete's sake, you're all such wimps. Just tell her!"

Colleen shot back a glare of anger, which Selese dismissed.

"No one? Fine, I'll say something," Selese said as she walked up to Gabriella, taking the crystal from her. It glowed a bright amber color.

"I have magic as well, oh my, what a surprise," Selese said in a sarcastic tone.

"Not the time, Selese," Luke warned.

"When would it be time, hunter? She just found out she's one of us. She has magic. I say, tell her everything. Let her decide."

Everything again fell silent.

"What magic do you have, Selese?" Gabriella asked.

Selese turned to see the innocence and genuine wonder in the woman's eyes.

"Me? Well, I . . . I . . ." Selese stuttered before pulling up her hood. "I can walk through shadows. So can Colleen."

"I'm going to kill you, Selese!" Colleen yelled.

"Why? For telling the truth?" Selese shot back, and pointed the crystal toward Colleen. Gabriella watched as it glowed a bright blue.

"Why is it a different color?" Gabs asked.

"It's because she"—he indicated Selese—"was involved with dark magic. The color indicates a possible danger," Luke told Gabriella.

Selese turned, giving him an angry stare. "Danger? Do you have any idea what I've had to go through?" She then threw the crystal at him, missing as Cayden deflected it.

"She should find out what she is—what she *truly* is. This whole thing about magic and non-magic secrecy sucks."

Selese again turned to Gabriella. "Not knowing, did this to me." And Selese turned herself into a copy of Gabriella.

"You can shapeshift?" Gabriella exclaimed. "Can I shapeshift?"

Amanda stood by. "I have no idea; this is still all new to me too."

Selese approached Gabriella. "She told you stories of her adventures and you believed her, right?"

Gabriella nodded. "I wanted them to be true."

Selese walked back with a smile. "You see? She would want to know. Instead, you hunters stop all that."

Gabriella looked around. "Hunters? What hunters?"

"The ones who hunt those of us who break the rules. Those hunters," Selese said, pointing toward Luke, Cayden, and Ken.

"But what about Amanda?" She turned to her friend. "Are you one of them?"

Amanda didn't know how to answer. She had thought about joining, but now with everything that was happening, she had to reconsider.

"They asked her, but I have a feeling she said no," Selese said.

Gabriella turned to Amanda. "Did they ask you?"

Amanda smiled, "Sort of, nothing official. But, I got to see their secret lair."

"Amanda?!" Colleen yelled.

Gabriella started laughing, "Oh, my gosh, you have the strangest adventures, Mandy. I wish I'd been there."

"Yeah, probably would have had to pull you out of one of the meetings or something," Amanda said, laughing.

Selese smiled, seeing these two friends laughing. "Now that's something. What are you hunters going to do now?" Selese said, pointing to Amanda and Gabriella. "You'd have to take both their memories to fix this. And I don't think your magic is going to work on Amanda, since nothing seems to so far."

"I don't know, Selese. I don't have a clue as to what to do here," Luke admitted.

"What do you think, Gabs; want your memory erased? That's what they do when you get out of line," Selese said.

"We don't even know if her memory *can* be erased," Colleen said. "We don't know what else she is yet. We might not be able to."

Selese picked up the crystal; it again shone a bright amber color. "Then maybe she should. Maybe you should help her find out what else she might be."

Selese's demeanor became angrier and saddened. "Maybe if she knows what she is, then she would make better choices."

The dark anger in Selese's eyes turned to true sadness as she turned to Colleen. "Maybe if I'd known what I was, this wouldn't have happened to me." Selese pointed to her heart as she turned back into herself before pulling her hood over her head and disappearing into the darkness.

Colleen felt her heart break. She never knew how much the wraith mage hurt Selese. Now she was regretting thinking she had always been bad.

A few moments went by before Amanda wiped tears from her eyes. "She has a point. What are we going to do about this?"

Luke looked at her. "I don't know, it's just . . . Colleen, can you track Selese?"

"She just left, so I should be able to. It's easier with Shrive along," Colleen replied.

"Cayden, Ken, you go with them. I'll work things out here," Luke said.

Within moments, they disappeared into the shadows.

"What about Gabs?" Amanda asked.

Luke walked over. "I don't know. But if she really wants to find out, I can bring her in to see the magistrate. They'd be able to tell you."

Gabs smiled, looking to Amanda. "When could I find out?"

Luke touched a symbol on his arm. "We could go now, if you like. We could take the fast way. Of course, I'll have some explaining to do."

Amanda nodded. "It's your choice, Gabs."

Gabs looked at him. "Okay, let's find out. I hope it's something cool. But, what about my car?"

Luke laughed, "We'll come back for it. Let's put some gas in it first." Within a moment, the car appeared nearby, the fog dissipating even more as Luke pulled the charm from his pocket. After filling the tank, Luke put the can in the trunk.

"Maybe we shouldn't leave it here," Gabriella said.

Luke sighed, "Okay, maybe we should drop it off on campus before heading to see the magistrate." Amanda and Gabriella nodded at the same time, making Luke laugh, and as he said a few magic words, the three, and the car, disappeared.

* * *

Unknown to them, Tyler had seen and heard everything. In a daze of disbelief, he walked to where they had been standing. "What the hell is going on here? People shapeshifting, disappearing, like magic?"

He almost lost his balance spinning around to see where everyone had gone and as he regained his equilibrium, he saw something glittering in the sand. Tyler dug the crystal from the ground and it glowed a dim amber color as he held it. Tyler seemed almost entranced as the fog now dissipated completely and he stood only a few feet from his car. He smiled, "Of all the things I've learned, I find out that magic is real."

The remaining darkness could not contain the laugh that escaped Tyler's lungs. And as he drove off, the night was the only witness to his words, "This is going to be so much fun."

When all that can move becomes surrounded, a choice must be made. There is nothing but intentions in all of life, all of existence, and all of magic. This is the power we all hold and protect.

- Sienna Russell

Chapter Eight
That's a Surprise

Luke had some explaining to do when he arrived with Gabriella. Amanda wasn't a problem; she was already known to the Circle. He explained what had happened, and Ken was led away, presumably for punishment. Although Luke suspected what was going to happen; he'd seen it before when other Raven Hunters had made severe mistakes. As a hunter, you take an oath to protect all, magic or not, and to do so with secrecy. That means if it isn't safe or the appropriate time to act, you wait. You report the situation to the Circle and the head magistrate. You cannot operate without authority. And that was precisely what Ken had done; he acted at any cost to stop someone who was using magic outside the safe area. Amanda stayed with Gabriella the whole time. They overheard Luke talking with Cayden when he arrived. She heard him say, "Looks like we'll be looking for a new trainee."

She was going to ask, but was more concerned with her best friend. Gabriella had just found out she has magic and was beginning to have second thoughts.

"What if it's something bad? What if I'm a monster or something?" Gabriella worried as she waited for the magistrate to decide how to proceed.

Amanda was also concerned. She had fought magic before, good and bad, but this was all new to her. There was so much she didn't understand. Amanda yawned and stretched; it had been a few hours since they'd arrived and it was almost midnight, according to her phone. Thankfully, it was Friday night, and none of them had classes tomorrow.

"How long do you think they'll make me wait?" Gabriella asked.

Amanda shrugged, but Luke answered her. "It should be soon; they haven't had to use the chamber in a while. It takes some time to power it up."

Amanda stood, stretching again. "Have you ever seen it working?"

Luke shook his head, telling her he joined them well after it was last used. Most people don't need to. "If someone becomes a problem, they usually make them forget."

Amanda didn't like that; it didn't give the person a choice. She was about to say something when the door to the chamber opened and a small light floated from the large doors.

"Oh my gosh, is that a fairy?" Gabriella yelled, jumping up. Amanda grabbed hold of her friend. She knew from experience that most magical beings didn't like to be tackled.

The light quickly flew toward them before stopping and laughing at Amanda barely holding her friend back. "Sorry, she's just excited."

The fairy flew before Gabriella and bowed. "This one is feisty and has no fear. So strong and mighty, we'll see what we have here."

Moments later, Dr. Brentwood walked through the door. "Ah, Amanda, meddling in our affairs again?"

Amanda stood. "Actually, I was brought into this because one of your people acted recklessly. Don't blame this on me. And besides, she's my best friend."

The doctor looked over her glasses toward Luke and Cayden. Amanda turned to see both of them looking away as if in trouble.

Dr. Brentwood walked up to Amanda. "I heard the report. One of them messed things up. Your friend wasn't even on our watch. If she does have magic, I'm sure it's minimal at best."

Gabriella looked at her and hastily said, "But it might be something good, right?"

Dr. Claire kept her demeanor and calmly turned to Gabriella. "Maybe. But you should not be so eager to find out." The doctor seemed to look around Gabriella into the room. "You showed no signs of any abilities, and you could have gone your entire life without knowing."

"Ah, well . . ." Amanda started.

Her statement caused the doctor to close her eyes in frustration. "Miss Supp, why do I have a feeling you're about to tell me something I don't want to hear?"

Amanda paused before telling her about how she met her friend, mentioning that there was a book that fell on Gabriella, and Amanda went to see if she was all right. The doctor listened, and her stare became more introspective as Amanda went on. When Amanda said, "There's always things moving or falling when she's around. You just get used to it," the doctor sighed heavily and looked at the fairy floating nearby.

"If her abilities are that prominent, then that means we missed her."

Amanda stood in front of Gabriella. "What do you mean, missed her?"

Dr. Brentwood placed her hand on the door as if supporting herself. "We've known about you, and your friends Linda and Ron, for some time. In fact, we've known about them longer than we have you."

Amanda reeled back, stunned by the doctor's statement. "I don't understand. You've known about them, how?"

The doctor turned to Amanda. "As you know, there are many magical creatures in the world. Some all magic, some part. Not all of them friendly." She paused, looking toward Gabriella. "Are you sure you want to find out?"

"Yes!" Gabriella yelled. "I want to know. How do I know if something like what happened to Selese will happen to me?"

The doctor became concerned. "You know what happened to Selese? How do you know what happened?"

Amanda stepped in. "We don't know *exactly* what happened, but whatever it was, it hurt her. I don't want something like that to happen to Gabs."

Dr. Claire shifted her weight and looked again into the room; she gave a subtle smile. "We'll have time to talk about your friends and Selese a little later. For now, if you're sure?" The doctor paused, looking at Gabriella.

Gabriella stepped forward. "Yes, I'm sure."

Dr. Brentwood motioned for them to follow. "Good, then we'll get you settled and figure out what to do from there."

As they entered, the light brought into view a large crystal. It was like a rainbow of energies swirling inside. Around it was a ring with crystals of different colors, some showing markings that Amanda couldn't understand. She pointed at one she recognized.

"That's fairy writing," she said, rushing over to see what it meant, and started to laugh when she read it.

"What does it say?" Dr. Brentwood asked.

"What, you don't know what it says?" Amanda asked.

The doctor shook her head. "It says *fairy*, doesn't it?"

Amanda was about to tell her what it said but could see Alicee floating behind Dr. Claire shaking her head and giving a wink. Amanda shook her head. "Sorry, I've been asked not to tell you. But it does say *fairy*, sort of."

The doctor turned to see Alicee giggling next to her. "I see. I think we'll have to see if we can translate it better later," she said, looking at Alicee over her glasses. The fairy merely looked innocently back at her.

Dr. Brentwood sat at the controls of the machine. Its glass-like surface glowed in different colors. "Well, if you're ready, shall we begin?"

Gabriella nodded and asked what she needed to do. The doctor told her to touch the crystal panel next to her and wait until the device was finished. When Gabriella asked how long it would take, all Dr. Brentwood said was, "You never know, it really depends on the energies in you."

The doctor tapped the display before her and all the crystals began to glow. When the screen that Gabriella touched lit, they heard her say, "That tingles."

"Does that mean anything?" Amanda asked as she approached the doctor. But the doctor didn't react.

"Whoa, this is really weird, I'm all tingly. You should try this, Mandy," Gabriella said.

Amanda stood next to the doctor. "I guess that means it's working."

The doctor looked briefly at Amanda. "It's not supposed to tingle; in fact, you're not supposed to feel anything."

"What? You have to stop it then." Amanda became concerned.

"Your friend will be fine, but looking at the readings, I have a feeling that she has multiple magic in her. That may be why she is feeling the sensation." The doctor thought, remembering when Selese had a similar reaction when scanned.

"You're not sure if it will harm her, are you?" Amanda said.

"Look, several of the crystals are lighting up. I have only seen that a few times before," Dr. Brentwood said in amazement.

Amanda became interested in what was happening, but still worried about her friend.

"I've never seen these so bright before," the doctor whispered, making Amanda ask what she meant.

"Amanda, the Circle has been around for a very long time. And we rarely come across something we haven't encountered. Your friend seems to be one of them."

When Amanda asked what she meant, the doctor pointed to more than ten of the crystals lit brightly. "We have come across others with multiple energies, but there is always a dominant one. She has several, and all very strong. I've never seen anything like this before."

Amanda looked at her friend, then back to the doctor. "So, what does that mean?"

The doctor tapped the display and the machine started to shut down, but as it did, several crystals around the main one remained lit.

"She has Elf, Banshee, Dryad, Korrigan, and even—"

The doctor was interrupted by Amanda. "And fairy!"

"Yes, even fairy. And very strong." The doctor turned to look at Gabriella, who was looking back at them. When Amanda turned she started to laugh, seeing her friend's hair standing up like it was charged.

"What? What's wrong?" Gabriella asked, her voice hinted of fear.

Dr. Brentwood kept her composure, trying to hold back a laugh as well. She had never seen anyone have this sort of reaction to the machine before. "My dear, I'm sure we can get a comb or brush for you if you like."

Gabriella turned to look at her reflection in the crystal behind her. She smirked, trying to push her hair down before laughing. "Mandy, I'm glad you brought me here. You sure have the strangest adventures!"

The doctor motioned for Alicee to help Gabriella as the doctor tapped Amanda's shoulder. "It was good that you ran into Selese, and brought your friend here. Who knows what someone would have done if they'd found out about her?"

The Feather has been in the shadows for too long. With our resolve, our leadership and our power, we will make the world as it should be.

- Paul Vikander's dying words

Chapter Nine
The Hunter and the Thief

Many voices were heard arguing but were interrupted by the sound of a gavel on stone. As the room fell silent, Dr. Claire Brentwood started to speak. "As you all know, the *Effigy of Tarnus* was returned after being taken from the archives."

"That damn thief of yours should be rotting in a dungeon somewhere!" a voice in the crowd yelled.

"That'll be enough. The criminal is under guard, and even though her reasons for taking the statue are unknown, we feel that she is truly sorry for her mistake."

Again, arguing could be heard among the others in the theater, many defending Selese, others demanding her blood. Dr. Claire sighed as she peered over at Cale. He sat forward, staring into the darkness of the room. She knew he was trying to decide what to do with his adopted daughter. Their relationship was no secret, but Selese's actions were now weighing on them all. *I'm with you, love. I wish they could see the good in her.*

Dr. Claire looked around the room as the guild's master of arms walked in. He walked with a substantial presence, yet his feet never made a sound across the cobbled floor.

"Any trouble with the patient, Tom?" Cale asked with more concern about the girl than present affairs.

"No, Lord Cale, she is secure. Even if she eludes the guards, she would not be able to leave the Sanctuary."

His words put Cale to ease, at least somewhat. The hunter still carried a burden of what to do with his daughter. He yet didn't know the reason she took the statue. She had mentioned she needed money, but he had helped provide for her, she should have had enough. *What was her real motive?*

He was brought back from thought when someone mentioned that the girl mentioned the Broken Feather was interested in the icon. But it had no purpose; at least that's what most thought. Cale, like the master of arms, knew otherwise. The likeness of Tarnus was what remained of the wraith mages that ruled centuries ago.

"May I suggest to the council that we place the statue in a more secure location? Perhaps in the Forge," Tom said loudly for all to hear, making Cale nod.

"Secure it in the Forge. We'll deal with 'our thief' shortly," Cale said with disdain.

"I'm not sure you are equipped to deal with the girl, Lord Cale." Dennon spoke forcefully.

Cale sat up and calmly asked, "And why is that, Dennon?"

"The girl came to you. She told only you that the Broken Feather was interested in the icon. She also mentioned something else when speaking with you. Would you care to share that with the rest of us?" Dennon then stood silent, awaiting an answer.

Cale smiled and gave a slight sigh. "No, I will not share what she said with you. It has no bearing on the situation."

"Then what was the reason for the theft, Lord Cale? Can you at least tell us that?" Dennon shot back.

Cale leaned back, his chair making an audible creak as he did. "No." His statement brought a murmur to fill the room around them.

"And why not?" Dennon demanded.

Cale took a breath. "Because she has yet to share that with me."

Dennon smiled as he looked around the room. "If my history is correct, Tarnus was a geomage, was he not?"

"What does that have to do with this situation?" someone from the room asked.

Dennon returned his eyes to Cale, stating, "Yes, Lord Cale, would you be able to enlighten us?"

Cale furrowed his brow and leaned his chin on his intertwined fingers for support, "Where are you going with this, Dennon? The council has wasted enough time today."

Dennon put his hands in the air. "But you only seem to want to protect the icon. And weren't you apprenticed under a geomage? You would know more of why the Broken Feather would want with the statue."

Cale leaned back. "Are you implying that I'm part of the Broken Feather?"

"Is that an admission of guilt, Lord Cale?" Dennon accused.

Cale laughed, "Not at all, Dennon. I'm no more a part of the Broken Feather than you are. I'm more interested in what and why my daughter has done this, so I can only laugh at your accusation. Besides, I'm only interested in putting the relic somewhere until we find out everything."

"I have served this council most of my life, and I—" Dennon was cut off when Cale spoke.

"Dennon Fierst, you have served this council with honor and integrity for some time. Although your methods can be a bit harsh, I am aware of the relationship I have with my daughter and her history. But her defying one of the Broken Feather is an action I can trust."

Dennon looked around, hearing the comments about the girl returning the statue to prevent the Broken Feather from getting it. He knew in his mind that any further questioning would start to bring reprisal.

"Yes, Lord Cale, you're right. I was merely thinking of the safety of the council." Dennon now sounded more reserved.

"Noted, Dennon." Dr. Claire interrupted Cale as he was about to speak. "Maybe we should return to the other business at hand."

Many agreed, and they again debated the council's agenda, none noticing that Dennon had walked out of the room, only to disappear into the shadows.

* * *

In the infirmary, Selese sat staring out the window, its glass covered by a field to prevent her from leaving. She smiled as she walked toward the door. Opening it, she attempted to walk through, only to feel her hands held inside the room. She stopped, noticing glowing rings of energy preventing her from leaving. Her body was outside, but her hands remain stuck within the room. She tried changing size, and watched in fascination as the rings mimicked the size. They remained the same distance from her wrists. After trying several times, she reentered the room and placed her hand in the doorway.

"Well, well, well, Tom, you've learned a few new tricks. I'll have to see if I can steal them from you; this could come in handy," Selese muttered with a smile.

As she admired the rings holding her captive, the floor before her darkened. She looked up to see Aaron Baskin, the one known as the blind guard.

"You're not trying to escape, are you?" Arron asked, his eyes seemingly staring off into the distance.

Selese smiled, "Actually, I was, but I can't."

Aaron smiled, "Tom's handiwork, right?"

"Yep." Selese headed back to her bed. "What can I do for you, Aaron?"

Aaron placed some food and clean clothes on the table beside her bed before returning to the doorway.

"Those are for you. Your other clothes were really torn up. I'll have your chest plate fixed soon." Aaron gave her a smile.

Selese held her hand to her chest, now realizing that her chest plate had been removed, making her suddenly felt insecure, and fear started to fill her mind. She pulled out the jacket Aaron brought and wrapped it around her.

She looked at Aaron. "I know you're not blind, Aaron, but how do you see where I am?"

The man pushed away from the door and back into the room. "Selese, I know you're afraid, and many are looking to imprison you for your actions. Why did you steal the statue?"

Selese curled further into the pillows, as if creating a wall around herself. "It's, it's personal. I just needed the money."

Aaron turned to look at her. "You should tell Lord Cale the reason. I know you won't tell me."

Selese placed her face into the pillow.

"You asked me how I can see you?" Tom whispered.

Selese nodded.

Aaron smiled, "A nod of inquisitiveness? That's good. But to answer, I can see the energy all around."

He bowed down toward her. "Even yours."

Aaron turned to exit. "Selese, you may have been touched by darkness, but that's not what I see. Your light is much brighter than you realize."

Selese felt warmed by his remark. "Thank you, Aaron. I needed that."

The man nodded, giving a smile before closing the door behind him. Selese looked at the rings as they faded from around her wrists. She still felt the warmth of Aaron's words and sighed heavily. Her entire life was changed when she was eleven, her family hunted, and in the end, she almost became a servant to those same pursuers. Since that day, and her survival, many took her as nothing more than a greedy fool. She had gone to the geomage, hoping he'd pay her for the energy she had. She had hoped to have enough so she could leave and go far away, far from being hunted. The geomage Jeffrey Britlan offered her that very opportunity, but as soon as she was restrained, he made his move.

His terrible voice once again echoed in her mind. "Elf, darkling, and fairy, your dark hair telling me which is most prevalent. I can use that for my purposes. So easy to take, and such wonderful energy."

Selese balled up her fists. She had been treated as a criminal ever since Aiden saved her life. All she wanted to do was be free from being hunted. Cale had even taken her in after Aiden's death. Unfortunately, the old geomage paid a heavy price in saving her. He was severely injured by the wraith mage while healing her. She watched the master protect himself and her while he worked. But in the end, he was exhausted, and so was Britlan. With no more magic and the last of his strength, she watched as the old man killed the wraith mage using his own hands. It was soon after that when Aiden succumbed to his injuries, and she had no way of repaying either him or Cale for their actions. That was, until now.

Selese lay back on the bed, her fists still tight as she pulled them to her chest. She let herself relax, hoping for a solution. And taking a deep breath, letting it out slowly, she calmed. *I'll give him what I have; maybe it'll be enough.*

* * *

In the dimly lit hall, a figure emerged from the shadows. Dennon removed his hood as he headed toward the sounds of short, high-pitched screams. He knew the music of a sylph being ripped from its ether.

"I hear that Tarnus has returned to his place of dishonor." The low voice carried from behind the wall of glass and wire.

"I fear our ruling lord will take to hiding Tarnus for the time being," Dennon responded.

A short man with white hair rose from his chair. "It doesn't matter. If there is no sun, the essence will start to emerge. The knowledge of the past will return on its own."

Dennon shook his head. "We need to act quickly. That damn thief threw our plans to take the Circle back months."

The white-haired man spoke. "Have you forgotten that Terrell being arrested set us back as well? I had to finish his work on the extraction methods."

Dennon nodded; he understood what the man meant. Raymond Terrell was the main authority on extraction of essences, and Dennon had just met the young woman who helped put that brilliant sorcercr away.

"That girl is here at the school. I had an unpleasant conversation with that troublemaker. I cannot believe that witch Brentwood is considering bringing her on as a Raven Hunter."

The small man removed his glasses and cleaned them; he looked unconcernedly toward Dennon. The hunter turned and tapped the glass to see if the creature inside was still alive. It never moved.

"That one had a good amount of energy and I was able to charge over a dozen staffs with it. Of course, they will only work for what I have made them for."

Dennon smiled, "That's good news, Jeffrey. Then perhaps all is not lost."

"Not so fast, Den. We would do best to wait until I have all four of the icons. Once I have all of the elements, we can use them to access the power of the Circle of Paragon," the man answered. "As for the girl and Dr. Brentwood, keep an eye on them. We do not want to bring any suspicion toward us yet."

Dennon gave a glance of annoyance, but knew the man was right. Without the elements, the secret of the Circle would be difficult to control. "It's too bad Brentwood has the key. It'd be so much easier to access the Circle without her to protect the chamber."

The small man laughed, "Remember, the power was passed to her, Den. She doesn't know how to truly access the power of the Circle."

Dennon nodded his head in agreement. Dr. Brentwood was a scroll witch; she was given the power because she had none of her own. The power of the Circle could only be gifted to those considered worthy by its current possessor, but not to anyone else.

The Raven Hunter smiled, again tapping the glass before him as he walked past the white-haired man. He stopped only to grab a small placard from the table.

"Paul Vikander? Is that what you're calling yourself?" Dennon asked.

"Yes, and I wish you would stop calling me by my former name. We wouldn't want anyone knowing that the head of the Broken Feather was still alive. Especially if Raymond said anything in his actions with that girl. After all, Jeffrey Britlan died when Aiden Hoff killed him."

Water and Magic are similar in nature. They are fluid, strong, and persistent. If not respected, you can drown in either.

- Donna Hessian

Chapter Ten
Something About Amanda

Amanda was surprised by her friend's reaction to what the machine found. She expected Gabriella to be in tears; instead, the opposite happened.

"I'm part fairy and elf? That is soooo cool! Can I jump through shadows?"

"Gabriella, you don't understand. This can be dangerous; in fact, I was hesitant to tell you. However, given recent happenings, we thought it best to inform you of your other attributes," Dr. Brentwood said. "I would recommend that you keep things quiet about what we found."

"Why?" Gabriella asked.

"Because there are some who may try to take advantage of them. And to be very honest, they can be extremely dangerous," Dr. Claire replied.

Gabriella looked to Amanda to confirm what the doctor was saying. When Amanda told her about Dr. Terrell, Gabriella became concerned.

"Will they be coming after me?" Gabriella asked.

Dr. Brentwood shook her head. "We have not told anyone outside this room, except for my Lord Cale."

"Can you trust him?" Gabriella asked.

"I'm pretty sure I can. We've known each other for a very long time," Dr. Brentwood replied.

Gabriella looked at her with suspicion.

Dr. Brentwood smiled as she looked at Amanda. "Yes, I trust him; we have been . . . together for almost that amount of time as well."

There was a silence between them all for a few seconds before Dr. Brentwood said, "Now you know a secret about me. I figured it was only fair, since we should keep what we know about you quiet as well."

Gabriella looked to Amanda. "So, what should I do?"

Dr. Brentwood sat on a nearby chair. "You don't have to do anything. We would be happy if you joined us here at the Sanctuary, but you are free to follow your own life in any way you choose. We only want to let you know that we will be around if you need help. And I'm pretty sure Amanda would be as well."

Gabriella again looked to Amanda.

"Your call, Gabs. Not that you can do much about being part fairy. I'm sorta jealous."

Gabriella's smiled faded. "I'm not sure I want to stay here."

"I—we—understand. Most people go about their lives not knowing what you now know. But we are around to help if you need it," Dr. Claire said sincerely.

Gabriella stood up. "I'll let you know."

Tyler had put together a makeshift lab in one of the vacant rooms of the computer science building. It housed old hardware and servers from years before. Over the last few days, the young man was working with the crystal he had found. He discovered that when pointing it at people, it glowed. At least sometimes it did, which was confusing. The color also confused him. Why was it amber for him and a few others, while for most it was blue and white?

He had made several devices that could use the energy the crystal gave off. He didn't know why it worked, but for some reason, the more he used the crystal, the more familiar its use became to him. That knowledge both frightened and fascinated him.

The room filled with the sound of typing, but when it stopped, all that was heard was, "Let's see if this works."

Tyler plugged the crystal into a small box and closed the lid. He tapped his phone, opening an application that synced to the box.

"So far, it seems to be working!" Tyler's voice filled the excitement.

Pointing the box toward himself hesitantly, he looked to the screen of his phone. A series of numbers changed and printed themselves across the screen. When he turned it away, the flurry of data disappeared.

"It works?" he yelled before looking at the door to make sure no one heard him. "I can't believe it works. I'm a genius!"

He again turned the box toward himself and watched the numbers rise and fall. "Now if I can only figure out what these numbers mean."

The young man spent the remainder of the night refining his device. The next morning, Tyler decided to try using the device on others on campus. Most classes were ending, but he was staying for summer courses.

Unlike most, Tyler didn't want to return home; his new father didn't want him around. Tyler was all right with that, and he had been trying to leave since his parents divorced a few years ago anyway. He was happy his mother's new husband was willing to pay for school, even if Tyler had to use school funding as well. But those thoughts drifted from his mind as he held up the small box and used it to figure out what things were.

Tyler was so engrossed with his project he did not hear someone walk up behind him.

"Tyler, you staying for summer classes as well?" Amanda asked.

Her question startling him he spun around, making Amanda step back. Tyler took a deep breath, placing his hand to his chest.

"You scared me!" He hurriedly put the small box away.

"You were looking at your phone, weren't you?" Amanda said.

Tyler nodded; he could tell her that he knew she had magic but instead came up with a plan to find out more about it from her.

Tyler had been focused on his creation for the last few weeks. But was still at a loss to what the information he had learned meant. Remembering that Amanda and the others were involved, he decided to see if maybe she had some answers. He offered to treat to coffee, wanting to know more about what she knew. Although he did wonder why Amanda always drank tea. He was surprised when she seemed apprehensive when he inquired. Tyler then said, "No reason, I like coffee better. I was just making conversation."

Amanda nodded she understood. She had seen him with others around campus, but he always seemed to be on his own whereas she seemed to always have friends around; Amanda almost didn't have a moment of alone time.

Amanda sipped her tea as they sat in the coffee shop, they talked about their classes, how they thought they did for finals—generally decompressing from the hectic final couple weeks. But as they spoke, Tyler kept looking at his phone, and he seemed puzzled.

"What's wrong?" she asked.

Tyler looked up. "What? What do you mean?"

"Your phone; something happen?" Amanda asked.

Tyler told her that he was working on a new app for something and was trying to figure out why it was doing what it was doing. His explanation made Amanda put up her hands and laugh, "Sorry, not that good with computers; not my field."

They both laughed, but a thought did cross his mind. *Why is it so easy to talk to her?* He had followed her several times and used the crystal on those around her. When he noticed that others who never met her interacted, they all reacted the same. They trusted her. Yet when he used the device to detect magic, she had none. Tyler was about to ask her about the magic but both were startled by a thumping on the window. Amanda was surprised and spilled her tea.

They both rushed to grab napkins to clean up the mess and Amanda looked up to see Gabriella standing there mouthing, "Sorry," before Amanda motioned for her to join them.

"Sorry, didn't mean to scare you guys," Gabriella said as Tyler carried the soaked napkins to the trash, making Gabriella lean in and whisper, "Am I interrupting?"

The smile on her friend's face showed she knew what she meant. As Tyler returned Amanda said, "No, we were just talking about the app he is working on."

Tyler sat down but looked blankly toward Amanda.

Gabriella sat and asked, "Is it a game? I love games on my phone."

Tyler shook his head. He thought about what to say but then looked at the crowd around them. "Well, it senses electricity in the air. But it's not working the way I thought it would."

"It's not a game?" Gabriella seemed disappointed, but asked why it wasn't working.

Tyler absentmindedly took out the small box and showed it to them. "You see, it's directional. If I point it toward something, it shows all these numbers." He showed her the phone as he pointed the box outside. "But when I point it toward someone"—Amanda flinched as he pointed the small box toward her—"I don't read anything."

"So, maybe it's broken for people," Gabriella said.

Tyler shook his head. "Not for everyone. If I point it toward another person, it sometimes reads data."

Hearing that, Amanda suddenly had a concerned look. She watched as he pointed it at someone in the diner, and the numbers again seemed to stream across the screen.

"What do the numbers mean?" Amanda asked.

Tyler looked at his phone. "I don't know; that's what I've been trying to figure out. They seem to be all over the place."

Gabriella reached out and grabbed the small box from him. Tyler went to take it back, but when he looked at his phone, he could not believe the numbers it showed. Seeing Tyler engrossed in the app, Amanda took the box from her friend. Tyler looked up from his phone, seeing the numbers change.

"Well, I think it's a battery problem. It was getting hot when I was holding it," Gabriella noted.

Amanda noticed it was warm but seemed to be cooling as she held it. She handed it back to Tyler, who smiled when he looked at Gabriella. "It got hot when you held it?"

Gabriella nodded, and Tyler felt it cool to his touch when Amanda handed it back.

Tyler handed it back to Gabriella and took it back from her a few seconds later. The case was indeed warmer. He set it down on the table and took a sip of coffee.

Seeing the smile on Tyler's face, Amanda became increasingly concerned. She had found out about Gabs's background earlier, and now this. Her instincts again were screaming, making her ask, "What kind of energy does that thing measure again?"

Tyler smiled, "You know, you're right; it may be a battery temperature problem. I think I know how to change something."

Tyler grabbed his phone from the table and rushed out the door. He only paused to knock on the window. "Hey, thanks for the help. I'll be seeing you around!"

Gabriella waved to him as he walked away. "He seems like a nice guy."

Amanda nodded, but something about that box, and everything that had happened recently, including finding out about Gabs, caused Amanda to feel in her gut that what Tyler was working on wasn't going to be good for anyone.

There are times when a bird flies against the breeze. This is akin to life. The same wind that slows the bird can change the course of anyone, anything, even mountains themselves.

- Alex Pertu

Chapter Eleven
Family Get-together

"Amanda, Gabriella, I see you're both still on campus!" Dr. Brentwood called to the two as they walked toward their apartments.

"Yeah, we're both starting next week for the summer session, so it didn't make sense to head home. And especially since . . . you know." Amanda nodded toward Gabriella.

"Ah, yes. That," Dr. Brentwood agreed. She watched as Gabriella's eyes widened.

"Anyway, I was wondering if either of you have seen Shrive." Amanda shook her head. Gabriella seemed to be thinking about it but also shook her head. Amanda noticed that Dr. Claire became concerned.

"Haven't you heard from her?" Amanda asked.

The doctor shook her head. "I'm worried that something may have happened."

"We can look for her if you like," Amanda offered. But Dr. Brentwood's wits kicked in and she declined Amanda's offer. Although the girl did insist that it would be no trouble, given

Amanda's recent dealings with the Raven Hunters, she felt it best for Amanda to remain out of their business.

* * *

Claire waved to them as they walked away. She remained brooding on what may have happened to one of her top hunters, but her musing was interrupted by someone behind her.

"You're actually out of your office at this time of day? Wonder of wonders."

She turned and laughed, hearing Cale's voice. Even though that had been together for years, they kept things professional in public. Even the Circle had its misgivings of their romance from the start but allowed it, since both were powerful allies. But her mind was still focused on Shrive being missing.

"Cale, have you heard from Shrive?"

He nodded. "Yes, I asked her to look into something for me; why?"

"What? Have you heard from her recently?"

"Yes, I just spoke with her; in fact, she's on her way back."

"What was she doing?"

Cale looked at her. "I heard a rumor that the *Deluge of Yves* statue was missing, I had tracked it down to a small museum in Michigan. But she couldn't get a close look at it. Normally I'd ask Selese to go, and she's much better equipped to . . . snoop. But she's sort of tied up at the moment."

Seeing the bundle of clothes he had under his arm, Claire tugged on a corner amusingly asking, what he was carrying. Cale laughed, "Actually, it's for our troublemaker."

Claire looked away as if in thought, "Hmm, now which one would that be?"

Cale smiled, "I'm going to see her. You want to come along?"

Claire nodded; she had been worried about Selese since she returned with her armor shredded. *No one should have to endure that sort of horror.* Claire asked what he had; her lover showed her.

"It's a mix of titanium and gold, tougher than the one she had." Cale admired his own work. "It's lighter too. I can't imagine wearing something like that; it'd be pretty heavy."

"You spoil that girl, and you know that," Claire shot back at him, making him nod.

"She's been through a lot, and I don't care what others think about her, she's not evil." Claire knew what he thought about Selese, and she agreed with him; that's why she fought against the council's recommendation to imprison her in the dungeons. After all, why would she tell them she committed the crime and who was after the statue?

There was a brief silence between the two as they headed toward the Sanctuary.

"You know, I knew she had armor, but I have never seen her wear it," Claire noted.

Cale noted, "She's been wearing it since I took her in."

"How? Something like that would be so stiff and heavy. It can't be comfortable."

Cale stopped to look at the golden armor he held. "This is a mix of titanium and gold. Besides, she's a natural geomage; this is like putty to her."

Claire turned in amazement. "You never told me she could do that."

Cale looked at her. "What do you mean? I thought you knew. I mean, she was always bringing in rocks that seemed to be melted and leaving them on the table. You mean, you thought that was me?" The smile on his face was priceless.

"I never put it together." Claire started to blush in embarrassment.

Cale moved closer. "She's a damn good geomage." He again displayed the armor to Claire before tapping it. She heard it make a metallic sound. "It's like that for anyone else, but for her"—Cale then twisted and rolled the metal as if it was made of silk before it returned to its former state—"this is nothing but a piece of cloth."

Claire stared in amazement. She had known Cale was a geomage for the longest time, but now finding out that Selese was one; that was an astonishment.

Claire touched the armor. "Do you think she'll like it?"

Cale nodded. "You're welcome to join me and find out."

Claire placed her arm in his and said, "Then, kind sir, show me the way."

* * *

Inside the Sanctuary, Cale knocked on the door where Selese was staying. She only turned to acknowledge his entry. He could see her staring out the window, but she didn't seem to be enjoying what she saw.

"Thinking about escaping?" Cale asked.

Selese shook her head. "No, I've got nothing to wear, and I'm not leaving here without protection." She then tapped above her heart and returned her gaze out the window.

There were several seconds of silence before Selese said, "I know you're disappointed."

Cale placed the wrapped bundle on the bed. He watched Selese turn and look at Claire standing in the doorway before she sat on the bed. She touched the packet. "I'm sorry. I didn't know the Broken Feather wanted the icon. I wouldn't have taken it if I knew."

Cale sighed, "Then why did you take it?"

Selese looked at Claire. "Is she here for the same reason?"

Claire shifted from leaning on the doorway.

"Selese, she has every right to be here as I do," Cale said firmly.

"I guess she does," she replied, before turning to Cale.

Selese didn't miss the sudden smile on Claire's face as she moved inside the room. She watched Selese place her hand on the bundle of clothes and slide the armor from beneath.

"Don't worry; I'm not running this time. The Broken Feather knows I betrayed them. I'm not stupid. And it's not like I've ever had people trying to kill me before or anything."

Cale pushed the armor under her hand. "That's good to hear, but you still haven't told me why you did it. I mean, you haven't stolen anything in such a long time. I know you've been working two jobs. Tell me—tell us—what's going on."

Selese placed her hand on the armor. "If it weren't for the armor you made me, I wouldn't be alive. Those cursed things would have killed me for this." She motioned again to her heart.

"Selese," Claire started to speak, but when the girl's eyes met hers, she could see the sadness.

"Aiden died protecting me. You took me in when I had everything taken from me . . ." Selese's voice faded. But as she pressed down on the hard metal, it became like soft fabric. "You did so much for me, I didn't know how to repay you, and since Aiden's gone . . . I . . . ."

Claire felt tears starting in her eyes as Selese fought to speak.

"I only wanted to pay you back. I stole before realizing it was wrong. I was working those jobs to make as much as I could. I figured maybe if I paid you for the gold it cost to make my armor, that, I . . ."

Selese paused to regain her composure. "I finally realized that I'd never be able to repay you; I know I can't repay Aiden."

Claire sat down next to the girl and put her arm around her after wiping tears from her own eyes. Cale cleared his throat, fighting back his own. Selese looked to them both. "I really messed up this time. I'm going to have to watch my back more than usual."

Selese then stood and, picking up the armor, placed it over her head as if it were a fabric shirt.

"You make that look so easy," Claire said, making Selese smile.

As she pulled another shirt over the armor, she asked, "Did you find out what that girl Gabriella was?"

Cale suddenly became serious. "That's none of your concern."

Selese looked out the window again. "Did you know that Amanda thought my name was really cool? And to be honest, I can see why they're friends."

Cale looked puzzled, as did Claire.

Selese looked to them both. "Really? She has things move or break when she gets excited. Strange things happen when she's upset. She likes hanging out in forests and loves plants. Not to mention she's as hyper as a hummingbird on caffeine." She huffed at the two of them staring at her.

"Oh, please, can't you see? It's obvious to me she's part fairy." Selese then smacked her forehead. "Dammit, I'm rhyming again."

Claire started to laugh and Cale looked at her. "I'd forgotten about that."

Selese pointed at him. "Someone's gotta watch over that girl. I nominate me."

Claire looked to Cale. "She would be perfect for the job. But she'd have to keep a low profile. She also has her own back to watch."

Selese looked at Claire. "It's the perfect job, can't you see? Nothing to rob. Just watch a girl part fairy." Selese put her hands up in frustration. "Stupid rhyming."

Claire laughed, "I've never seen her like this, does it happen often?"

Cale shook his head. "Nope, only when she gets really excited or happy."

"It's not nice to make fun of people, Lord Cale. It shows that you're lower-class," Selese shot back with a smile.

Selese moved toward the door and was stopped when her hands became stuck.

"You're not going anywhere until Tom removes those restraints, and he's in class giving exams all day today."

Selese smiled, and with a flick of her wrists and some shapeshifting, Selese slid the restraints off. She twirled them on her finger above her head. "No worries, I figured out how to take them off hours ago. Let's go."

Selese walked out the door and started down the hall. Claire and Cale emerged from the room. "That's one tough girl we've got there."

Cale nodded. "Yes, she is. Let's hope she stays out of trouble."

There is more to leadership than power, and there is always more than most anticipate. A leader understands the power they hold. It can be given, taken, and misused like all things in life. You only have your conscience and your heart to show you how it should be used.

- Dr. Clair Brentwood

Chapter Twelve
How does it Work?

Tyler had returned to the lab and closed the cover on the small box holding the detector. When he turned it on, he was startled as what seemed like lightning jumped from the light on the table. He watched as a thin line of electricity stayed connected, and the light fought to remain lit.

"That's interesting."

He looked at his phone and the display showed 122, 60.

"What the hell is that supposed to mean?" Tyler griped.

He examined the small filament of energy connected to the light and touched it. His hand was in pain as he felt a shock.

"Stupid, stupid. Don't want to kill myself with this sh—" He paused, suddenly remembering he felt something similar when he touched the inside of his computer while it was still on.

"Wait, those numbers. This thing measures energy. It can't be voltage and frequency, can it? It can't be that simple?"

He grabbed a nearby meter and touched its leads to an open outlet. It read the same thing: 122 volts and 60 Hertz. Tyler then carefully turned the device and held it in his hand. He again pointed it at the lamp and was surprised at the result. This time there was no spark, but the reading was the same.

Then Tyler pointed it at himself, and several numbers came up. He recorded them before looking at the lamp again. He then pointed it at himself, and the same readings appeared. Tyler then started to laugh.

"This is more than a detector; it's like a computer! It's outputting data. Oh, this is incredible, it's a crystalline computer of some kind!"

He placed the box on the table and sat, covering his face with his hands. The only sound that could be heard was his quiet muttering. "I've got to figure out how this thing works. Why did it spark like that?"

Tyler placed his hand where the box lay and felt the surface. As he tapped it, he realized that it was made of metal. There were stories of Amanda's adventures. He remembered that iron affected magic, and the characters had used it several times to subdue creatures. But why was the box connecting to the electricity like this?

He inspected the table further; it was made of stainless steel, but a section of the table was dark and scuffed, almost as if someone had tried removing something from it. He took his phone and looked up what would discolor stainless steel, chuckling to himself. *If it stains, then it's not stainless.* He spent several minutes scrolling through his phone when he came across something.

"That's it, silver nitrate."

However, Tyler didn't know how to test for silver nitrate. But he had a thought; if silver was grounding the electricity, what would happen if he placed it on the table and pointed the box at himself? Tyler did just that.

Looking at his phone, the readings were all zero.

Tyler stood. He was happily excited at this discovery, and now he'd found a way to see if the readings were human-made or magic. "I can make this work. But where can I test it?"

* * *

Amanda was rummaging through her car; she had been searching for her sketchbook for almost twenty minutes. She couldn't find it in her apartment, and the back seat of her car was the only other place she could think of. She was focused, and hadn't noticed the figure walk up behind her.

"Everything all right?"

Amanda spun around, startled but ready to fight before seeing it was Shrive, who slowly placed her hands up and took a step back.

"Didn't mean to startle you."

Amanda took a breath. "Sorry, I'm trying to find something."

She mentioned to Shrive that she was working on some pictures for Ron's latest story, "An Apple Tree in the Forest." Shrive looked at her, puzzled.

Amanda took a moment. "It's about an apple tree that if you eat the fruit, it gives you the abilities of any animal you wish."

Shrive crossed her arms. "So?"

Amanda smiled, "And eventually, you turn into that animal." Amanda sighed, "Sounds like they are having fun without me."

Shrive rolled her eyes.

"Anyway, it was a cursed tree made by someone who likes animals more than people."

Amanda looked at Shrive, who seemed unimpressed by the story. But Amanda said, "Well, I guess you don't get it, since you're, um . . ."

Shrive raised her eyebrow, glaring at Amanda before Amanda said, "There's no way for me to finish that sentence in any good way, is there?"

They both started laughing. Shrive knew what she meant and was playing along for the moment. When she asked Amanda if she needed help finding the book, Amanda was happy to accept.

Within moments, Shrive covered her eye and spoke the same words she used when investigating the museum's theft. She looked up and down the car but was interrupted when Amanda tried touching her face. Shrive swatted her hand away, only to glare angrily at her friend.

"What? I want to see if it had a physical presence." Amanda pointed to the circle that looked like a monocle.

"Wait, you can see this?" Shrive pointed to the very same, making Amanda nod. Shrive shook her head and said, "Keep forgetting. You can see magic."

Amanda smiled, "Yeah, well, not like I've never encountered it before."

Shrive resisted laughing as she continued to search for the book. When she came across what looked like a silhouette next to the driver's seat, she asked, "Did you check between the seat and the console?"

Amanda turned, reaching into the vehicle, only to emerge with the lost book. She held it up, thanking Shrive for her help.

"Can I see the drawing?" Shrive asked. Amanda thought for a moment and reluctantly opened the book, making Shrive say, "You don't like people looking at your unfinished work?"

Amanda shook her head. "I'm not sure you're going to like it."

Shrive told Amanda that she loved reading the *Haunted Maples* stories. It's what got her to become a Raven Hunter. And when she saw the picture, Shrive was astounded at the detail of the drawing Amanda showed her. The tree, the woods, the person turning into a cat . . .

Then as Shrive looked closer, she turned to give Amanda a stare of annoyance. "Why is my face on the woman?"

Amanda looked around. "I have no idea what you're talking about. That is a random face on that figure." Amanda played innocent before starting to laugh. "Actually, I wasn't sure I was going to use you in there, but it's not like I've seen many cat-girls in real life."

Shrive looked at the picture again before smiling. "You know, I read your adventures and loved them. I had always wanted to be a part of them someday." She handed the book back to Amanda. "I guess it'd be fun to be in one of the stories."

Amanda smiled, "Thanks, I didn't want to have to redraw the character."

A few minutes went by as they talked. Amanda asked why she was there. As far as Amanda knew, Shrive lived off-campus, and classes were done for the semester.

"Actually, have you seen Selese?" Shrive asked.

Amanda hadn't seen Selese since that morning when she dropped by to say hello. She had meant to ask. For some reason, Selese seemed to be hanging around them both a lot more than she used to before.

The two continued to talk, and both realized that Gabriella wasn't around.

"I wonder. Maybe Gabs and she went somewhere together," Amanda said.

Shrive looked at her friend. "That's not good. You don't know Selese."

Amanda became worried and asked why. Shrive told her that Selese was a thief and not a very trustworthy person. But Amanda disagreed; she was able to read people fairly well, and there was nothing off about Selese to her.

"You're a very trusting person then."

Amanda nodded. But she did worry about Gabriella. "Why do you think she's bad?"

Shrive reminded her that she has no heart, that she sided with a wraith mage, was a thief, not to mention she can look like anyone.

"That doesn't make sense. From what I learned, Selese was tricked by the wraith mage. And the stealing, that's not something everyone hasn't tried at one time or another."

Shrive looked at her. "Steal? You've stolen things?"

Amanda rolled her eyes. "It's not like I'm doing it for a living. I did stuff when I was younger. Like toys, dolls, things like that. I usually felt bad and brought them back. It's not like I've never done anything like that ever."

Shrive continued to stare at Amanda, who was beginning to feel uneasy. "What? You've never taken anything?"

Shrive shook her head.

"You're kidding. You've never taken anything?" Amanda was surprised.

Shrive now looked at her friend with suspicion.

"Oh, for the love of . . . Not everyone's perfect, Shrive. I'm not a thief, and you have no reason to judge someone because you think they are bad," Amanda scolded her.

Shrive understood and relaxed. "Sorry, I've been finding bad people for most of my life. You're right. I'm sorry. Let's forget about it, okay?"

Both of them agreed. Amanda then said, "Maybe we should look for both of them."

Shrive agreed.

But after several minutes, they didn't know where to start, and their conversation came back to Selese, with Amanda asking, "Why did the wraith mage choose Selese?"

"Because of her energy."

"What energy, magic?"

Shrive replied, "Yes, the magic in her."

Amanda asked what was so special about the magic in Selese.

Shrive's only answer was, "You didn't know? Selese is like your friend."

"What?" Amanda yelled.

"Selese has multiple ancestries, including darkling, but mostly fairy," Shrive replied.

Amanda was astounded. She hadn't known that Selese was part fairy and other things. She now knew that it was more common than she had thought. It also explained the concern that Dr. Brentwood had when she told them. To Amanda, things were starting to make sense.

"Wait, you don't think someone would do something like that to Gabs?" Amanda was now very concerned.

Shrive shook her head. "No, she doesn't have any darkling. Also, now that she is known to us, the hunters will watch over her."

Amanda didn't like that answer. The thought of always being watched made a chill run through her. But as she thought about it, she muttered, "Hmm, two people who are part fairy. Where would they go?"

It was spring, but Gabriella's car was still in the lot. They weren't anywhere on campus. Then Amanda realized where there might be. "I think I know where they are."

When Shrive asked where, Amanda replied, "Well, I'm going to need your help with that. I'm not able to shadow-walk, yet."

Chapter Thirteen
Is This Magic?

Inside the Sanctuary walls, several large screens showed people all over the campus coming and going. The screens included the surrounding areas and safe houses. The long panel with gems and lights twinkled. For the most part, they were dark or glowing a whiteish-blue.

As one of the people stared down, not paying attention, one of those crystals turned a dark amber red. The light flickered for several minutes from white to red and back until the operator looked up and saw the last change. What the hell is that? Costa whispered before turning to another operator to confirm what he was seeing. Within a moment he hit a button and an alarm sounded in the hall where the Raven Hunters gathered.

Dennon had returned from meeting with the leader of the Broken Feather, his disappearance bringing several of them to question where he was. He only delayed their suspicion by telling them he was investigating the theft of the *Effigy of Tarnus* statue. He was the first to arrive at the station giving the alert.

Costa looked to his side as Raven Hunter approached, "Someone's using magic on campus again. I thought all the students had left for the week!" the man told Dennon.

The hunter sighed with almost a growl. "Do we know who the offender is?"

The man at the display shook his head, his pointed ears showing when he turned. "No, it's in one of the closed labs. Whatever or whoever it is, it's reading as very strong, but there's something odd. It keeps changing from light to dark magic. It may just be a crystal flaking out on us."

Dennon looked around. "Have you ever known one of the detection crystals to flake out?" His tone was annoyed.

The man looked forward. "No, sir. But we had something similar in the library a few hours ago. The team couldn't find anything to substantiate an investigation. But it flickered just like this, only much shorter. We thought the protection around the *Effigy of Tarnus* was failing, but it wasn't."

Dennon was becoming angry. "Was anyone told?"

"Yes, sir, we had several people check the library. The only thing they found were students studying. No activity, and the protection spells were at full strength."

Dennon rubbed his face. "All right, I'll deal with it. If it's something serious, I'll call for backup."

"Sir, I'll alert some of the others and have them on standby," the man told Dennon.

"No, let them be. I'll deal with the issue," Dennon said as he walked toward the Shadowed Hall.

Within seconds, Dennon appeared in the shadow of one of the walls of the academic building. He could hear a young man laughing, obviously excited at something he was doing. Dennon pulled out a detector crystal and it flickered, amber to blue and back again.

"What the hell?" Dennon looked toward the sound of the laughter. As he approached, he noticed that the light in the room flickered on and off. At first, he thought maybe it was just one of the students having some fun, but when he heard, "It works, I can't believe it works!" he had to investigate.

The old hunter approached stealthily. If it was something innocent, he didn't want to interrupt. Dennon had been a hunter for many years, during that time the world had changed. He had hoped long ago that things would have become easier, that he'd have made a difference. Many including the head of the Feather, seemed to him, to be too patient. Although, subtlety wasn't his style; he was becoming tired of working with Paul. Dennon preferred action, that was one reason he agreed to join the Broken Feather. However, he remembered what his mentor said about not bringing too much attention to himself or the Broken Feather. So, if this was something innocent, they would have a pass for today.

The hunter stopped outside the door before carefully looking around the corner. Off in the far side of the room, he could see the light flash and flicker. He could see a young man obviously happy with what he was working on, so Dennon decided to get a closer look.

Silently, he entered. The young man focused on a small box and his phone. Dennon watched as the young man tapped the table and a long spark of energy flowed from the light toward it. He then watched as the young man held the box to accomplish the same feat.

"Curious, this seems like magic, but it's science. I wonder what he's made," Dennon muttered, and he decided to keep watching.

Dennon waited silently. Any good hunter knows that their prey sometimes would have to wait. He was about to leave, thinking it was just some kid messing with science that mimicked magic. He turned to leave but stopped when he overheard, "Now, why did that statue give such a high reading? I wish I knew more about it."

Is he talking about the "Effigy of Tarnus"? Dennon thought. Now the old hunter had to step in. He raised his wand and fired a sleeping bolt, only to watch the magic drawn into the small box— the sudden flash and sound making Tyler fall from his chair and duck under the table. Luckily, he managed to hang onto the box and his phone.

Tyler went silent, looking from beneath only to see the shoes of someone walking toward him; he scurried through to the next row. Tyler watched, hoping to see an opening so he could escape. The footsteps were slow, methodical, almost expecting to see his target on the floor. But as Dennon made his way around the table, he found nothing.

Immediately he pulled out a small vial and threw it toward the door. It broke, releasing a transparent film that seemed to be filled with electricity.

"I know you're still in here. That field won't let you escape," Dennon said with confidence.

Tyler had made it to the door and when he touched the field it gave him a shock. He couldn't help but cry out. He watched as some of the energy flowed toward the box.

Hearing his cry, Dennon rushed toward the door.

In a panic, Tyler held the box to the field and pushed the switch. It did nothing. But as he flipped the switch to the other side, the area's energy drained away quickly and he was able to escape.

Dennon watched as the young man rushed out the door toward the end of the hall. "That's impossible! No one can dispel that without a key." He followed.

Tyler ran, sliding as he turned the corner; he was panting from running. He had only been in the building for a few weeks, and Tyler had spent most of his time in the lab and not exploring.

Right now, he was in unfamiliar territory. He slowed his breathing for a moment to listen for footsteps and when he heard them, he started running again. Tyler found himself in a room and closed the large metal doors. Unfortunately, he did not realize that it was a dead end.

"Great, I'm in a room with no exit and one light. This is something like in a horror film. First, I find that crystal, and now I've got some lunatic firing lightning trying to kill me. I should have never gotten involved with this magic stuff." Tyler chastised himself and leaned against the door.

He felt the hard metal hit his back as the hunter pounded on it to open the door. Tyler reached up to made sure the door was locked. He felt several more strikes before they stopped. The young man was still trying to catch his breath when a man walked into the light from the shadows.

Tyler sat silently, staring at the older man as he removed his hood, revealing his graying beard and sunken eyes, which were now staring straight at him.

"How did you remove the field? You're too young to be a master. Who showed you that spell?" Dennon commanded an answer.

"No-no one. I used this." Tyler held the box up, showing it to Dennon.

"I understand if you do not want to cooperate. Just know that I do not want to kill you," Dennon said as he raised his wand, firing a sleeping bolt.

He watched as the small box absorbed the energy of the bolt. Tyler was surprised as well, making him drop it, and it now pointed toward Dennon. Tyler remembered his phone, "Great, I can call for help." But as he opened his phone, he saw the numbers on the screen and where the device was pointing. He flinched as the old man fired again, only to see the small box absorb the energy.

Dennon paused, standing in disbelief, but remembered that the library's detector seemed to indicate that the protection spell failed. He watched as the young man scrambled for the door and tried pulling on it, forgetting it was locked. Dennon pounded his hand flat against the door, making Tyler move to the wall.

The hunter picked up the small box and looked at it before firing a sleeping bolt toward the device and watched as it was absorbed.

"Curious." He pointed the crystal he had toward the box, and it glowed.

"This is not magic; what is it?" Dennon asked, looking at Tyler.

Tyler was terrified. He had just made an incredible discovery, and this man was interested in it. But his sense of worth gave him some strength. "That's mine, old man. I figured out how to use those crystals." The young man grabbed the box from the hunter's grasp, before jumping back against the wall.

"What crystals?" Dennon asked, surprised by his empty hand.

Tyler pointed to the box.

"Boy, that is a detector crystal. It only shows energy, and whether it's light or dark leaning," Dennon growled.

The hunter fired another sleeping bolt, only to see it again disappear into the box.

Tyler became braver. "See, you can't hurt me while I have this."

Dennon glared at him. "I don't need magic to hurt you, boy."

Tyler felt the fear in his chest. "Well, if you're going to kill me, then at least tell me if you know what these readings mean."

Dennon looked at the boy's phone, seeing the numbers scrolling along the screen. He looked at the crystal he held. "This is magic. It is a stone, nothing more."

Tyler shook his head. "I know it's some kind of crystal, but it's like some sort of crystalline computer."

Dennon was in disbelief. He looked at Tyler as he held up the crystal. "You mean you can read information from this?"

Tyler nodded.

The Raven Hunter placed his wand back into his side pocket. "What's your name?"

Tyler refused to answer. Dennon could see the fear inside him. "At least tell me if you were at the library earlier today."

It took a few seconds, but Tyler nodded. Dennon smiled, and his demeanor became more welcoming. "Well, that was easy, wasn't it?"

Tyler became confused.

"Sorry for the theatrics, my boy. We were chasing down people using magic on campus. But what you have there, this could help us." Dennon gave his best convincing smile.

"What do you mean?"

Dennon pointed the crystal he held toward the young man and it glowed a light amber. The small box prevented him from using any magic on the young man. But Dennon was quick. If this young man caused the failure of the protection spell, perhaps he would be of use to the Broken Feather.

"You attend school here, don't you?" Dennon asked.

"Yeah, but I have summer classes, just not that many," Tyler replied.

"Why not?" Dennon asked.

"I don't have the money, and—wait, why are you asking me questions like this?" Tyler objected.

"Do you know about magic?" Dennon asked.

"I know it exists now, thanks to this," Tyler said, holding the box up.

Dennon smiled, "You're right, it does. As for those numbers," the hunter paused, "I have never seen anything like that before. But perhaps a colleague of mine could help. Would you like to find out what they mean?"

Tyler relaxed as the hunter spoke; something inside him felt as if this older man was a kindred spirit. He couldn't explain it, but what the Raven Hunter was offering was worth exploring.

"I'm listening."

Dennon told the young man that magic did exist, but that the Raven Hunters kept it secret from the rest of the world. Including the fact that if Tyler could use the crystal so quickly, he was a natural magic-user. That cemented the young man's trust when he said, "You have figured out more about these crystals in a few weeks than I dare say our scholars have in millennia. And what you have here could make almost anything possible."

Tyler held onto the box and asked, "How much would the job pay?"

The question made Dennon laugh, and he told Tyler, "My boy, what you have discovered will make you—and all of us— wealthier than in your wildest dreams. I'd say it would cover your tuition several hundred times over."

As they walked from the room, all Dennon thought was, *Have I found something that will help us move our plans along quickly? Oh, Paul, I have someone for you to meet.*

* * *

Amanda and Shrive appeared in the Shadowed Hall, only to be stopped by the guards. Thankfully, Dr. Brentwood had given them orders to allow them through. Once they were inside the Sanctuary, Shrive asked, "Okay, now where do you think they are?"

Amanda smiled, "If you were a fairy, where would you go?"

Shrive smiled back, "The Grove."

Within moments, they were headed toward the Grove. Amanda looked up as the dark hallway turned to sky. Off in the distance, they could see two people near the trees, a dozen or so fairies flying all around. They walked up and were met by Alicee, whom Amanda greeted warmly.

"Hey, Gabs?" Amanda yelled, and watched her friend spin around in a circle before stopping.

As Amanda walked up, she told her friend, "Easy on the spinning, Gabs. You'll make yourself dizzy. I know from experience." Amanda thought back to when she used to spin with Roween, making her laugh when she was younger.

Shrive joined them, seeing how happy Gabriella was in the Grove. "You're definitely part fairy. But how did you get here?"

"Oh, Selese brought me," Gabriella replied.

"Where is she?" Amanda asked, making her friend crane her neck, looking around.

"I think she went over there by the tall trees."

Shrive appeared perturbed. "No one's supposed to be by those trees; it's to stop from harming them."

Reluctantly, they headed toward the tall oaks that were in a line. They could see someone lying on the ground, flowers all around her, almost as if there was a bed of soft petals beneath her. "Is that Selese?" Shrive asked.

She was about to yell when her lips were held shut by a small fairy holding her finger to them. "A small room they tried to keep and hope to hide, she asked to sleep under the open sky."

Shrive gave a muffled, "What?"

Amanda laughed, "They kept Selese in a small room to keep her safe and hide her from the Broken Feather. It was like a cell, according to Selese." Her words made the fairy nod.

Shrive looked at Amanda as she said, "What, you've been around them your entire life, you should know what a fairy is saying." Amanda then asked the fairy if she could talk to Selese.

The fairy flew toward Selese, hovering above her before turning to the others and motioning for them to follow. As they got closer, Shrive saw another fairy sitting on Selese's forehead, as if standing watch. All she could think was, *I've had her all wrong the entire time.*

Amanda knelt as the fairy on her friend's head watched them vigilantly. Selese lazily opened her eyes. "I was enjoying my nap. What do you guys want?" She looked at Shrive. "Don't tell me you've come to arrest me again."

Shrive turned to Amanda. "I think you're right. I've been wrong this whole time."

Selese sat up, crossing her legs before looking confused at the two of them sitting there. "What?"

Amanda shook her head. "It's not important, but we did want to see how you were doing."

Selese gave a subtle smile before saying, "Oh, just hiding, but I am free. The sun is shining. It's good for me." She then hung her head as the fairy who was sitting on her head giggled. "It's not funny. I hate speaking in rhyme," before she started laughing.

Amanda joined her, then looked to Gabs. "I don't think I've ever heard you speak in rhyme, except when you had to."

Gabriella disagreed. "Oh no, remember I told you I had to go to speech therapy? I was always talking in rhyme before we met. I hated those lessons."

Amanda nodded. She did remember. "Wow, forgot about that. Although it does explain a lot."

Selese stretched and again asked what they wanted. But this time, Shrive answered. "We really were looking for you. We wanted to see how you were doing; I also don't know if Gabriella told you what happened at the diner. Amanda was telling me about the small box."

She looked at Shrive, then to Amanda. "You know that guy Tyler. He had some kind of box. He told us that it measured electricity in the air, but . . ."

Selese put up her hand. "Yeah, Gabs told me. Not interested."

Amanda shook her head. "You don't understand. It only worked when he pointed it at Gabs. When he pointed it at me, it did nothing."

Selese replied, "So?"

Amanda continued, "When Gabs held it, it started to heat up. I think it detects magic."

Selese suddenly started to become interested. "You mean like the detector crystals?"

Amanda nodded. "Yes, like them. I think he found a way to read information from them."

Shrive looked at Amanda. "You didn't tell me that."

Selese was now hanging on her every word. "But if he can detect magic, without the crystals, then . . . Well, what can he do with it?"

Amanda shrugged; she didn't know either.

Then Gabriella said, "You know, he was acting really weird when he walked by that statue in the library section of the museum."

"What statue?" Selese asked, genuinely concerned.

Gabriella motioned with her hands, "That twisted thing that looks like mud and a person stuck in it. I think that thing's sort of creepy. But he was able to take the glass off of it and touch it."

"What?" Selese yelled. "When? When did he take the cover off?"

Gabriella shifted backward and stuttered, "Wh-When I was in the library a few hours ago. I was expecting an alarm to go off or something but it must have been turned off."

Selese jumped to her feet. "Come on, we have to tell Cale."

"Why?" Gabriella asked.

"Because that security spell is tough to break. I had to trick the sensor gems when I took it the first time," Selese told her.

"You mean you stole it?" Gabriella sounded hurt by Selese's admission.

"I gave it back; I didn't know who wanted . . . Oh, never mind. I gave it back, all right?" Selese told her new friend.

Shrive followed after her as they walked from the Grove. Gabriella waved to the fairies as she left.

"I don't get it, Selese. Why do we have to tell Lord Cale?" Shrive asked.

Selese turned. "It took me days to figure out how to bypass that spell. If he figured out how to nullify it—"

Amanda spoke up. "That means anyone can take the statue."

Selese nodded. "Yes, even the Broken Feather. Come on. They have to know."

Gabs tapped Amanda's arm. "What's going on?"

Amanda said, "In summary, bad guys are trying to steal a magic artifact. Don't know why. Tyler may have found a way for them to do it easily."

"But why are we tagging along to tell Cale about it?" Gabs asked.

Amanda smiled at her friend. "Hey, this is every day for me, remember? We might have information they could use. Besides, weren't you the one who told me you wanted to go along on an adventure?"

Gabs nodded.

"Well, we're off to one now," Amanda replied with a large grin.

What the world sees is nothing more than illusion. From war, to victory, to selfless acts and hope. These are all things that we perceive. With magic, it is much more so. The balance of life and power are intertwined within our dreams. And, that is all it is, a dream.

- Author unknown. Manuscripts of Talin recovered by the Circle

Chapter Fourteen
Answers and Clues

It took some time, but Selese and the others convinced the council to find her father. Dr. Brentwood was nowhere to be found in the Sanctuary. They had hoped to allow her to hear their story as well, but when they finally found Cale, he was willing to listen.

"We're swamped, Selese. You'd better not be wasting my time." Cale sounded annoyed.

"You know, I've never heard you like this, what's wrong?" Selese asked.

Her father sighed and sat back, staring at his desk, which was now covered in paperwork. "Sorry, Limerick had a break-in last night. They attempted to steal the *Shard of Lenton*."

"Sir. Why are you telling this thief?" the hunter standing next to him scoffed.

Selese remained unphased by her remark as Cale turn to look at her. "*This thief* would probably have done a better job and actually taken the *Shard*, Collins. Besides, with the recent activity, we may need her expertise."

The woman seemed appalled by her master's response. "How can you not think it was her?"

Cale shifted in his chair, giving a smile. "One, she was on campus and in the Grove for the last twenty-seven hours. Two, she hasn't been to Ireland in over two years."

"How can you be sure?" Collins protested.

Cale stood, sternly pushing the new Raven Hunter out of his way. "Because her hair isn't blonde."

Amanda looked at Selese, pointing to her hair, making her nod. "Yeah, every time I step foot in Ireland, my hair turns lighter. Don't know why. It lasts for weeks."

That made Gabriella ask, "I wonder if that'd happen to me. I've never been to Ireland. Maybe we should go."

"Easy, Gabs, one adventure at a time," Amanda told her.

The new hunter again began to protest.

"And three, I believe she would have done it much more surreptitiously. Not to mention that we wouldn't have found out until some time later. Whoever attempted this was very amateurish. I don't even think they were looking to steal the *Shard*."

The new hunter stood her ground, protesting Cale's observation. But when he asked what theories she had on the criminal, the young woman stared back at him blankly.

Cale leaned on his desk and again asked what was so important. Selese tried to explain, but she looked to Amanda for the full story. When Cale asked, all Amanda said was, "I have a theory," and she continued telling him what they had experienced. She gave as much detail as possible, and seeing the concern in the man's eyes, Amanda knew she had the right story to tell.

"If you're right, then perhaps the *Shard* was an attempt to test something, not steal the artifact," Cale surmised.

This made Collins looked at her master with doubt. When she asked, "Do you think it was the Broken Feather?" Cale dismissed it.

"It has no value to them. But it does have a similar protection spell cast over it." Cale thought aloud. "Collins, go find Luke and Cayden, I know they're around here somewhere. They are supposed to be patrolling the school grounds."

Cale turned to Amanda. "And aren't you supposed to be in class soon?"

Amanda could see the sun setting and pulled out her phone. "Six forty-two? I've gotta get going. Masters' Techniques class was changed since they had the water leak in the building. Shrive, you coming?" She started toward the Shadowed Hall.

"You won't be able to go that way without someone who shadow-walks, Amanda!" Cale called after her.

Amanda pointed to Shrive. "Same class as me." Shrive waved as they disappeared into the shadows.

"Well, that leaves the two of you. Do you have any further information for me?" Selese smiled and looked toward Gabriella, who shook her head.

"Well, if that's the case, you may be able to help me make sense of this crime scene info. I could use a new point of view." Cale looked at Selese.

"Well, I was enjoying a nap in the Grove, and Gabriella here, I think, was enjoying the place as well. So . . ." She looked at Gabriella, who pointed at the mountain of paperwork, then shook her head. Selese smiled and told Cale that she couldn't help right that moment, but if he was really stuck, to send someone to find her in the Grove. But as she turned to leave, Luke and Cayden entered the office.

"Ah, just in time. I have a job for you two. You need to show Collins how to file this type of report. I'll be here, so don't think I'm passing this off on you."

Just then, Selese gave a subtle wave to the two, and Cale watched Cayden wave back, making him pause for a moment before shaking his head.

Selese felt Gabriella pull on her arm, but Selese turned away. "Maybe I should stay and help."

Cale looked at her and toward the two young hunters, again shaking his head.

"Hey, Gabs, if you want to go back to the Grove, I'll take you and come back," Selese mentioned.

Gabriella tapped her friend's arm. "I'm good. I should probably head back to my place. I've been at the Grove for the whole day. I like it there, but it is a bit boring. Maybe I'll catch up on my reading. And I have some commissions to finish up so I can keep going here. You go ahead and stick around."

"Sounds like a wise choice. Collins can walk you to your apartment. I'm sure she wouldn't be interested in the menial organizing we'll be doing till she gets back," Selese said as she looked playfully over Cayden's shoulder at the box of papers he picked up.

Gabriella smiled in agreement, and Collins took her straight toward the Shadowed Hall. Collins seemed very quiet when she reached the room, making Gabriella ask her if something was wrong.

The young hunter looked straight ahead and mumbled, "I've known Lord Cale for a few years, and every time someone mentions the Broken Feather, he seems to dismiss it."

Gabriella looked at her. "So what? Maybe they aren't always the problem."

Collins scoffed, "Whatever is going on, I'd stay clear of it. I've heard rumors that he was a member of the Broken Feather. And with all of the times they have been mentioned he hasn't gone after them . . ."

Gabriella asked, "What are you saying?"

Collins remained silent for a moment before saying, "I think he's with them."

Gabriella looked at her. "I think you're wrong, I don't care if you've heard rumors. From what I've seen, he can't be one of the Broken Feather."

Collins looked around and again told Gabriella to stay clear of whatever was going on. She thought that Selese was still a thief and bad news.

"You're wrong about her as well, Collins. Oh, what is your first name?" Gabriella asked.

"Ember. My first name's Ember."

"Ember? Wait, really? Okay, wow, Ember Collins." Gabriella paused for a second. "Just because you heard something like that doesn't mean it's true. You have to find the facts. Otherwise, if you get people wrong, you can screw things up."

The new hunter looked at her in disbelief. Gabriella continued to talk as she closed the door, leaving her in the hallway, listening to the sound of her lecturing through the door. Collins shook her head. "They did warn me I'd come across some strange things when I accepted this job."

"This doesn't make any sense. They had the Shard, free and clear. Why'd they leave it?" Selese mumbled. "Also, they damaged the display, including the gift shop, on the way out."

"What doesn't make sense?" No one noticed Dr. Brentwood standing in the doorway before she looked to Selese, seeing her perched on the back of the chair and said, "It's not safe sitting like that, dear."

The doctor greeted everyone and told them she wondered why everyone was here so late and had decided to check. She also mentioned that she would be back. She had to see the council. They were dealing with a rogue elf that just popped in.

Cale looked over his desk at Selese sitting on the top of the chair. "That's the question. And I wish you wouldn't do that."

Selese looked around. "What?"

"Balancing on the top of the chair like that," Cale scolded her.

Luke looked over; her chair was back-to-back with Cayden's as he continued to write out their findings. "Selese is right. This doesn't make sense. The only artifact that was touched was the *Shard*. I mean, it's a broken sword. Besides, there are a lot of expensive things there to steal. A collector would pay top dollar for this stuff."

Selese looked back. "That's it. My next job, you're coming."

"Really, Selese? We have enough trouble trying to train honest hunters," Luke chided her.

She turned to see a less than amused stare from her father, so she decided to be less playful. She knew her father was right; they could have taken the *Shard*, but a similar spell also protected the *Effigy of Tarnus*.

"What's so special that the *Shard* had to be protected like that?" Selese asked.

Cale stared at her but said nothing. She knew that it must be serious if it was protected with such care, but she had to know. "Is it something similar to the *Tarnus* statue?"

Her father again remained silent, but after a few moments, he told them, "The sword was used to slay the last fire-breathing dragon."

"But there are dragons still, and they're on the council," Cayden spoke up.

Cale looked around the room. He had trained both Cayden and Luke, Selese was his daughter, and he knew she was right; the problem was the *Effigy of Tarnus* and the *Shard* had something in common.

With a deep breath, Cale told them why the sword shard was protected. "Yes, we have dragons still, but if you haven't noticed, they no longer breathe fire."

Selese looked straight at her father as he spoke. Cayden nodded.

"The sword was used to slay the last of the chaotic dragons, the only remaining who could breathe fire."

"Why did they have to kill it?" Selese asked.

"Because all the dragon wanted was to have complete chaos. It only cared that humans, fairies, or others were around for one reason. To fuel its flames," Cale told them.

"You mean it drained magic?" Cayden asked.

Cale shook his head. "No. Worse."

Luke looked at him. "It ate them to consume their magic?"

Cale nodded.

"So, why is the *Shard* so dangerous?" Selese asked.

Cale slumped in his chair. "It would give it's bearer the ability of fire-breathing. The only downside is that you have to consume magical creatures for their power."

The room was silent for a few moments before Selese said, "Right, make sure it's not stolen, got it. That makes it even weirder that they didn't take it."

The rest nodded. But when Selese asked, "What's so special about Tarnus?" all Cale did was shake his head.

"I don't know."

His response made Selese uneasy, almost as if he was lying.

They continued to examine the photos and other evidence, but they still came to the same conclusion; the artifact should have been taken. Selese looked at the picture of Tarnus. "You know, we should get Amanda involved with this. She and her friends have had some experience with hunting down stolen artifacts. Maybe get a fresh perspective."

Cale shook his head. They had been at this for hours, and even he was starting to tire. Luke and Cayden were already lounging on the furniture. The only one still wide awake was Selese. Cale looked at her again, sitting on the edge of the chair, poring over the investigation notes.

"If only you had put that much study into your schoolwork," Cale chided.

Selese remained focused on the papers in front of her. "Who said I didn't?" She then looked at him with a determined gleam in her eye.

"You know, I think Amanda could help, but you'll have to trust her," Selese told him. "I mean, I trust her."

Cale looked at her quizzically.

"Do you know she asked Shrive to bring her to find me so that she could see not just how her best friend was, but how I was doing? She even thinks my name is cool. I mean, I think she actually cares about people, human or not."

Cale rubbed his face. "I'll consider it. Besides, it's late. Let's look at this tomorrow morning with rested eyes."

Cayden looked at the clock on the office wall. "It's two in the morning. It's already tomorrow. I'm officially calling out from work and sleeping in."

Selese laughed, pointing to herself. "Ha! Part darkling, don't need sleep. I love the night."

Cale stood. "That's it, everyone go, get some sleep. We'll look at this sometime tomorrow."

With that, Cayden moved the box of paperwork to Cale's desk, Selese put what she had on top, and Luke wrestled himself off the couch where he had just fallen asleep. They said good night, leaving Selese behind as Cale sat laying his head down on the desk.

"You going to tell the truth now?" Selese asked.

Cale raised his head to see the serious look in his daughter's eyes.

"I'm good at lying. It gets me in places, and I know when someone is lying."

Cale stared at her; he could see the determination in her stance. He knew she wasn't going to let this go. "It's for your own protection. I can't tell you."

"Why?" Selese protested.

Cale took a minute to gather his thoughts, and they all came to one conclusion. Selese may be able to help him.

"All right, all right, you're correct; the icon is similar to the *Shard*," Cale said.

Selese stood her ground. "And what else?" But after she asked, she could see the torment behind his eyes. Whatever it was, it was something dangerous.

"Wait, never mind. If it's that bad, I don't want to know."

Cale felt pride in seeing Selese like this. He knew she wasn't evil, as most saw her. That's why Aiden saved her. All she wanted was to feel safe. Cale looked at her and took a deep breath. "I'll share the secret of the *Tarnus* statue if you promise not to go looking for trouble with it. Or tell Amanda about it either."

"Why, does it involve her?"

Cale shook his head. "No, but I have a feeling if you're right about her, she may ask us to destroy it."

Selese suddenly felt a lump in her throat. "I'm not going to like this, am I?"

Several moments went by as Cale thought how to explain what the *Effigy of Tarnus* was. "Aiden shared the secret with me before he died. I never thought I'd have to tell you this. It's why the wraith mage took your heart."

Selese grabbed her chest and fell to her knees. Within moments, she looked up at him, tears streaming down her face, but said nothing.

"I can't . . . let's call it a night and just get some sleep." Cale's voice cracked wearily.

"No, tell me," Selese pleaded.

Cale remained silent, regretting giving in to her question in the first place. But Selese's pleas brought Claire to her side. "Is everything all right?" She immediately knelt next to Selese, who pushed her away.

"You have to tell me. Why did he take my heart?" Selese pleaded again, but Cale remained silent.

"It's all right, Selese. It's all right." Claire tried comforting their adopted daughter but again was pushed away. Although she accepted Selese when Cale had brought her home, Selese never seemed to be as settled. Claire regretted not being there for Selese after receiving the responsibilities as head of the Circle. Her husband was left mostly on his own to care for her after Aiden saved her. She also knew it was why he spends so much time at the Sanctuary instead of their house. Claire felt the weight of their world as her mind stated the obvious, *that night changed everything for all of us?*

As she knelt on the floor, Claire looked to Cale. She could feel the pain in his silence, but when she looked at Selese, her adoptive mother knew the girl had to know.

"Tell her, Cale. She must know. You've come this far." Claire's words sounded hurt, almost angry.

Cale leaned on his desk; he saw them both staring back at him.

"The *Effigy of Tarnus* is not actually a statue; it's a repository. It contains the essence of Tarnus," Cale told her.

"And?" Selese demanded an answer.

"Aiden told me what the statues were before he died. The wraith mage was looking to take over the Circle; they needed a geomage vessel to contain the essence to use it against us." Cale paused as Selese looked at Claire.

"You mean he was going to use me for that?" Selese said.

Cale shook his head. "No, he was going to use your body; that's why he took your heart. He would have been in control of your body and, essentially, in control of the essence of Tarnus."

Selese stared blankly at Claire, as the weight of the information sank in. When Claire could see the tears forming in Selese's eyes she pulled her close and held her. Selese balled up her fists, her nails scratching the stone floor though the carpet. She had only believed that Britlan had wanted her energy. She hadn't known he was going to use her body as a vessel. The girl finally understood what had happened, and what Britlan was going to do with her.

Cale exhaled as if a weight was lifted from his shoulders, and he sat on the floor next to Selese and his hand covering her balled up fingers.

"I'm sorry, Selese. I'm sorry I kept this from you. But I didn't want to hurt you any more than you already were,"

Selese peeked around Claire to see tears in her father's eyes; she thought, *it must have been killing you to withhold that from me.* She now fully understood what Aiden and Cale had done for her. And what they did to protect everyone.

It took a few minutes for the three to return to almost normal.

"So, I guess Tarnus was a geomage?" Selese said.

"Actually, he was much more than that; he was *the* geomage," Cale replied.

Selese looked to him to explain.

"The Circle was founded long ago; you know your history, right?" Cale asked.

Selese nodded. "Yeah, by the five pillars. The masters of elements. We all know that."

"Yes, but you only know them as the five pillars, Earth, Air, Fire, Water, and Spirit. But do you know their actual names?" Claire asked.

Selese shook her head. She never thought to ask. Claire told her, "The original five pillars were Donna Hessian representing water; her statue is the *Lament of Hessian*, her tears representing Water. Sienna Russell and the *Conflagration of Sienna* signifying Fire; a woman in the desert surrounded by flame, she seems to be reaching for the sky to escape. Alex Pertu and the *Flight of Pertu* embodiment of Air, a figure suspended on a spiral, representing air magic. And of course, the *Effigy of Tarnus*, Earth, symbolized by a man fighting a stone snake, drowning in mud."

"All very creepy-sounding if you ask me," Selese said, making Cale laugh. "But there's five; who's the fifth?"

Claire spoke up. "Shaun Benoit, the first non-magic person to head the Circle."

Selese shook her head. "No, there are stories of the magic he did. He was part Fae."

Claire shook her head. "No, he wasn't. The five pillars have always remained in some form. The icons were protected and hidden, but there is always one pillar that remains in plain sight."

Selese looked at her. "You're head of the Circle."

Claire leaned back as she spoke. "I was gifted the key of the Circle by its predecessor, Bethany Hoff. Just before Britlan killed her, trying to steal it."

Selese couldn't believe what she was hearing. "But you have magic. How can you be just human?"

"You make that sound as if it's a bad thing, dear. Remember, I'm a scroll witch," Claire said.

"That didn't come out right, I'm sorry. I meant you, you were . . ." Selese went silent.

"What's wrong?" Cale suddenly became very concerned seeing a look of sadness on his daughter's face.

Selese looked at them both, tears again starting to fall down her face as she hugged Claire. "I wasn't the only one cursed by that mage when he took my heart."

Claire pulled her closer. "I've never taken this as a curse, my dear. When I finally learned what it really was, I was even happy."

Selese looked at her. "What do you mean?"

"My life before this, before I met Cale, was, for lack of exposition, minimal. I had no prospects, and was even in danger of losing my freedom." Claire remembered the first time she had met Cale; she had just stolen a briefcase from him on the bus. She had spoken with him several times before and had gained his trust. She had opened it to see what looked like large gems. Seeing the prize, she felt happiness for the first time in years. But her euphoria waned as she felt guilt, and wondered how she was going to sell them. Her feelings turned to shame as she looked up to see Cale's eyes staring at her. She asked for forgiveness when he reached out his hand to her. She believed him when he said, "you have a talent for making people trust you. Maybe I can help you do something with that."

Dr. Brentwood felt the remorse of her past as she said, "Cale showed me there was something more to the world. I learned that I could help not only myself but others when I became a scroll witch." Claire reached for Cale's hand. "And with the key, I found I could do so much more."

Cale explained, the pillars were used to create The Circle of Paragon, the source of the Sanctuary's power. It also allows us to remain unnoticed, and allows Scroll witches to use magic. It is the source that keeps us all hidden from the rest of the world. And what keeps magic from overwhelming us all. If Britlan had procured the icons, he could have undone everything we have worked to build."

Cale rubbed his eyes. When he returned to look at Selese he could see that she understood. "Now you know the secret of the Circle, and now you have to keep it a secret from everyone else. Unless, of course, you'd like your memory erased," Cale told her.

"Very funny, Cale, very funny," Selese mocked him.

But when she saw the expression on Claire's face, she understood he wasn't joking.

Chapter Fifteen
A Girl Walks in to a Bar

The next morning, Cale returned to the Great Hall sometime after 10:00 a.m. The late night had caused him to oversleep. He had just arrived when he was alerted to a possible incident on campus. He headed to the detection room, asking for the day's status.

"Dennon left late yesterday to investigate a glitch we had on the sensor crystals," Costa told him.

Cale looked toward him suspiciously. "A glitch?"

He explained the events and that Dennon had returned much later than expected. When the man pressed for his report, all Dennon told them was that he had spent most of his time chasing a false lead. It turned out to be student working on a science experiment; the device he'd made mimicked magic.

Cale looked curiously at the report. He had known some science to border on magic, but had an uneasy feeling that Dennon was not telling the whole story. Handing the report back to the man, Cale told him, "When Dennon gets in, have him see me. I want to talk about his report." The man nodded and returned to his post.

It was a few hours before Dennon arrived at the Hall. He had spent the early hours speaking with Paul and his new apprentice, Tyler. They put together a look-alike box with a stone crystal that gave the illusion of magic as the power was turned on. When Dennon was ordered to see Lord Cale, the hunter dutifully complied.

The two spoke, and when asked, Dennon produced a small box similar to the one Tyler had created. When he turned it on, the detector in Cale's office flickered.

"You see, it's not magic. But it's close enough for the detectors to pick it up," Dennon told him.

Cale gave a relieved sigh. "Good to hear it was nothing. I'd hate to have to restructure the whole system."

Dennon laughed, which to Cale seemed out of the ordinary. The hunter was as serious as they come, and seeing him laugh made Cale very concerned. He began to wonder if something had happened to the student. When he pried, Dennon had an answer.

"Well, I overheard that Paul Vikander was looking for help in his repair shop in town." Cale looked expectant, as if he was waiting for a better response, making the hunter sit tiredly in the chair. "You may think I'm hard on people, Cale, but truthfully, I can understand that boy. He was having trouble paying for school, and I knew about the job. He seemed like a fit for helping out."

Cale stared at Dennon before saying, "Are you really Dennon, or do we have another shapeshifter to worry about?"

Dennon laughed, seeing the amusement in Cale's words, but quickly reverted to his usual no-nonsense self. "Lord Cale, you do have a sense of humor. I can go grab some delinquents if it makes you feel better."

"I'm serious. What have you done with Dennon Fierst?" Cale asked.

The Raven Hunter sighed. "I could see the look in his eyes. It reminded me of myself when I was younger. I'd say he was a kindred spirit, in a way. He seemed to find enjoyment in what he was doing, and I decided to help."

Cale looked to the wall. "Is he dangerous?"

Dennon shook his head. "No, he was bored. He discovered this by accident." He pointed to the box. "I took him to see Vikander, and do you know what happened?"

Cale turned with interest.

"They started talking. That boy knows more about computers, electronics, and so many things that I don't understand. He and Paul, they were speaking a language I couldn't comprehend." The hunter leaned back. "He offered the boy a job right there. And the best part is that the money he'll earn will be going to him so he can continue to attend school. It was truly amazing."

Cale smiled, "We do have to think of our students."

Dennon smiled, seeing the tired eyes of the man across the desk. As a hunter, he looked for weakness in an opponent. "You look tired, Cale. Everything all right?"

Cale leaned back. "We were up all night working on the Lenton case."

When Dennon asked who was helping, Cale mentioned everyone, including Selese.

"You have a thief working on a robbery?" Dennon looked at him with an air of irony.

Cale smiled, "Well, as you know, we sometimes have to bring in people with expertise in a matter."

Dennon nodded. "Of course. You're right, sometimes we do."

The rest of the conversation focused on the recent involvement with the Broken Feather. Every time Cale brought up the box, the hunter changed the subject, only saying, "It isn't worth time worrying about it."

After their meeting, Dennon left with a feeling of accomplishment, his mind thinking of the meeting between Vikander and the boy. He knew they would have something to test soon. As the hunter mused his recent finding, he chuckled. "Tyler Fenris; that is a somewhat prophetic name. Not quite Fenrir, but perhaps he can help us take over the Circle." The hunter pulled up his hood and vanished into the darkness of the Shadowed Hall.

* * *

A few weeks had passed, and Amanda was finished her semester projects. She was writing an email to Linda about recent happenings. She was concerned that the hunters were monitoring emails going out from the school. Amanda had asked if that was the case, but never got a straight answer from anyone associated with the Circle. She decided to use her phone and service when she sent information about the goings-on around campus. Amanda had hoped Luke would tell her something when he stayed. He only nodded, but changed the subject when she pressed the issue. Amanda looked at the wall realizing Luke left his jacket on the stand by the door. She gave a subtle romantic sigh as she returned to her email.

Her latest message was filled with a lot of information, including discovering a possible magic detector that Tyler had created, although Amanda was worried that she had not seen him for a couple of weeks. When she asked one of the professors, she was told Tyler had still been attending classes.

Amanda was surprised when Linda and Ron said it would take at least a week to head up to see her if she needed help, and that for the moment, she was on her own. Linda informed her about a possible theft of a magical artifact in Cleveland, which Ron was still looking into. But if Amanda needed help, they would be there as fast as possible.

Amanda became upset, realizing that they continued to investigate strange happenings while she was away. Ron had supposedly been out for a book signing, but when Linda mentioned that Ron swears he saw a woman with cat-like features disappear into the shadows, she laughed. "Have to ask Shrive if she was in Cleveland."

Amanda decided to make the most of things. The weekend had finally arrived, and the two-week break was coming. She looked forward to heading back home for a few days and see her family and friends, especially Roween and Jinx. Amanda stared out the window, lost in thought, and was startled when there was an excited knock on her door. When she answered, the door flew open and she was thrown off balance as Gabs rushed past her.

"I'm done my projects; I am so excited!" She paused a moment to take a breath and look for Amanda. "You finish yours yet? I'm here to help."

Amanda shook her head, laughing, "Sorry, Gabs, already done."

Her friend looked at her as she processed the statement. "Oh, that's great. We're both done. That means we can do something else!"

Amanda could see the look in her friend's eyes. She seemed to be a woman with a plan. Seeing what was obvious, Amanda asked, "Where are we going?"

Gabs told her about the Struder House. It was a bar, and was supposed to have great food. Amanda smiled and said, "What else?"

Her friend looked innocent. "Maybe we can get some company to go with us?"

Amanda felt herself blush as she realized who she was talking about. It was no secret that Luke and she had been seen together a lot since they'd met. Both Selese and her had seen them together several times. Gabriella even mentioning that she had seen Luke leaving sometime early before dawn from Amanda's apartment. Gabriella's mind wandered, as she remembered Selese laughing when she mentioned him leaving.

Amanda snapped her fingers and chuckled bringing Gabriella back to the real world, "Okay, let's go see if we can find them."

It was only a few minutes before they came across the two hunters. Luke waved as they approached Amanda, who returned the gesture. When they asked if they wanted to go, Luke hesitantly responded, "We're on patrol tonight. Can't." Amanda felt disappointed, but as Luke moved closer, he whispered, "Maybe Thursday? They have us running around here recently with all the activity." Amanda felt herself feeling warmer than usual as he moved nearer.

As she stepped back, he asked, "Where are you heading, anyway?"

"The Struder House; her idea," Amanda replied, pointing to Gabriella.

Cayden smiled, "You know they don't even check IDs there. You should be able to get in pretty easy. But I wouldn't try getting alcohol; they're pretty strict."

Gabs looked innocent and told them that they weren't planning on it. Cayden smirked and said, "Just warning you."

As they started to walk away, Luke reached for something in his pocket. "Amanda, wait."

The two girls stopped as Luke walked up. "Here, been meaning to give you one of these." He handed her a detector crystal.

Amanda took it and gently pulled it away from Luke's grasp. She noticed he seemed to hold onto it a bit longer. It appeared to be like any ordinary piece of crystal.

Gabs plucked it from her hand and it started to glow a shimmering blue as she looked at it. Amanda looked annoyed and held her hand out. Gabriella's eyes opened as if she had done something wrong and gently placed it back in Amanda's hand as she mouthed the word, "Sorry."

Both Amanda and Luke laughed as it was returned; the crystal again shone clear.

"You know this doesn't work for me, right?"

Luke nodded. "Yeah, but." He paused. "There have been some weird things happening. I figured it wouldn't hurt. Besides, you do know that two icons were stolen, right?"

Amanda shook her head. "When?"

Luke told them both about the Water icon's theft and that the Air icon was almost taken. If it were not for a lucky guard, it would have been. Amanda was now certain there was more going on than they knew. She was wondering if she should leave for break. Instead, she was contemplating staying and helping. But as she stared at the crystal, she felt her necklace shift, as if being tugged, and she felt a sudden need to get away.

Luke watched as she stared past him. "You all right?"

Amanda smiled, "Yeah, I think I'm going to have to head home for the break." She produced the small wooden ring she wore.

The hunter nodded. "Ah, got it."

Amanda held the crystal out to him. "Still doesn't work for me."

Then Cayden spoke up. "Maybe not, but we heard that they tend to light up when there is something else around."

"Like what?" Amanda asked.

Cayden shook his head. "Don't know. It happened at the place where the theft was."

"That is interesting," Amanda muttered as she placed it in her purse. She looked to Luke. "Next Thursday, then?"

Luke smiled and nodded.

"Okay, your loss today, fellas. We'll see you later," Gabs said as they walked away.

* * *

Amanda and Gabs arrived sometime after 9:00 p.m. and were surprised at how easy it was to get into the bar. However, it did seem to have somewhat fewer people than they had been told. As they walked toward an open table, they heard a familiar voice. "You two look like you're looking for trouble." Amanda turned to see Shrive standing by the pool table. She quickly joined her two friends.

"So, no company?" Shrive looked at Amanda, who replied, "Nope, they're working."

Shrive smiled, "Well, their loss. First time here?"

Amanda nodded.

"Order what you want, I'm buying," Shrive told them.

When the server asked what they wanted, Amanda only asked for a soda. Gabs tried convincing her to get something else. When Amanda refused, saying, "Nope, I'm driving," Gabriella ordered a beer, as did Shrive. And as she placed her hand down on the table, she felt something soft and wet. The server laughed, "Yeah, you might be better by the bar. I haven't had time to clean the table yet."

Amanda wiped her hand on the napkin the server handed her and they walked up to the bar. To her surprise, Selese turned to greet them.

"Oh, these are some seedy characters. Gonna have to watch them," she joked, motioning to the bouncer by the door, making the man smile.

"Selese, you work here?" Amanda asked.

"Yeah, bartend a few nights a week." She leaned in. "I don't sleep much, as you know."

They spoke for a minute before Selese asked what they were having. Amanda told her a soda, and Shrive ordered a beer, as did Gabriella. Selese poured the drinks and as she was about to place them down, said, "We have one rule here. Unlike other places, you pay after your glass is empty."

Amanda thought that was strange and glanced next to her, seeing Shrive fighting to hold back a smile. They picked up their glasses and toasted each other, but as they went to drink, the beer in Gabriella's glass vanished. She stared through the bottom only to see Selese staring back at her, her chin against her hand, her elbow on the bar. "No good, Gabs, you're not old enough."

Both Shrive and Amanda laughed. "Your doing?" Selese shook her head.

"Nah, new guy's trick, not mine. But I helped think it up," Selese told them.

She pointed to the tall man behind her. "His name's Morley Waymire."

Amanda thought he looked familiar, and when she heard his name, she figured it out. "Wait, isn't Cayden's last name Waymire?"

Selese smiled, "Yep."

Morley leaned over, pointing to Selese. "She's a smart one, but since she needs looking after, they sent me. Besides, I've been looking for some extra cash. We don't get paid much by the Sanctuary."

Shrive spoke up. "Nice trick with the drinks; she didn't even get a chance to taste it."

Morley looked at Gabs. "She's not old enough, so no, she didn't." He leaned back and smiled at Gabriella. "But, you still gotta pay, you emptied the glass."

Amanda started to laugh, holding her full glass up high. "Cheers, girls. But the joke's on Shrive, she's paying."

Shrive laughed as Selese handed Gabriella a soda. They had some fun, and as Shrive put her glass down, Amanda said, "Heard there was a theft."

Shrive looked at her. "How did you find out?"

Amanda smiled. "You weren't by chance in Marshal, Michigan, or Cleveland, Ohio, recently, were you?"

Shrive stared, stunned. "How did you know where I was?"

Gabriella looked perplexed as well. "Yeah, how did you know? All Luke said was that Shrive was investigating."

Amanda smiled back at them both. "Worked it out from the clues."

Shrive laughed, "Hell, break's coming up. Next assignment, you're going with me."

They all laughed, and Amanda again felt a tug on the small wooden ring. She pulled the chain and thought for a moment. "I don't think I can. At least not this time."

When Shrive asked why not, she pulled out the chain that held the ring and they all watched as it seemed to pull to one side.

Selese saw as well. "Oh, no. You're going where that wants you to go."

Amanda looked at her and Selese said, "Trust me on this, if you want to see bliss."

Selese then slowly banged her head gently against the bar. "Just a rhyme, nothing to see. It's just rough, being part fairy."

Within seconds, they all started laughing. Amanda nodded. "She's right. I think I'm needed elsewhere."

Silence in one's heart is to listen to their spirit. For it is when we hear no thoughts, no anger, no distraction is when you find peace and the strength you possess.

- The Circle

Chapter Sixteen
A Secret About Her Friends

Amanda smiled as the sign for the interstate passed by her as she drove. She had been on the road for a few hours and was getting close to her destination. She had called to let her parents know she was heading home and was glad she did. Her mother was in Washington, and her father had headed to Europe for business. Jinx was with the neighbors, so Amanda would have come home to an empty house. Instead, she was heading to see her friends.

Amanda missed them almost as much as she missed her family. Linda, Ron, and the others had become a part of her world, especially Roween. And that was something she had wondered about for some time. Amanda had heard the stories of fairies and how they faded as children grew older. But here she was, heading back to a place where her friends were with her fairy friend daily. Not to mention Amanda had found many like them at the school she now attended.

Tired, Amanda stretched, waiting for the light to change to green before taking the last turn to head to the cabin. It wasn't long till she would see them and hear the familiar, comforting rhyming of Roween's words. She sighed, realizing that even as she was growing older, the world still held magic.

The sun had set; Amanda felt reenergized as her car's headlights lit the small mailbox in front of Linda's house. She could see the glint of the crystal Roween insisted they install. Since they had taken on the responsibilities of stopping evil magic, it seemed a necessity. Roween had placed a spell that hid the house and those in it from anyone wishing to harm them. She had done the same at the cabin where Amanda stayed. But as Amanda stopped, she felt a heaviness within herself as she placed her hand on the gift she'd brought for her friends, and it took a moment for her to get out of her car.

As she turned to see the carved wooden door, she felt that heaviness lift. "It's good to be back," she muttered as she took a breath to smell the familiar flowers that were in the front yard.

When she reached the door, she knocked. The frame glowed a subtle golden color at each tap. "Looks like Roween upgraded the spell on the door again."

It was only seconds before the door opened and she saw Ron standing there, his arm in a sling. She immediately hugged him gently and asked what happened. "Work-related injury." Ron was trying to make a joke but then said, "Welcome back, kiddo."

The commotion brought Linda to find out what was going on and she saw Amanda standing there holding onto Ron. She felt her eyes blur with tears as she walked toward them but gasped as Amanda reached out to hug her. All of them hearing Lind say, "Have you gotten taller?" After a short embrace, Amanda pushed away. She tried to speak but couldn't find the words. Ron smiled, "We missed you too." They spent the next few minutes talking as they made their way to the main room.

"We were expecting you earlier," Linda said.

Amanda sat and replied, "I got a late start; had to help someone with a problem."

"It wasn't something serious, was it?" Linda asked.

Amanda shook her head, saying, "No, Gabs locked herself out of her room again," making them all laugh. She then looked around as if searching for something.

Linda noticed. "She's not here at the moment. She was expecting you earlier, but you know how she can be."

Amanda looked disappointed, but Linda was right. Roween had other responsibilities. She looked at Linda, asking, "Many things to do?"

They all chuckled at her joke, It was something Roween said every time she had to leave. When they finished, she looked at Ron. "So, tell me what happened. You hurt yourself working in the garden?"

Linda smiled, "I wish! I wouldn't have been so worried if he had."

Amanda looked at him with a determined stare, making Ron reply, "I'm sure I'm not the only one with interesting stories to tell."

Ron mentioned hearing about the Circle and the *Pertu* statue and that someone was trying to steal it. That it contained magic, and how he convinced the museum he was researching a story and he wanted to look at the statue after hours. He was surprised when they said he could, before overhearing them say, "You've read his stories. If he writes a story on this, we can insist that he use the museum's name. That way, we can make some money from this stuff."

Amanda scoffed, "Was that all they wanted, to make money from it?"

Ron nodded. "Yeah, but while I was examining it, I heard something behind me, and then my feet left the floor. I found the wall pretty solid when I hit it."

"That's when you broke your arm?" Amanda asked.

Ron shook his head, "Fractured, but no, that happened after." He continued to tell his story.

"I was dazed, but stood up. There was a bright flash, and I heard an explosion. In the light I saw three people standing in the room, apart from the guard who was with me."

Ron rubbed his arm. "I did this saving the guard."

Amanda hung onto his every word. He mentioned the column breaking and how he pushed the guard out of the way and into the three people; how the column clipped him as it fell, fracturing his arm. He told her that when he pushed the guard, he fell into two of the robbers and must have injured them because the last one panicked and started dragging them backward.

"When I stood up, I rushed toward them but found nothing but darkness behind the display case. I turned around and I thought I must have hit my head because I swear, I saw what looked like a cat-girl looking at the statue. She had a white patch on her left ear."

Amanda smiled but held her words.

Ron continued, "I watched as she waved her hands, and there was some sort of light around the statue. I watched her walk backwards, but as I went to see who she was, there was no one there. When I tried to move the statue, it wouldn't budge. I know there is something else going on here."

Linda saw Amanda's smile. "You know something, don't you?"

Amanda nodded. "Yeah, there have been some thefts going on, and that cat-girl was probably a friend."

Ron raised his eyebrows.

Amanda reached into her pocket and produced a crystal. "I do have a story to tell you and wanted to show you what they used to find out that Gabs was part fairy."

"Wait, Gabriella is part fairy?" Linda interrupted.

Amanda nodded. "And a few other magic things. Apparently, she's descended from a bunch of other magical beings."

"Wow, that's a surprise to hear!" Ron said as she handed him the crystal to look at. And as he held it, it glowed a bright blue-white.

"Um, is this supposed to do that?" Ron asked, holding crystal away from himself.

Amanda jumped up and took it from him; it again was just a crystal. She looked at Linda and motioned for her to put her hand out. When Amanda placed it in her friend's hand, it also glowed a bright blue-white. Linda handed it back to her quickly.

Amanda stared at the crystal. "How is it working for you two?" She cradled the crystal in her hands. "It's not supposed to work for people who are not . . ." Amanda stopped and looked at her friends. They watched as a big smile appeared on the girl's face, confusing them both.

Amanda started to laugh. "That's why they knew about you before me!" She then handed the crystal to Ron, and it again glowed a bright blue-white.

"What are you talking about, Amanda? Who knew us before you?" Ron asked, holding the crystal up.

Linda stood. "I'm going to make some tea. I have a feeling we are going to be up for some time tonight." She took the crystal from Ron. She held it up to Amanda as it glowed brightly. "And I believe Amanda is going to tell us her story when I get back." She handed the crystal to Amanda, who meekly took it from her. "And I hope she has a lot to tell us."

Amanda could see the sternness in her friend's eyes and she turned away to see Ron staring at her before she said, "Oh, I have a lot to tell you. but, maybe some of it should wait until Roween gets here."

Amanda told them about the bar and that the glasses were enchanted. Linda laughed, "Serves you right; you're too young to be drinking." Amanda told them about the Grove and all the fairies and other creatures she had met. But, as she was about to tell them about the crystal, she felt herself being lifted off the chair. She turned to get her bearings in a mild panic and could see Roween floating next to her. Within moments her fairy friend zipped around her, and Amanda could see her head bobbing and searching all around her. Moments later, she felt herself flop into the chair, Roween holding her head tightly to her nose.

"No bruises or breaks, and face looks fair. No ruses to take, friend took care. Welcome back from where you roam, welcome back to this old home."

Amanda felt tears of happiness hearing her friend's voice again. "I missed you too, Roween."

There were a few minutes before things settled. Roween was sitting on Amanda's shoulder as she sipped her tea. They spoke for a bit. Ron again mentioned, "Who knew about us, and how did they know that Gabriella is part fairy?" That question perked Roween's attention as well. Amanda produced the crystal and handed it to Ron.

"Dr. Claire said they knew about you before I met you," Amanda told them.

Ron had a look of concern on his face. He held up the gem and was about to ask something but could see Roween staring at the crystal, shaking her head. "What is this?" he asked Roween.

The fairy gently flew over and he handed the crystal to her. It glowed a bright white. In fact, it shone so brightly that they had to shield their eyes. Roween dropped the crystal to the floor and Ron picked it up. It again glowed a bright blue-white. He suddenly dropped it. "Damn, that's hot." He picked it up again and tossed it between his hands to cool off.

He looked at it. "You said someone knew about us before you met us."

Amanda nodded. "Yes, according to the doctor, the Circle knew about you before I met you both."

Ron almost seemed angry. "Why would they know about us?" He held the cooled crystal tightly. "Because of this?"

Amanda shook her head as Roween landed on her shoulder to comfort her. "I don't know, okay? She just told me."

Ron calmed himself. "Amanda, I'm not mad at you. It's just that there has been a lot of magical activity recently and with the last thing"—he pointed to his arm—"you're telling us that the Circle is real and they are doing these thefts?"

Amanda sat wordlessly but shook her head. "No, not them, someone else." She knew as much as they did, and Roween touched her face.

"Amanda, my dear, do not fret. Things will clear, just not yet," Roween said.

Ron looked at her. "Do you know what's going on? Why they knew about us?"

Roween floated toward him, but drifted between him and Linda. She used her magic to take the crystal from Ron and give it back to Amanda before giving a sigh and saying. "Gabs is fairy, this I know. Light and airy, like shining snow." She looked to Linda. "There are things that humans miss, like songs of sylphs that drive the mists."

They watched as Roween floated before them, her wings seeming heavy, as if burdened. They watched as she flew before Amanda, who held her hand out as she landed.

"That thing that glows is what they used, and secrets show and rights refused." She looked at Amanda. "You have no magic of your own, but look at how much you have grown. The friends you have, please don't be wary, for both of them are, yes, part fairy."

The room was silent for a few seconds before it was filled with Ron asking, "What?"

Roween looked at them both, their eyes wide in disbelief. She turned to see Amanda staring at her. "Are they really?"

Ron grabbed the crystal from Amanda and held it as it glowed once again. He handed it to Linda, who was now standing beside him. She said, "You knew?" to Roween.

Roween nodded. "That is why you can see, others' magic and this fairy."

Linda and Ron stood stunned by the news. As Ron took a breath, he said, "I'm not as surprised as I thought I'd be. It sort of makes sense. Why didn't I see it before?"

Linda looked at him, concerned. "You knew before? How?

Ron sighed, "When I first met Erant and Josclyne, she said, he has eyes, not of this world, that's not good for us." He paused. "I didn't put it together till now."

Amanda looked a little sad, making Linda ask what was wrong. she answered, "I'm just a human without magic; I don't have anything special."

Roween flew before her, a surprised look on her face, and was about to speak when Linda interrupted. "How can you say that? You may not be like us, but you can see Roween. You are almost twenty and can still see her. You have friends that are apparently part magic. Not to mention you are going to an art school that has a secret lair of an organization that houses and protects magical creatures. How can you say you have nothing special?"

Amanda rushed toward her and hugged her as Roween floated nearby. "You're right, I do have something. I have all of you."

Ron laughed as he rubbed his eyes after looking at the clock. "It's been a long day. Maybe we should all try and get some sleep." He paused. "Probably not going to be able to, but whatever."

Linda agreed, "You had a long drive, and this has been exhausting. Ron's right."

Roween nodded before floating to the window, where a new ginger blossom opened for her to land. She was tired, and she knew Linda was right. She had been busy all day, and now there was a secret about her friends that was just revealed. Her magical mind raced. The Circle knew about her friends, and she heard them say that the statue was being protected. Roween had stayed away from the Circle for most of her existence. But she knew other magical creatures that had interacted with them before. She was now concerned that if they knew her friends, then Ron was right. This was part of something much larger.

We have brought ourselves into the light. Through magic, and hope all the world will be as it will. For our path is with theirs, our legacy, our dream, and our duty.

- Translated from Darkling texts.

Chapter Seventeen
Missing the Adventure

The next few days were uneventful. Amanda contacted her parents, telling them she made it to the cabin safely. She had planned to spend a few days before heading back to school. It was only a month till she would be home for the semester. Amanda worried about Jinx and had called their neighbor to check on him but was surprised when they told her she would have to come to pick up Jinx since they were going on an impromptu vacation.

When she informed Linda, her friend offered to pick her cat up, and he could stay with them. Linda smiled, seeing the subtle glare from Roween, but still insisted on bringing Jinx home. Ron had offered to drive up to the school but changed his mind seeing Amanda, Linda, and Roween staring back at him. His mind was made up when he felt himself lifted from the floor and flopped onto the couch, with an annoyed fairy floating before him shaking her head.

"I'm guessing you don't want me to go?" Ron mocked. Roween didn't remain silent, explaining why. Ron heard her out, and he agreed. She made a good point that the Circle had known about them and was probably watching. They all knew there was something much larger going on and they needed to know much more before getting involved.

Amanda did not have much information, and so far, she had several people around her that seemed to be protecting her from the bigger problem. But, as with all mysteries, they would need to find more information. That was one of the reasons. The other was that Ron was still injured and needed to heal before getting involved. Both Linda and Roween were sure of that.

Amanda had moved back to the cabin; she was lucky no one was staying there since it was turned into a rental. She smiled, hearing Erant complain that these humans need to learn manners. Amanda sat on the worn chair and smiled; she had missed the everyday, magical happenings she had experienced over the last few years.

Amanda worked at the table, drawing her latest illustrations for Ron's stories. Apparently, even only able to partially use one hand, Ron was able to type very quickly. Linda had made sure to include several pictures of the area and the creatures they had come across.

Amanda didn't spend the entire time working. She visited friends and others she knew from the area. Of course, she needed to stop into Paragon Rising to make sure Ron wasn't getting into trouble while Linda was picking up Jinx. Amanda was stopping in to have lunch with him and to check in on him as per Linda, and she was amused seeing Ron trying to juggle the register and bagging with one arm. It was a few moments before she offered to help.

As Amanda walked in, she noticed the person Linda had hired on her phone in the corner of the store. She told Ron, who was asking where she had gone. Amanda told him she'd take care of it.

Amanda did just that, standing before the woman about the same age as her when she interrupted. When the woman told her to go away, Amanda turned the tables.

"I guess the call is more important?" Amanda asked.

The woman nodded. "Someone saw Amanda Supp earlier. I'm trying to find out where she is so I can get this signed." The woman held up a copy of *Karakkon's Keep*.

Amanda smiled, remembering that adventure. Karakkon was a low-level wizard that had lost himself in his own maze. It took them all less than a few hours to find him and put the creatures he had released back into suspension. That's not what annoyed Amanda, however. The person the woman was searching for was now standing right before the clueless woman.

When Amanda asked where they said they saw her, she was surprised. "Someone saw Amanda Supp her the weir over on 73. Probably looking for another creature." Amanda laughed. She hadn't been anywhere near the weir; she had been across town at a friend's.

"Amanda? Did you find her?" she heard Ron yell.

"Over here!" she replied, and seconds later, Ron appeared around the corner after locking the front door.

Ron became curious as to why Amanda was standing before his employee who was crouched against the wall, making him ask, "Everything all right?"

Amanda nodded, telling him that his employee was looking for Amanda Supp, the artist. Her words brought a pleasantly humorous look of confusion from the man standing next to her.

"Kylie, um, it's lunchtime. I'm locking up. You don't need any help, do you?" Ron asked.

The woman glanced up briefly and shook her head before returning to her phone. Ron resisted laughing at what was happening. Amanda stepped forward and after tapping the woman's phone, asked, "Can I see your book?"

The woman handed the book to her and Amanda opened it to see Ron's signature. She asked Kylie if she had a pen, and was about to sign the book when Kylie protested.

"Stop! Don't write in it. I'll help out, just don't ruin it, okay?" Kylie jumped up, grabbing the book from Amanda before looking toward Ron. "Sorry, I really wanted to get her autograph. She's just so hard to find today."

Kylie looked at the book and opened it before glancing at the photographs of Ron, Linda, and Amanda at the cabin. Amanda watched Kylie. "Do you really think they have adventures like these?" The employee then looked up and saw Amanda staring back at her, and noticed the picture. Kylie looked at Amanda and then to the book a few times.

Ron started laughing, followed by Amanda. "Amanda, will you sign the poor girl's book already? I'll finish closing up for lunch."

Amanda continued to laugh as she took the book. "Kylie, right?" She signed the text next to her picture and handed it back. "I guess it's lunchtime." Amanda looked around.

Kylie remained focused on Amanda and saw Ron walking away behind her. "Kylie, you still have class in an hour, right?" The woman nodded. Ron told her she could go; she didn't have to rush to class today. As Ron started toward the back of the shop, Kylie still stood in the corner. She turned to see Amanda walking past him as he said, "Kylie, I'm locking up, so unless you are planning on staying . . ."

The employee snapped out of her surprise and told them to wait until she grabbed her stuff. She thanked Amanda and asked if she could take a picture with her. Amanda laughed but agreed.

Kylie left after gathering her things and was on the phone as she got into her car. She seemed to be having an exciting conversation with someone as she drove off.

"Hope she doesn't get into an accident," Ron said, holding his hand out seeing a few drops of rain on his palm.

* * *

They were sitting in a booth at Reanard's Grill and Ron was doing his best to hold his burger with his injured arm as Amanda laughed at him. "You are stubborn," she noted.

Ron looked over his burger at her. "You know, Linda says the same thing. I have no idea why."

Amanda chuckled at his sarcasm. It brought back memories of their adventures. Ron asked about the crystal and she tapped her purse. "There is this guy, Tyler, who has one like it, but he put it in a box with some electronics. It heated up when Gabs held it."

Ron put his burger down and listened.

"No one's seen Tyler for the last few weeks, but all of his schoolwork has been turned in. It's bizarre," Amanda said, perplexed.

Ron leaned back. "Who's Tyler, a new boyfriend?"

Amanda looked at him and stuttered, "N-No, he's not. Luke, maybe. Wait, what was I talking about?"

Ron leaned forward, his eyebrows raised. "Luke? So, his name's Luke?" He placed his hands under his chin to support it as he leaned on them, favoring his fractured arm. "You know Linda, not to mention your parents, have been dying for an update since the year started." Ron looked at her with a discerning glance.

Amanda looked at him. "You're making this weird, you know that?"

Ron laughed, "Yeah, I know. Don't worry, I won't say anything. Well, maybe if Linda tortures me, I might. And of course, maybe another being who may want to know. I can't exactly say nothing to her."

Amanda thought for a moment, realizing that he was talking about Roween. "Oh yeah, no. You can't keep anything from her. She'd pull it out of you if she has to." Her statement made them both laugh.

"Ah, good times. Do you miss it?" Ron asked.

Amanda looked outside, her eyes focusing on the puddles caused by the rain, and nodded. "Yeah, every day. That's probably why I accept what's happening at school so easily."

Ron nodded. "I get it. But you wanted to finish up school. That's important."

Amanda agreed. She'd wanted to be a commercial artist since she was young, and was well on her way. She did miss the adventures they had, and Ron could see her thinking about her decision.

"School's important, and it's not like you're going to make a lot of money from magic and ghost hunting." He paused for a second. "Maybe a treasure here or there; but nothing that'd make you very rich."

"Wait, treasure? What treasure?" Amanda asked.

"You missed that adventure. We could have used you to get into some places. I was too big to fit in, so Linda had to do it. She was covered in webs when she unlocked the door, and I couldn't stop laughing," Ron told her. He then raised his glance, before muttering, "Then again, maybe not" Ron Realizing that Amanda was now taller.

Amanda then asked, "How much did you find?"

Ron thought for a moment. "Enough to keep the shop open for a long time." Amanda noticed he lingered on *long* for a few seconds. She made a mental note to ask Linda later how much they found.

They stayed for a bit longer, but finally decided to head back to the house.

* * *

When they arrived, as soon as Amanda spoke, Jinx bounded into the entryway. When he leaped onto Amanda, he nearly knocked her over.

"Wow, Jinx, you've gotten heavy! What have they been feeding you?" Amanda said as she ruffled his scruff, something Jinx only allowed her to do. Ron could hear him purring from the main room as they walked in. "Was there any trouble getting him here?"

"No, he went right in the carrier, and I swear he was moving it toward the door himself when I arrived. Guess he wanted to get out of there," Linda told her.

Jinx lay across her lap as she continued to ruffle his fur. She brought up the treasure, which made Linda look at Ron, who replied, "I just mentioned treasure. I didn't say anything else."

Linda answered the same as Ron had, making Amanda laugh. But when Linda replied, "Not just the shop; the house, the cabin, maybe a few thousand trips around the world," Amanda looked surprised.

"How much?"

Ron nodded. "We got lucky."

Amanda smiled, "Now, you have to tell me what I missed."

The next couple of days went quickly, and Amanda was packing again to head back to school. Jinx lay on the front room desk as she stopped in to say goodbye to her friends. Amanda picked Jinx up, bringing him with her, and placed her backpack on the table along with Jinx. She rifled through her bag to get out the drawings she had done while there. She could see Jinx looking at her, his tail wrapped around him as he stared.

"I wish I could take you with me, Jinx, but they don't allow pets in the apartments." She sounded sad, and hadn't noticed Roween flittering behind her. When she turned around, her fairy friend surprised her with a hug on her nose. She pulled away from Amanda. "He's a cat and many winks he'll see, he's not a brat, just leave Jinx to me."

Amanda picked up Jinx one last time. "Hear that, Jinx? Roween's going to watch over you, so you be good. No trying to eat her." She then lightly tapped his nose. Jinx flinched, but then raised his paw and did the same to her.

Seeing this, Linda said, "Looks like he understands more than he lets on."

They all laughed, and Linda took Jinx as Amanda handed Ron the remaining artwork before scratching Jinx one more time.

"I'm going to miss him," Amanda said.

Linda smiled, "We'll take good care of him till you get back. He's welcome here. Besides, I told your parents he's here now, and they weren't sure when they could come and get him."

Amanda looked at her phone; it was getting late. She would have to leave soon to avoid the heavy traffic. She said her goodbyes, ruffling Jinx's scruff one last time before she closed the door and started back to school.

Chapter Eighteen
You Never Know till You Miss It

Amanda turned the car off and sat silent for a moment. It had been a long ride back to school, and not just because of the traffic. That same feeling of leaving those she cared about behind again weighed on her. She moved her hand as if scratching Jinx in her mind before she opened the door.

Amanda could see the shadows formed by the lights that dotted the parking area. She wearily grabbed her backpack and suitcase and headed up to her apartment. She was careful to remain quiet, as it was sometime after 1:00 a.m., and anyone still on campus was probably sleeping.

Amanda unlocked the door and tapped the light. The room was as she had left it; nothing seemed out of place. Her foot slid on something as she stepped forward. Looking down, she could see several folded pieces of paper littering the floor. Clumsily, she knelt to pick them up and almost lost her balance with the heavy backpack.

Amanda looked at the notes. She recognized the handwriting as those she was friends with. The notes were mostly from Gabs and Shrive, asking to get in touch when she returned. A few were from Selese, mostly saying Gabs was all right.

She then came across one she didn't recognize. It was written on a small, torn piece of paper. It read, "Call me when you get back."

"It'd be nice to know who you are," Amanda muttered. The note did not indicate who had written it. Amanda shook her head and went to shuffle to the next message when she saw the name under her thumb.

"Luke left me a note?" Amanda felt the air around her warm as she stared at his name. She smiled, placing the note on top.

Closing the door, Amanda dropped her backpack; it made a dull thump as it settled on the floor. She looked around before again looking at the note she held.

"Probably a bit late to call him," she muttered, but then thought, *maybe he's working tonight*. She shook her head and placed the pile of papers on the table. She relaxed in the chair and took a deep breath. As she did, she wrinkled her nose.

"Air's stale; I should probably open a window for a few minutes." Changing the air in the room was something she did every couple of days. It was just something she did, even back home. It's also why she preferred being outside most of the time.

Amanda opened the window a crack and went to the kitchen. She was tired and thirsty. She filled a glass with water and gulped down, then started filling the glass again. This time she slowed herself and sipped, turning to head back into the room. She choked, being startled by a small, glowing fairy flying before her. Alicee smiled. Amanda couldn't help but notice that it was the same type of smile Roween had when she was playing tricks.

"You are back, no need to hack. It's contrary to this small fairy," Alicee said, continuing that mischievous smile.

"Alicee, thanks, it's good to be back. How did you get in here?" Amanda asked. The small fairy pointed to the window.

"You have the notes, all that wrote?" Amanda took a moment to realize what she was asking before nodding.

"Adventures unfold, and notes not told. A friend named Shrive so did strive, with friend Gabriella, to find a stela," Alicee said.

"Wait, what are you talking about? You're not making sense," Amanda said, making Alicee cross her arms, before using her magic to show her a picture of a stone with markings. She didn't notice what they were at first, but when the fairy ring she wore glowed, the markings became clear. The rock said, "Museum Ro . . ." the rest was broken and unreadable.

Amanda thought for a moment and realized that the stone looked like part of a column. "Is that from the museum in Michigan?"

Alicee nodded. She told Amanda that it was found in the Shadowed Hall. It had been moved aside, near one of the columns. Gabriella had tripped over it when Shrive brought her home from visiting the park. According to Alicee, there was no record of any travel to that area, except for Shrive and later Luke when they investigated the attempted theft of the Pertu statue. Amanda looked at the note Luke had left before wondering if that was because of what they found. The messages from Shrive might be as well. Amanda jumped when she heard someone say, "Oh good, you're back."

Amanda looked toward the person, ready for a fight, but as she walked out of the shadows, Amanda took a breath and was surprised when her senses filled with a pleasant fragrance.

"You know you don't just appear in someone's place, right? How about a little privacy?" Amanda grumbled, making Alicee motion for her to be quiet.

Selese smiled, "You were talking to this fairy, and you just walked in the door. I only jumped in because I heard Alicee talking to you."

Selese walked up, nodding to Alicee. "You tell her about the stone?"

Alicee nodded and turned to see Amanda looking less than happy with them both standing there. "You know I just got back, right? It's late; what are you still doing up?"

Selese looked annoyed. "Night's my best time, remember? Besides, I'm off work, checking in on Gabs. And to make sure you got back safe."

Amanda realized that Selese was worried and became glad that she was checking up on her friend as well. But Amanda was tired. The drive had been long, and she desperately wanted to get some sleep. Selese noticed. "Look, it'll just be a few minutes, then we'll get out of here and let you rest."

Amanda became concerned that Selese was suddenly serious and asked, "What else has happened?"

Selese sighed, "Someone stole the Hessian statue. And that foiled attempt on the Pertu was a lucky break."

"The Hessian statue?" Amanda asked.

Selese sighed again, "Okay, maybe it'll be more than a few minutes."

Selese told her about the pillars of the Circle and the statues' names, going against everything her father had told her to keep secret. Selese felt vindicated when Amanda said, "The pillars probably help power the Circle. Probably not a good idea to destroy them."

Amanda paused, sniffing the air. "New perfume?"

Selese nodded. "Cayden got it for me." Amanda nodded, giving an understanding wink.

Amanda told them how Ron was at the museum and that he saw Shrive when she arrived. Selese seemed almost amused and said, "You mean cat-girl got caught?"

Amanda smiled, "Yeah, he watched her do something to make the statue challenging to lift." Amanda told her how a piece of the column injured Ron as it fell. He was hit pushing the guard out of the way.

"That explains the piece of the column. It probably went through when whoever was there shadow-walked out of the museum," Selese said.

Amanda looked at the image again. "What's this symbol?" The fairy ring she wore allowed her to read different writings, but the symbol seemed written in chalk. When Selese examined it, she didn't know what it was at first, but then she realized what it was and told Amanda.

"That's an element, a scroll witch symbol. I don't know what it means, though; but I know someone who might," Selese said.

Amanda looked at it again and grabbed her sketchpad. She quickly copied the symbol, showing it to Selese. "There, that looks pretty close."

Selese looked at the symbol. It wasn't close. It was identical. When she asked Amanda how she copied it so well, all Amanda said was, "I'm just able to," before pausing. "Also, what's a scroll witch?"

Selese told her about humans being able to use magic, even those without magic blood. Those humans were known as scroll witches. They used symbols to access the magic, but it was limited. She mentioned that most use it to travel or unlock places within the Sanctuary. Others, like Luke and Cayden, use them to do their jobs.

"Wait, Luke doesn't have any magic in his life, uh, I mean, background," Amanda said, making Selese smile. She had known the two of them had been seen together, and she suspected that the two might have been more deeply involved. Amanda's words only confirmed she had feelings for the hunter and that, Selese found humorous.

"Yes, Amanda, your boyfriend is a scroll witch. Anything else you need to know?" She moved closer. "I can do some research for you, if you like."

Amanda seemed to pause for a moment before shaking her head. She was tired from the trip, and still wasn't in a mood to get into things with Selese. She was able to manage a timid smile.

Selese watched her fight back a yawn and took pity. She knew Amanda had been driving for hours, and they did pop in with the surprise information.

Selese waved to get Alicee's attention before looking to Amanda. "Was it a long trip?"

Amanda nodded. "Yeah, traffic was bad; could have used a portal. Think this would let me?" She held up the sketch.

Selese snickered, "I don't know. I'll find out. We should let you get some sleep." She turned to leave and noticed Amanda staring at the symbol. She decided to say something. "Hey, don't start messing with that. You don't know what it does yet."

Amanda looked up. "I know better than that. I learned the hard way when I set off a trap in one of the keeps we visited. I was just wondering why it was there."

Selese nodded. "I'll let you know what I find. Get some sleep." Selese then looked toward the door. "I'm sure Gabs will be here bright and early when she finds out your car is back in the lot."

* * *

The next day, Amanda met Shrive at the pizza shop they had started using as an unofficial meeting place. As Selese predicted, Gabriella was with Amanda since early morning and had already updated her on what they found when she tripped over the stone. She showed them the sketch of the symbol, but none of them knew what it meant.

As they were heading back, Amanda brought up the museum. "Hey, Shrive, did you notice Ron when he was at the museum?"

Shrive replied, "Who? There was no one there, just the guard."

Amanda looked into the rearview mirror at Shrive. "You mean you didn't see the guy in the tan jacket watching you while holding his injured arm? He told me that he was wondering if he was seeing things when he saw your ears. He told me about the magic you used to secure the icon too."

"What? You can only see those when I'm changing or in sneak-shift. I remained like this the entire time!" Shrive protested, pointing to herself. "And what do you mean he was standing there? The only other person in the museum was the guard. I'm still trying to figure out how he didn't get crushed."

Amanda smiled, "Ron pushed him out of the way; that's how he fractured his arm. You mean you really didn't see him?"

Shrive looked annoyed. "He wasn't there. I'm pretty much invisible when I want to be."

Amanda looked at her. "Sneak-shift?"

Shrive leaned forward between the seats. "Yeah, mostly cat. Quiet and deadly." She smiled, showing her cat-like teeth. Then she continued. "Ron wasn't there; you're making this up."

Amanda smiled back, "The spell you used was pretty effective. He couldn't lift the statue off the pillar."

"Yeah, it was an attachment spell." Shrive's eyes widened. "Wait, he really was there? And I didn't see him?"

Amanda nodded.

Shrive leaned back. "I still don't think he saw me. He must have gotten there later and tried to move the statue after I left."

Amanda smiled, "He mentioned that small white patch on your left ear."

Shrive reached up, touching her ear. "You can only see that when you're up close. I still don't believe you."

"Remember, I could still see the shimmer," Amanda told her.

Shrive replied, "That's impossible, unless . . ." She paused and looked annoyed. "He has a fairy ring, doesn't he?" she said, making Amanda nod.

"Dammit, I knew you were trouble when I met you," Shrive joked, making everyone in the car laugh.

Amanda waved to someone they passed when they arrived back on campus. He had been walking by the entrance of the lot. When they stopped, Shrive headed back to the main building to check if she had another assignment while Amanda and Gabriella headed into the dorms. None of them noticed that the man they passed was now standing off in the distance, watching them.

Tyler tapped the small box and his glasses dimly glowed, the display scrolling numbers. He moved the thin wire running down to the small, patterned box in his pocket. A smile crossed his face as he watched the three women heading their separate ways. Only the night heard him mutter, "She is an elf, feline magic. It may possibly be a curse; I've been meaning to ask Mr. Vikander about things like that." He turned to the two walking toward the dorm. "One is human, and the other a fairy and assorted mix." He laughed, "The boss is going to love the new upgrades I've made for the detector. I hope these people aren't dangerous, though, and I'd hate to have to take their magic away."

Tyler's smile disappeared as he looked down to his wrist and scrolled through the display on his watch. He stopped on one of the symbols before turning to walk toward the shadows. His last words heard by the darkness were, "That cat-girl is pretty cute, though," before disappearing into the shadows.

Humans and things are what magic all brings. When strife and all is hurried and scary, then life is a ball, when you know a fairy.

- Fairy saving

Chapter Nineteen
The Plan Moves Ahead

Things had quieted as the new week of classes settled; the new semester brought new people and more work. Amanda had taken on a job as an illustrator for work credit; unfortunately, she found more work than she could handle. Thankfully, Gabriella and Shrive were willing to help. They had just finished the job when Gabriella seemed happier than usual as she walked in. She had been gone for the last few hours, leaving Shrive and Amanda to finish the previously paid illustration.

"Gabs, you seem cheery, what's up?" Amanda asked as she placed the artwork in the container, ready to ship. Gabriella turned to see Amanda standing there and felt a little guilty for leaving them to finish up. She had a reason, and it involved her friends. She had also finished her semester project well ahead of schedule. They all had been there for more than a year, and she was going to celebrate. In her mind, this had to be done.

Gabriella pointed to Amanda and then to Shrive. "The three of us are lucky today."

Shrive looked over at her, jokingly saying, "Oh, I don't like the sound of this."

Gabriella smiled and held before her three tickets for the Struder House. "I got these. One for each of us." She handed Amanda one of the tickets. As Amanda looked, she became excited. "Gabs, are these real? Where'd you get them?"

Shrive took hers quickly as Gabriella handed her the ticket. When she inspected it, she couldn't believe what she was seeing. "This was sold out; you really got tickets to Two Times Crazy Violin Cult. How?"

Gabriella smiled, "Selese. They're playing this weekend at the Struder House." She looked a little disappointed. "Still had to pay for them, though."

"Selese got you tickets?" Shrive asked, unconvinced. But when Gabriella nodded, she said, "You had that girl all wrong."

It wasn't long before the short celebration ended and they headed off to get some sleep. Amanda complained that she had to get up early for the exam in Art History.

Amanda's mind started to drift as she looked at her phone. The deadlines for both courses and the jobs were beginning to pile up. She had done nothing for the *Haunted Maples* stories as she had promised, and even wondered if maybe she should have taken the entire summer off and worked on the illustrations for Ron. But as she stared at the unfinished work of her semester project, she realized that she probably wouldn't have time for that.

* * *

The weekend arrived quickly, and Amanda was sitting with Shrive at the Studer House. They were both waiting for their food before looking for Gabriella.

"Where'd she go? The band's gonna be on soon," Amanda asked before seeing Gabriella through the crowd. She hugged her as she arrived at the table, making her almost spill the drinks she was carrying. Amanda grabbed a coupleof them as Gabriella sat down.

"I can't believe you forgot to order drinks," Gabriella said as Amanda handed one to Shrive. Gabriella held her glass up. "To us."

After a quick toast, she paused. "Don't worry, ladies, the drinks won't disappear this time. At least not on their own." They laughed as the band was setting up and the server put down the tray of food they ordered.

"Oh yeah, pizza fry night. Never thought I'd like this sort of stuff," Shrive said, jokingly wrestling Amanda for control of the food before she shoved a handful into her mouth. She scowled as Amanda laughed at her, gulping down the fries.

After the band started, they enjoyed themselves, and Amanda finally asked Gabriella where she had been all day. She could barely hear her friend through the crowd and loud music, but she replied, "I had to speak with my counselor, something about my tuition. I wanted to pay for the year but didn't have enough. I'm still not making enough money to pay for everything," Gabs said. She complained that she'd probably still owe money, and her grant was delayed being approved for next year. And now she was worrying about food. Amanda smiled and handed her a bowl of pizza fries. "Don't worry, we got ya covered."

As the band wound down, the crowd started to thin out. The three were planning on staying a bit longer, maybe meet the band, but they were out of luck. Selese told them that they already left. They had another gig a few states away and had to hit the road. She also told them that Tyler was in the crowd.

Amanda had known Tyler was back at school. He only had a few classes, and from what Selese found out, he was working for some eccentric professor. When they did finally see him, he was surrounded by people, well-dressed and popular. They were cautious, making sure they had people between them and the computer artist. Selese and Shrive tried to find information on his employer; even Lord Cale was unsuccessful, which made Amanda worried. When Gabriella saw Tyler, she couldn't help but feel jealous.

"Another college dropout makes millions," Gabriella said, making Amanda tell her, "That's not important."

Gabriella felt a bit resentful and said, "Some of us don't make money from the artwork they do."

Amanda looked at her. "At least not yet. Your stuff's been doing good online. You paid for most of this semester, didn't you?"

Shrive interrupted, "Besides, he's not making millions." She pointed to him. "There's something else; he's wearing some sort of tech glasses."

Amanda thought for a moment, remembering the box he had been working on earlier. She was suspicious. "What if those are connected to that box he made?" Her words brought the small group of friends to silence. As Tyler turned away from them, Amanda casually pulled out the detector crystal and pointed it toward Tyler. Selese was close by, and they both watched it glow a dark amber, making Amanda look concerned.

"What's that mean?" Gabs asked.

"It means he's been messing around with dark magic; that's probably why he's got money now."

Shrive hit Amanda. "Stole my idea, girl! I wanted to say that." But as they joked, Selese watched as Tyler touched his glasses and started to turn around. She quickly pushed Amanda's hand with the crystal away.

"Ow, what was that for?" Amanda asked, rubbing her hand.

Selese continued to watch Tyler. "When I tell you to, point the crystal at him again. Do it."

Amanda nodded and as Tyler turned away, she again pointed it at him briefly, and he again touched his glasses and turned toward them. Amanda quickly put the crystal away.

"That's unexpected. Looks like he can detect the detector crystals," Amanda said. The three of them looked concerned while Selese smiled. "I'll be right back."

They watched as Selese moved through the crowd, winding up behind Tyler. She did so with stealth and was standing close to him in the group. She did her best to see if she could see the back of his lenses. She was rewarded when someone bumped him and they were almost knocked off. She quickly had a chance and could see the words that were on the lenses. Being part darkling gave her excellent eyesight, and she could make out the words: "Human 30%, Troll 15%, Fairy 10%."

She quickly moved away while Tyler fumbled to put his glasses back on when she reached the table. "Bad news, girls, Amanda was right. That thing can read magic. In fact, I think it does the same as the crystal circle."

Amanda appeared even more concerned as Shrive turned to look toward Tyler and Selese said, "Did you hear that two icons have gone missing in the last few weeks?"

Amanda shook her head. "When?"

"Last week, just before Tyler came back. The *Conflagration of Sienna* went missing."

"So, the fire icon was stolen." Amanda confirmed Selese's information. She was now sure there was much more going on.

As Dennon walked into the room, he could see the circle of light created by the overhead lamp as Paul worked at a control panel. The hunter had delivered the icon for Paul to test the recent mechanisms Tyler had helped create. Dennon looked over to see a drunken man, half-conscious, sitting in a cage of copper and steel, something the old mage certainly noticed.

"Found him homeless; no one's going to miss him. You know that boy is a genius. He has a gift for combining magic and technology." Dennon continued to stare at the half-drunk man, now standing in a circle of light. "All I have to do is press a button and—" The old mage turned to Dennon. "This is the best part."

The cage glowed yellow and the man started to convulse until his eyes became vacant. Paul approached the cage, asking, "Whom do you serve?"

The man, without hesitation, replied, "You, the mage of my creation."

Dennon looked confused as Vikander cheered giddily. "I would have had to rip his heart out and store it. Now with a little magic and the press of a button, I can make as many servants as I desire. And the best part is, it doesn't just work on humans."

Dennon was surprised. "Other creatures as well? How'd you get the boy to do it?"

Vikander laughed, "Those with enough brains to understand, yes, any creature. But it does take longer. As for how I convinced the boy? I told him we take away the powers of those who are dangerous. I didn't go into detail as to what else I would take."

Dennon chuckled, turning to see the *Lament of Hessian* statue on the table as Vikander said, "Here's a new trick."

Vikander placed the statue into another chamber and attached it to the cage. "I've successfully transferred energies from one to another." He pointed to a small sylph in a glass jar. Dennon could see the lightning it fired from his hands. Paul looked pleased as he said, "I took the powers from a lightning Raiju and placed it into one of them. It took me only a day to do so. I think we're ready to move on to the icon."

Paul continued to work as Dennon watched. The wraith mage pressed buttons until the cage around the statue started to glow again. He called Dennon over and pointed to the crystal on top of the panel.

"You see this? It indicates the power level being transferred. As it falls and grows dimmer, it indicates the power remaining. That was the old way of how I used to take powers." He then pointed to a small display. "This shows you in increments. The boy even created a simple percentage display."

Dennon could see the joy in his master's eyes and in his heart, he knew that with this new technology, they would be able to fulfill the taking of the Circle. But as he stared at the display, he noticed nothing seemed to be happening.

"Is this working?" he asked, making Vikander look over the panel.

The wraith mage looked concerned and rushed toward the cage holding his new slave. "The power is transferring, but . . ." The old man paused before rushing back to the panel. Dennon was startled as Vikander slammed his hand onto one of the buttons. The old man sat and leaned back into his chair as Dennon looked concerned.

The mage smiled, "I was too excited and almost ruined my own plan."

Dennon watched as the old man grabbed a book and started writing furiously. His master looked at the panel several times before returning to his notetaking.

"What is it?" Dennon asked.

Vikander held his hand up as he continued to write. Dennon could see an expression of relief on the old mage's face.

"Dennon, you have served the Broken Feather for some time. And I would be a fool to allow what we have achieved to be ruined by a simple mistake," Paul said as he placed the book down.

The Raven Hunter looked curiously at the scribblings and could see numbers where the man had written.

Paul stood and walked over to his new slave. "We didn't lose much, my friend." The old man sighed as Dennon listened, "I had theorized that due to the powers the pillars had, it would take a little time to transfer them to another. It seems that they were more powerful than I had anticipated."

Dennon asked, "Was the power lost?"

The wraith mage smiled, "As I said, only very little. It seems it will take about five hundred thirty-eight hours to transfer that power for us to use."

Dennon looked disheartened. "The slave will die before then. This machine is no good to us."

The old man laughed, "Oh, my friend, you are not a patient man." He walked over, putting his hand on the hunter's shoulder. "I'll have to make a support system to feed and keep the subject alive. It will only add a few weeks to our plan."

Dennon seemed relieved by his master's words.

Vikander nodded. "It will give us time to retrieve the remaining icons in the meantime. And after we have them all, we'll take the spirit."

Dennon felt the pang of victory as he heard his master. He, as did all senior hunters, knew that Claire Brentwood held the Key of the Spirit and the last secret of the Circle.

Chapter Twenty
You've Been Banned

Over the next few weeks, things quieted down within the Sanctuary. Amanda still hadn't had a chance to check on the symbol, since only hunters and members of the Circle were allowed in the Sanctuary, for the moment. The added security also meant that the campus was quiet as well. It was a welcome change, since mid-terms had finally arrived, and most students were studying—or at least trying to.

As the end of the week arrived, Amanda had just finished her last exam and was heading out when she felt a tap on her shoulder. Weirdly, she turned to see no one there. Amanda looked around, then noticed a familiar fragrance. "Selese, what do you want?"

"Wait, how'd you know it was me?" Selese said as she came around from behind Amanda.

Amanda smiled, then gently sniffed the air. "Same perfume."

Selese looked suspicious. "I put on too much today?" making Amanda nod before they both started laughing. They continued to talk as they headed out of the building. Selese asked if she'd join her in the campus museum. When Amanda asked why, Selese said, "Because I want to check up on the Tarnus statue. And if I'm by myself, they may think I'm trying to steal it." She paused. "Again."

Amanda took a moment before she laughed. "What makes you think they'll let me near it? They may think *I'm* trying to take it." They both nodded as they walked toward the museum.

When they arrived, they discovered that the display had been removed. Amanda face showed a stern look of concern seeing someone now cleaning the glass that once held the icon. Luckily, they ran into Shrive as she walked out of the shadows. Selese startled her as she walked up, making Shrive turn, slashing out at her. Selese jumped back.

"Easy, Shrive, me friend. No scratch." Selese then grabbed the nearby spray bottle and spritzed toward the cat-like face glaring back. Amanda could see the anger growing on Shrive's face and grabbed the spray bottle from Selese, telling her, "I don't think she likes that."

Shrive started yelling, but Selese stood her ground before Amanda stepped in. "Enough. Let's take this someplace more private." Amanda looked at the people staring at them as she dragged the two with her. "Too many witnesses; you can kill each other without an audience."

Shrive calmed, realizing that Selese was trying to make a joke, and Selese apologized, since it wasn't amusing. Shrive told them that the icon had been taken somewhere safe and that only a few people knew where it was. Selese thought for a moment before saying, "It has to be the Forge."

"The Forge?" Amanda asked.

Selese leaned in and quietly told them both, "It used to be where they made magic weapons, well before the school was built." She then continued. "They used it to make some of the lampposts that ring the campus. They're supposed to stop feral magic creatures from entering."

Selese told them how the Forge was the most impenetrable vault in this part of the world, and how it became a place to house some of the most potent artifacts they had.

"Wait, how do you know all this?" Shrive asked.

Selese looked almost regretful, telling them how she used to spend a lot of time in Brentwood's office when she wasn't in class. "It was after I got my . . ." She pointed to her heart. "I didn't know how to use it, so I was usually in some form of trouble. When I was bored, I decided to read." She told them that she learned about the history of the school and the Sanctuary. She knew more about places around them than even the higher members of the Circle.

"I figured I would learn about this place and when I was ready, to escape," Selese said.

Her friends looked puzzled as Selese again seemed regretful.

Selese sighed, "I felt like I was a prisoner. I didn't realize this place would become like home." She looked at Shrive. "Now, I think it's in danger."

Amanda held onto Selese's arm, making her smile. "You know, we should go check it out, make sure everything is secure."

Shrive shook her head. "The Sanctuary is still on lockdown. You'll never get in."

Selese noted, "You got in."

Shrive protested, telling them that she couldn't bring them in with her. But when Selese said, "I think I may know a way," Shrive became cautiously interested.

Selese told Shrive to go in and meet with Cale. "Tell him that his daughter has a concern and that he is to wait for her by the meeting rooms in the west hall."

When Shrive asked why, Selese told her, "Tell him I'm bringing a friend." She then pointed to Amanda. Shrive reluctantly agreed and disappeared into the shadows.

Selese turned to Amanda. "We'll give her a few minutes, then we'll head down."

When Amanda asked where, Selese said, "You'll have to trust me," and she pulled Amanda toward the hall door. Amanda followed, and they stopped before what looked like the stone foundation of the building. Amanda could see the archways that supported the structure above. Selese smiled as she looked around the darkened room.

"I know it's here somewhere." She turned back toward Amanda. "Tried it when I first found out about it. I wonder if it's still open." Selese held her hand to the wall and spoke the same phrase she did when she escaped from the Broken Feather. Amanda watched as her hand passed through the stone. Selese pushed her arm through until she felt a breeze.

"Oh good, it's not blocked. It would have been a short ride if it were," before smiling nervously as her hand pulled from the stone.

Selese turned to see Amanda staring in awe and cautioned, "Whatever you do, don't flail around. You'll thank me for it. The ride's going to be rough enough."

"What are you talking about?" Amanda asked.

Selese looked serious. "We're going to be going against the current." She grabbed Amanda and placed her before the wall. "I'm going to turn us both intangible to get through the wall. Afterward, it gets a lot more fun."

Amanda took a breath. "This is a magic air shaft?"

"Yep. You ready?" Selese asked, and as Amanda nodded. she turned them intangible. Amanda could feel Selese push against her back, and the sensation of passing through solid rock was a frightening experience she hadn't considered. But as she exited the other side, she felt the warm air against her skin. Moments later, the world around her lit brightly and she watched glowing air currents rush past her, and the ground beneath her fell away. Amanda felt herself tossed around, and the sensation of falling faster and faster. In the rustling air she heard Selese yell, "When we get to the end, don't forget to roll!"

* * *

Cale had joined Shrive by the meeting rooms and was less than happy. He and the other hunters had been busy fortifying the Sanctuary.

"Shrive, I have a whole team of people locking this area down. This better not be a prank from my daughter," Cale grumbled, less than amused.

As he turned to look toward the empty hall, he felt a sudden rush of wind. A moment later, Amanda appeared from the solid stone, followed by Selese. Shrive heard grunting and thumping as they both rolled across the floor.

Cale yelled for backup and jumped out of the way as Amanda rolled by. He felt Selese's back come to rest against his leg. She looked up, giving him an innocent smile. "Hello, Father."

Selese turned to look at Amanda to see her on her hands and knees, looking a bit queasy. "You all right?"

Shrive rushed over to help her up, and as Amanda stood, she said, "Just waiting for my stomach to catch up with me."

Selese looked at her father and put her hand to her ear. "Hear that?"

Cale looked confused; the only sound was the shuffling of Amanda's feet as she walked over, still off-balance from traveling through the air shaft. He asked her what she was hearing, concerned she might have hit her head.

"No alarm. We got in without setting anything off," Selese noted.

Cale became furious. "This isn't some joke, Selese. I have a team of people securing this entire place."

Selese looked sternly back. "So do I." She then put her arms around Amanda and Shrive.

Cale looked at the wall. When he'd used a spell, he wasn't able to detect the entrance. "How did you get in?'

Selese continued to brush herself off. "This used to be the work area for the Forge and there was an air shaft. They used an intangible tunnel to bring in fresh air. The stone turns the air intangible, and it exits in the alley between the buildings."

Shrive looked quizzically at Selese, who said, "What, you never wondered why that alleyway was always windy?"

Selese continued telling him that the shaft was right under where the Tarnus statue was placed. It was too close for comfort for her liking. She then grabbed her father's arm and turned it intangible, pushing it through the stone. He believed her as he felt the warm air moving away from within the wall.

Cale looked at her and then toward Amanda. "And she is here why?"

Selese huffed, "She's good at figuring things out. Maybe she can bring a new perspective."

The sound of footsteps suddenly filled the hall as a group of hunters, including Luke, rushed to help Cale as he looked sternly toward Selese. "No, you're leaving. Both of you."

"But we can help!" Selese protested.

Cale disagreed and ordered them to be taken out through the Sanctuary. "By the front way, please." As they were escorted away by the other hunters, Selese heard Luke ask if Amanda was all right.

Everyone stared as Amanda and Selese were being escorted through the Sanctuary. Arianne looked concerned, seeing them accompanied by the number of hunters with them.

"Tell me they didn't hurt someone," Arianne whispered.

From beside her, she heard, "Nah, just bruised someone's ego." She turned to see Raymond standing there watching as well. He had a smile on his face as he said, "They found a way that none of the council thought of. They're parading them through here as a warning. They don't want anyone to know they were caught off guard."

"How do you know that?" Arianne asked.

The quiet man pushed his shoulders back. "Because not much escapes me when it happens in the Sanctuary. I'm glad they showed them; even I didn't remember that entrance still existed." Raymond then walked away and faded into the darkness of the Sanctuary hall.

They reached the door, and one of the hunters pushed Selese out somewhat ungentlemanly, making her turn back in anger. As the same hunter grabbed Amanda's arm, Luke stepped in, pushing it off. "I've got this," Luke growled quietly before walking Amanda out the door.

He apologized to Selese for her being thrown through the doorway, making her say, "At least you did it right," before looking back at Amanda, seeing her smile.

They talked for a few minutes until one of the other hunters arrived and whispered something to Luke. When he left, all Luke said was, "They've banned you both from the Hall."

Selese asked, "What about the Sanctuary? I've gotta have someplace to go if the Feather comes around. Her too," she said, pointing to Amanda.

"I'm sure it's temporary; it's not like you two are criminals," Luke said.

Selese looked at him. "Wait, you don't think I'm a criminal?"

Luke gave a sheepish smile. "Selese, you're not. It took me a while, but I understand why Lord Cale insisted you weren't. I'm sorry."

Selese looked puzzled and was about to ask why he changed his mind when she saw him holding Amanda's hand. "She changed your mind, didn't she?"

Luke looked to Amanda and nodded. "She trusts you, and she's known you the least of all of us."

Selese felt a warmth in her chest, something she'd missed for some time. She then looked toward the Sanctuary; she had resided there until she was old enough to live on her own. It didn't hold the most pleasant memories, but what she felt now eased her spirit, at least some. Selese rolled her shoulders and looked around.

"I should probably get going." She turned to walk away. "You know, maybe you should escort her home, just in case more criminals are roaming the grounds." She then pointed to herself before waving as she disappeared into the shadow of a tree.

Both Amanda and Luke smiled.

Luke looked to Amanda. "You know, my shift is over. Do you want to grab something to eat? I know a great place nearby."

Amanda nodded nervously and accepted. She gripped his hand tighter as he pulled her along.

It wasn't long before they stopped and Luke pointed to a simple, gray door. Amanda looked up and read the sign. It was faded and said, "The Silver Palette."

"That's an interesting name for a restaurant," Amanda said.

Luke looked at her, confused. "It reads 'For Rent.' How do you see the actual sign?"

Amanda grabbed her chain with two fingers and wiggled it gently between them. Luke laughed and told her to try the door. As she turned the knob, she found it wouldn't budge. When Luke placed his hand over hers, it turned to allow the door to open easily.

"A magic lock." Amanda smiled at him. "There's one on the door of my friends' back home."

Luke sighed, then joked, "You're making it difficult to impress you, you know that?"

They were both laughing as they entered.

They spent a few hours together; the food was excellent, and Amanda told him stories of some of her adventures. Several people even greeted them as they enjoyed their time. But Amanda could see others staring, some making comments between themselves. Amanda overheard one of them and said, "Hope you don't get a reputation or anything from bringing me here."

Luke smiled, "Considering most of them know who you are, probably."

The two spent a little longer together before Amanda looked toward Luke and suggested, "Maybe we should head back?"

Luke agreed. "I'll take you home."

As they walked toward her apartment, the once brightly lit sky had turned to night. She held onto his hand, and once in a while, swayed lightly, pressing her body against his. The pace they took was slow, and the night just warm enough. Amanda looked up to see the moon partially full as it lit the sky. She turned to look back at Luke and noticed the small symbol on his collar.

"Oh, wait, I wanted to show you something." Amanda hurriedly pulled a small piece of paper from her purse and used her phone to light it.

"It looks like a scroll element. Where'd you see it?" Luke asked.

"I was doing some research and found it in a picture," Amanda told him, conveniently not saying where.

"This isn't research on the icons, is it?" Luke asked, concerned.

Amanda nodded. "It was at the museum where you checked out the attempted theft."

Luke handed it back to her. "I think it's a misfortune element. They're sometimes used to guard artifacts." He noted, "You probably shouldn't be carrying that around with you."

They continued to talk as they walked through the darkness, the waxing moon lighting the path before them. When they made it back to Amanda's place, he kissed her, but gently pulled away as she opened the door. Amanda gently pulled him back, and as they were about to kiss again, down the hall, they heard a door fly open. The sound echoed through the hall as Gabriella came rushing toward them, holding a stack of papers.

"Good, you're back, we just had a rush job come in." As she was just about to reach them, Gabriella looked up to see Amanda and Luke staring back with their faces awfully close together. All Gabriella could do was stare at them in silence.

"Yes, Gabs?" Amanda said, somewhat annoyed.

Gabrielle still stood silent. Her eyes switching between the two people before her. Luke chuckled before there was a loud alert from his phone. He looked at it. "I can't believe it."

Amanda asked, "What?"

When Luke looked up at her, their eyes lingered for a moment, but she could see his disappointment. "They just sent out an alert. Something's happened; they're calling everyone in."

Amanda was disheartened until Luke leaned in and kissed her again. She followed his lips back as he pulled away as his phone again pinged.

He sighed, "I have to go."

Luke hesitated as he turned before continuing to walk away. There was an evident expression as Amanda watched him leave. As Luke pulled his hood up, he jokingly said, "Told you; you probably shouldn't be carrying that around." She watched Luke disappear into the shadows. Her look of disappointment morphed to annoyance as she turned to stare at Gabriella.

Gabriella had been standing silently, finally able to utter a simple, "Oops?"

Moments later, Amanda sighed as she crumpled up the paper before tossing it into the trash can in the hallway. "C'mon, Gabs, what you got for us?"

When the sun is low, and you're on the ground. Like winter snow, can a fairy be found.

- Fairy saying.

Chapter Twenty-One
Checking out the Competition

Dr. Claire Brentwood appeared in the shadow of a large oak tree. She looked around as if confused. "That should have taken me to the front of their house." Instead, she found herself across the street. She walked across and was about to touch the gate to the yard when her bracelet vibrated.

"Protection magic, very strong. It seems our records are lacking on these two," Claire muttered quietly before opening the small gate. Claire knocked politely before gently placing her hand on the large wooden door. Her bracelet again vibrated, the gem now glowing red. She quickly pulled her hand back in fear. "Very strong magic."

She smiled as the door opened and Linda stood greeting her.

"Hi, I'm looking for Ron Wilt," Claire said.

Linda felt the door tug against her grip and she became cautious. "How can I help you?"

Claire smiled, "My name is Claire. I'm here to see Ron, if he's around."

Linda looked the woman over, feigning a smile. To her, the woman standing at her door did not seem threatening, but the house seemed to think otherwise. It took a few moments before she allowed her inside.

"Come in. I'll get him," Linda said as she allowed the woman to enter. She felt the door pull from her grip, nearly slamming on Dr. Brentwood as she swiftly moved out of its way.

"Sorry, oiled the hinges recently. It sometimes does that." Linda smiled as she motioned for the woman to follow. Linda led her to the main room, tapping a small wooden box on the shelf by the door as she walked by.

As Claire entered, she could see the old woodwork mixed with new furniture. The room seemed brightly lit for having such small windows. And she noticed the house felt as if it was alive.

"Is Ron here?" Claire asked.

Linda continued to watch Claire before saying, "Let me get him. Please wait here."

As Linda started to walk out of the room, Claire wanted to see what she was hiding and said, "Tell me how Ron was able to avoid our operative." The doctor then started to use magic. Her actions were met by the sound of a small wooden box scraping from the shelf and the wisp and twang of wood fibers suddenly constricting around her. The tension of the wood wrapped around her made it difficult to breathe, but as she fought to extricate herself, she realized what was holding her.

A fairy box? I've only seen pictures of these, she thought, before yelling, "Let me go!"

The commotion brought Ron downstairs, his one arm visibly in a cast and the other holding a wooden bat. He could hear the woman demanding to be released and looked toward Linda.

"I see you have things tied up here," Ron joked. "And who is our mystery guest?"

"Claire Brentwood, by my guess," Linda said.

Claire looked surprised when Linda knew who she was and became concerned as the red-haired woman watched her.

"Amanda spoke about you while she was here. You're exactly like I imagined," Linda said.

Claire stopped struggling and said, "I am not a threat to you."

Linda stood tall, unconvinced. "The house seems to think you are."

They watched as the woman looked around. "There was no indication the house was enchanted in our records."

Linda smiled, looking to Ron. "She asked about how you avoided being detected by the cat-girl."

Ron smiled, "Beats me."

Claire huffed, "I am no threat. I only came to speak with you. Please release me. This thing is quite uncomfortable."

Ron touched the fibers and it again turned into a small wooden box. He placed it back on the shelf as the woman fixed her clothing. "I doubt I'd be able to harm either of you if I wanted to. Given your precautions."

Ron smiled, offering her a seat, which she happily accepted. Ron sat away from Linda as the woman said, "My name is Claire Brentwood. I've come for some information. And, possibly, your help." Ron and Linda agreed to listen to what the doctor had to say.

"It seems you have some internal problems back at the Sanctuary. Why are you coming to us?" Linda asked before saying, "And how long have you been watching us?"

Dr. Brentwood sighed but responded, "You both have been under the Circle's watch for about ten tears, and certainly since you had Terrell arrested. Your actions, and being able to survive the incident, caused the need to research you further." She paused before saying, "I don't know if you are aware, but you have magic within you."

Linda nodded. "We're aware, unfortunately. Those crystals you use seem a bit intrusive."

Claire looked puzzled. "How did you come across one? Only Raven Hunters have them." The doctor closed her eyes as she answered her own question. "Amanda has one, doesn't she."

Ron nodded. "I presume she wasn't supposed to."

Claire nodded before telling them that only hunters are given them due to the ability to detect magic. She also informed them that Amanda had promised to stay out of the affairs of the Circle. And that she had kept her promise, so far. But then she told them, "Since she seems to have a detector crystal, she may not be keeping her promise." That fact worried Claire. She had so far kept Amanda out of things, but with the two recent thefts, the situation was becoming dire.

Claire again took a breath and thanked Ron for stopping the theft of the Pertu icon, and explained that the reason his injury was difficult to heal was that it was caused by magic. She clarified that it causes misfortune to anyone trying to take the icon.

Claire suddenly became reserved, as she realized she had never answered Selese's question when she was asked earlier. *What was I thinking? I should have told Selese what the element was when she asked.*

Dr. Brentwood continued to tell them about the icons and that Amanda was not prepared to deal with a matter of such a massive scale. What they were up against amounted to a group trying to take over the world using magic.

Ron agreed, "That sounds like Amanda's thing. She seems to like getting into impossible scenarios."

Claire looked worried. "This is not a simple matter."

Ron agreed, telling her, "You're right, it's not. We've had to protect her from similar things before."

Claire looked at him strangely.

Ron leaned forward in his chair. "There were things we encountered that we made sure she never heard about."

The doctor listened intently. She had read the files on them both, and knew of only the smaller encounters. When she asked, all Linda said was, "This is not the first time someone has tried taking over the world using magic. You ever hear of a sorcerer known as Oliver Tassam?"

Claire had led the Circle for over fifteen years. She knew the names of all sorcerers that had attempted to threaten the world. All were killed or taken by the Circle. She pressed them for more information, and Ron was happy to oblige.

"Yeah, real charmer that guy. Ripping out people's hearts to make them slaves." Ron paused as if looking for words. "He got what he deserved."

Claire could see Linda's reaction to his remark, and she seemed less than pleased. But as his words sank in, Dr. Brentwood became defensive. Noticing her sudden change in demeanor, Linda asked if she was all right. The doctor took a moment before asking for some water. Linda saw her composing herself as she walked by. When Linda returned, she realized that neither Ron nor she had spoken since she left.

Linda handed her the glass and placed her hand on the woman's shoulder, asking her, "What happened?"

Claire felt she could trust Linda and said, "I didn't want to think there were others who would do that." The doctor wiped a tear from her cheek as she said, "My daughter—well, adopted daughter—was a victim of one of the wraith mages."

The two were astonished by the doctor's reveal and consoled her. As Claire fought back tears she explained, "She's alive. A friend of my husband was able to save her by making a golden heart for her."

Ron and Linda were elated at what they heard. Ron nervously said, "She must be nice. She literally has a heart of gold," bringing a glare from Linda.

Claire laughed, "Actually, she's a handful, but her intentions are usually meant in a good way." She paused. "Amanda seems to trust her."

"Then she's a good person," Linda said. Ron agreed with her.

There was silence for what seemed an eternity as Ron looked over toward Linda. Claire could see her nod slightly before Ron said, "Let us know how we can help. Of course, we'll stay out till you ask for us to jump in. But if things get out of hand . . ." Ron didn't finish his statement, making Claire smile.

"The help would be welcome at the appropriate time. For now, though, I need to get back to the Sanctuary," Claire said, and was about to use magic. She hesitated and turned to look at the shelf. "I was going to leave you some files to go over but I need to retrieve them using magic."

Linda smiled, telling her that she could. Ron happily took them from her right after they appeared before asking Linda to get the journal from the Tassam incident. "Get the one from the cabinet. It's the copy."

Ron and Claire talked while Linda went to get the journal. "Do you keep a log of all of your encounters?" Ron nodded. "Just in case something happens. There are some crazy things out there."

Linda overheard the last statement as she walked back in carrying the journal. "He keeps duplicates, in case a certain young lady gets her hands on them."

Claire nodded.

As Linda sat next to Ron, she warned the doctor, "Make sure Amanda's not getting involved with something like this, if it's this serious."

Claire nodded as she looked up from the journal. "I have been doing my best to dissuade her."

* * *

Paul Vikander was admiring the icon he held. The woman cowering in the cage nearby could see the smile he had on his face. Her eyes, surrounded by dry tears of fear, continued to stare at him. Paul continued to admire at the figure of a woman being consumed by a pillar of fire.

"Such craftsmanship. I always loved art. It is something that warms me." The old man looked out toward the rest of the room as if reminiscing.

"You know, I am quite an artist myself. All of these you see, I did."

The woman stared at the horrifying images, a mixture of figures and pictures that ran across the room. Some looked like photographs. In fear she tried to scream, but there was no sound from her at all. Paul Vikander again returned to admiring the statue he held.

"It's beautiful, isn't it?" Paul muttered before turning to look at the statue encased in metal and glass in the extraction device nearby. He turned his attention to the display and could see it almost finished transferring power to his recent creation. The white-haired man looked back at the woman with a subtle smile. Seeing this, the woman again screamed, but no voice was heard, the silence interrupted by the sound of the cage as she pulled at it. The metallic sounds were seemingly music to the old man's ears.

"Don't worry yourself, my dear, your time will come very soon." He looked at her over his glasses with an evil smile. "You won't feel a thing."

Chapter Twenty-Two
I've got a Plan

Dr. Brentwood appeared within the Shadowed Hall; the guards acknowledged her as she stepped before them. "Any travelers since I left?" Claire asked the guard, who slowly shook his head.

Claire raised her brow. "Not even Selese?"

The guard again shook his head slowly.

Claire felt relieved at the report and ordered no one to be allowed past the entryway of the Hall. She then passed through the archway, making the protection magic shimmer as she stepped through.

On the other side, Dr. Brentwood could hear the council arguing and felt their frustration. Like Lord Cale, she knew the Forge was the best place to store powerful and dangerous artifacts. There was no safer place, except the hidden city off the coast of Ireland. She could hear that very argument as she walked in to see the council heatedly debating what to do with the *Effigy of Tarnus*.

"Members of the council, the icon is safe. I realize that the others have gone missing. Hunters are out now looking for clues as to where they were taken!" Cale said, yelling over the continuous debate.

Claire smiled at her husband when he noticed her walking into the room. She heard one of the members saying, "Tarnus is safe, but the icon of Spirit has gone missing. It is nowhere to be found within the grounds!"

Claire took a breath and forcibly said, "The icon is not missing, Councilmember Harris. It was merely at a different location."

The council member glared toward her, then calmed. "I withdrawal the request."

Cale shook his head as she sat beside him. Leaning in, he asked, "Where were you?"

Claire smiled, "I was investigating an alternative to using the Raven Hunters in finding the icons."

* * *

On campus, Amanda felt the cold air of the season against her face as she ran. It was the weekend, and she had decided to go for a run. Since she had started hunting monsters with Linda and Ron, Amanda knew it was a good idea to stay in shape, just in case adventure came around. She had stopped to take a drink from the bottle she was carrying when she heard her name from a distance.

Amanda turned to see Luke running toward her.

"You out for a run this morning?" Amanda yelled to him.

Luke nodded and between breaths said, "Yeah, figured I'd get some in before heading home."

The two talked for a few minutes before they decided to finish their run together. Their last stop was by the apartments. Amanda liked the feeling of Luke being around and invited him to stay. Luke reluctantly declined, telling her, "I'd love to, but I'm still on call."

Amanda understood, but was disappointed. They stood in the cooling wind as they talked. Amanda eventually brought up the symbol she had found. "I threw it in the trash last night after, you know . . ." She motioned toward him, making him smile.

"You're still investigating, huh?" Luke said, knowing she never stopped. That was something he liked about her; she was persistent. He was also surprised when she turned down being a hunter when asked.

Amanda looked to the ground. "I need to know more about that symbol. It's driving me nuts. I know it's the key to this. I just don't know how yet."

Luke caught his breath. "If it is bothering you that much, maybe I can offer something."

Amanda moved closer to Luke and said, "Go on."

He kissed her and said, "You know I'm a scroll witch, right? Well, maybe I can get you in, and we can both see what that symbol means."

Amanda put her arms around Luke, who did the same. "And how would you do that?"

* * *

Amanda was startled when Luke produced a set of magic cuffs. After his saying only a few words, she found herself disoriented as they appeared in the Shadowed Hall. Before her stood two large guards, neither of which Amanda recognized.

Luke stood proud. "Luke Grainger, bringing in a subject to identify an artifact."

The guards looked at him and then to Amanda, fighting to escape the magic bonds on her wrists. "You didn't say you were arresting me!" She went to kick Luke.

The guards smiled and allowed them both through. Amanda continued to fight, attempting to pull away from Luke as they walked toward the repository. When they reached the room, Luke released the magic bonds holding her wrists and looked at her. He could see the anger in her eyes.

"You could have let me know. I thought you were arresting me!" Amanda said.

Luke moved close. "That'd be no fun. Besides, if I had told you, it might not have been as convincing. They may have thought we were together." He then gently kissed her.

Amanda returned the kiss and as they parted, said, "Next time tell me, or I'll hurt you." Luke chuckled as he pulled her into the room.

Amanda could see the walls high with books. Several stones glowed to give the room light. She placed her hands on the small podium that held an old-style inkwell. She held her hand over it and the ink seemed to move, as if it was alive. She continued to look around and could see books with different symbols and words, some she recognized. There were a few tables with small piles of books sitting on them. She watched as one floated up toward the shelf before putting itself away.

Luke climbed the ladder that rolled around the entire room. It magically extended as Luke reached upward. He looked at a few books and took some from the shelves. She watched him slide down.

"We can start here." Luke handed her a book, placing the other on the table. Amanda's eyes followed another book as it left the table, floating toward the shelves.

"You see that?" Amanda said, amazed at the sight.

Luke nodded. "Yeah, if you leave them for a day, they put themselves away."

Amanda giggled, "You realize you were just rhyming."

Luke looked around the room. "Well, it was enchanted by the fairies."

* * *

Outside the repository, Dr. Brentwood was walking from the meeting hall; she could hear some voices in the room ahead. Her head was pounding from the frustration of the council. "Please don't let it be someone trying to find an anti-drunk element."

Claire stood in the doorway and could see Luke reading, but didn't know who was with him. When she turned the corner to look closer, Claire smiled, seeing Amanda flipping through one of the book's pages. A thought filled her mind. *You are a lot like me, you won't give up, will you?*

She waited a few seconds before clearing her throat, the sound making the two turn with guilty stares. She could hear Amanda say, "Uh-oh, busted."

Claire entered. "Weren't you ordered home to rest, Mr. Grainger?"

"Uh, yes, Dr. Brentwood," Luke replied, realizing he was probably in trouble.

Claire looked at Amanda, who stared back. "And why are you here, Miss Supp?"

Amanda smiled, "I was looking for a symbol to learn about it. I know it's the key to this whole thing. I don't know how yet."

Dr. Brentwood sighed, "I thought you wanted to finish school before getting into this line of work?"

Amanda responded, "I do, but I thought maybe I could help."

Claire looked at the two of them and smiled. "You were ordered to get some rest. We may need hunters if something happens." She pointed toward Luke, who looked embarrassed.

She then looked at Amanda. "Don't worry. You're not in any trouble. I'd have to arrest myself for breaking the rules."

Amanda looked to the doctor to clarify, which she eventually did.

"I went to see your friends."

Amanda asked, "How are they? Ron still have his sling on?"

The doctor nodded, then returned to scolding them. "Neither of you should be here."

Amanda began to protest but Dr. Brentwood spoke before she could begin.

"I've just come from a long meeting with a lot of people arguing." She pointed to Luke. "You, go home and get some sleep. And you," she pointed to Amanda, "you are coming with me."

Luke was about to protest, but the doctor cut him off. "I'll take her out of here. You used the Shadowed Hall. Besides, my office is closer. I don't want anyone to know she was here."

Luke walked away sheepishly as Amanda turned to see him slump toward the Shadowed Hall. Claire turned to Amanda. "Don't worry, he's not in trouble. I don't want anyone thinking you were being arrested. I presume that's how you two got in here?"

Amanda was amazed. "How'd you know?"

Claire chuckled, "That's how I would have gotten past security."

Amanda grinned as she walked alongside the doctor. Dr. Brentwood told her that she asked Ron and Linda to research some things and that they were terribly upset that Amanda was getting involved in the thefts and recent Circle business. She even told Amanda that Linda was angry for her putting herself in danger.

"I don't believe you," Amanda said.

Claire replied firmly, "I was just there, and they said to make sure you were not getting involved with any of this."

Technically the doctor wasn't lying, but she was emphasizing Amanda's involvement so far. Like her friends, she wanted to protect Amanda. Dr. Claire knew that the thefts of the three icons were serious. She had also promised the council that she would remain in the Sanctuary until things had settled; instead, she left to see Amanda's friends without telling anyone.

When Amanda asked about the symbol, Claire told her, "Selese brought it to my attention earlier. It's used to protect important artifacts from being stolen. It causes misfortune to anyone nearby before the item is taken. It's normally quite effective" Claire said, before adding, "I meant to tell Selese before I left. But I forgot."

Amanda seemed to understand.

Claire led Amanda to her office and ordered Colleen to follow her back to her apartment. "Make sure she gets there."

Amanda was angry when she made it to her apartment. Colleen had thought about asking security to help her, seeing her friend act as she did. Colleen was startled when Amanda pounded the desk, complaining about Ron and Linda not trusting her.

Shrive had arrived and shook her head. Seeing Colleen trying to calm Amanda, she decided to help.

It took a while, but after Amanda calmed, she decided to call Linda, who confirmed that Dr. Brentwood was there and assured Amanda they were ready to help if needed. Ron had to get on the phone to repeat what Linda told her before Amanda realized that Dr. Brentwood had lied.

By this time, Colleen looked to Shrive, who said, "I've got her from here." Colleen appreciatively thanked her and headed back to the office.

"Why would Dr. Brentwood tell me that they were angry?" Amanda said as she threw a bottle of water to Shrive. Just before she took a drink, Shrive said, "Maybe she thinks it's getting too dangerous. Also, we need to find out how Tyler is involved with this too."

Amanda agreed, then looked out the window. "We have to find out what those glasses really are."

* * *

Shrive's words lingered in Amanda's head. "Was Dr. Brentwood lying meant to keep her safe? Was the situation so dire that she wanted others to stay away from it? Amanda tossed and turned, having a restless night, only to fall asleep sometime in the early morning. Amanda groggily rolled over to see the time on the clock.

"Crap, I'm late," she mumbled as she fought her way from beneath the covers. She had never heard her alarm and was going to be late for class. Her apartment was a flurry as she readied to leave quickly. She closed the door and had to unlock it, having almost forgotten her portfolio.

As she hurried toward class, she looked at her phone and felt relieved, seeing she was going to make it in time. But the world stopped as she felt the impact when she walked into someone standing in the hall. Amanda tumbled to the ground, as did the person she hit.

Amanda gathered her things and went to stand, apologizing to the person she walked into and asking if they were all right. She could see the papers and books strewn around the floor and felt terrible for walking into someone probably working on a project. She bent down to help, and the voice she heard made her freeze.

"Amanda? I'm fine. You walked into me." Amanda looked up and was staring at Tyler.

"Tyler, I haven't seen you in class. Where have you been?" she asked before noticing him desperately searching for something. Scanning the floor, Amanda looked up to realize that his glasses were missing. Amanda started helping him pick up his papers as she again asked where he had been.

"Working." He paused. "Uh, work-study program." Tyler stumbled on his words. Amanda knew he was hiding something, but she continued to help collect the papers all over the floor. When she grabbed one, she revealed his glasses beneath. Amanda watched as Tyler's hand was about to grab them. Amanda needed to examine the glasses. In a spontaneous moment, she jumped toward Tyler, knocking him to the side.

"I'm sorry I'm really sorry. You're not hurt, are you?" Amanda said with an improvised frantic sounding voice she could muster. As she shook Tyler, she used her foot to kick the glasses behind her. When Tyler looked around to where he saw the glasses, he found nothing.

"Oh, my God. Were you wearing glasses? I'm so sorry. Let me help you look for them." Amanda said as she pushed Tyler away from her. She swiveled around and, with her other hand, swiped up the glasses to get a look at them.

As she inspected them, it was easy to see these were no ordinary glasses. The small boxes on the sides looked like some of the smart glasses she had seen, but one side had a crystalline tip poking out from it. She held the glasses toward Tyler and could see the display. It read, "23% darkling." Amanda squinted, trying to see what was in the background of the lens. She was surprised when she saw pictures of Shrive.

Tyler turned to see a blurry Amanda holding something out toward him, and he reached out for it. Amanda hesitantly handed the glasses to him. She watched as he hurried to put them on.

"They don't look broken. I didn't see any cracks," Amanda said.

Tyler looked over at her with fearful concern. "You looked through my glasses?"

Amanda nodded, then stood. Tyler followed suit. There was silence between them for a few seconds before Tyler spoke. "What did you see?"

"You have a display in your glasses. Is it for some sort of game?" Amanda tried to lie, but Tyler saw through it.

"You know what's going on here, don't deny it," Tyler said coldly.

Amanda tried to look innocent.

Tyler pulled up his sleeve and tapped the display on what looked like a watch with an extended display. The element symbol flashed before opening the application connected to the glasses. He looked at Amanda. "You're human, but . . ." Tyler looked at someone down the hall and the display changed. "He is not completely human."

Amanda said nothing as Tyler continued, "I saw you with them. I know this is all real. People have been lying about magic not existing."

Several people stared as they walked past the two arguing. Tyler moved closer. "You knew about all this. Those adventures of yours are real, aren't they? I even watched you disappear with them." She could see the determination behind his glasses and she nodded slowly. Tyler became angry. "Are you with them?"

Amanda shook her head. "No. They asked, but I haven't said I'd join."

Her words confused Tyler and he said, "Wait, you said no, and they let you live? Keep your memory?"

Amanda asked, "What are you talking about? Most everyone I've met is nice. Not some bloodthirsty monster. This isn't one of those games you've been working on."

Tyler seemed more angered by her response and showed her the display. "These things are running around unchecked. They're dangerous."

"No, most aren't. Well, some are. Arghh, Tyler, you have to be careful; this isn't some game. Something serious is going on here."

"You know what it is? Tell me." He seemed eager to understand.

"I don't know for sure yet. I know some don't want me to get involved, others want me to help them." She moved in and whispered to him, "You have to be careful. This isn't like the adventures I've illustrated."

Tyler stepped back and said, "Vikander understands things around here. He's helped me more than you and the others have." He turned to look at a woman walking by and as Tyler tapped the large touchpad on his wrist on the display, it read sylph 3%. "You see this? These things are running around, and no one knows it."

Amanda again warned, "You don't know what you're getting into."

Tyler defended himself. "And you do? Tell me. What is all this?"

Amanda shook her head. "I'm not involved. I was thinking of, but I'm not. I don't know what this is all about yet."

Tyler smiled smugly. "Well, if I find out, I probably won't tell you." Amanda watched as he pulled out a wad of money. "Some of us know how to make money from what we know how to do." He gave a nervous chuckle. "My boss has been telling me all about things. And he has been trying to save humans from them."

Amanda stepped back from Tyler as he stared at her. She paused before saying, "Be careful, Tyler. I'm not sure what's going on yet. Please watch your back. From what I've found, your boss may not have your best interests in mind."

Amanda arrived late to class and sat next to Shrive, who could see Amanda was upset. When she asked what was wrong, Amanda waved her off, only saying, "Later."

Class finished; Amanda had not taken any notes. She had been thinking of what Tyler said, and wrote only one word on the paper before her. "Vikander." Amanda decided to note the symbol she had seen on the display before she headed out, the one just before the application opened. She started to sketch and was about to finish when Shrive's hand pushed hers from the page.

Shrive leaned in. "Are you crazy? That's a casting element. You trying to zap yourself?"

Amanda looked dazed toward Shrive. "I was just sketching what I saw."

"If you finished that here without another element, your notebook would've probably gone up in flames," Shrive warned, making Amanda quickly pull her hands away from the page.

"I ran into Tyler before class," Amanda said, making Shrive extremely interested.

"What happened?" Shrive asked.

"I had a chance to see what he was working on; he even showed me." Amanda hesitated. "We were right; he did make a magic detector. But it does much more."

Shrive smiled, "Yes, we were right. We have to tell Selese. Did you get anything else? How does it work?"

Amanda followed her reluctantly as they headed out the door. She told her the numbers and that it works on anyone. Amanda took a breath before she said the rest to her friend. "On a side note, he had you as a background. I think Tyler has a thing for cat-girls."

Shrive turned to Amanda in disbelief. "What?!"

Through might, through knowledge and through persistence. There is no credence that will alone cannot divulge truth.

- Caleeon of Doft. Last of the Chaotic dragons

Chapter Twenty-Three
What does this do?

The day seemed to take forever to end. Amanda met her friends at the pizza place. She told the others what she had discovered after her run-in with Tyler, confirming what they had suspected about the glasses. She gave as much detail as possible, even mentioning the background pictures of Shrive.

"Tyler has a thing for cat-girls?" Selese mocked Shrive. "In games, maybe, I could see that."

Shrive growled as she said, "He thinks I'm anything like those games, I'll slash those glasses off his face." Amanda could see Shrive's whole head of hair seem to fluff.

They all heard, "Easy there, Shrive, don't want you ruffling your mane there too much." She was surprised to see Colleen walking up, accompanied by Luke.

"Wow, to what do we owe the pleasure?" Selese joked.

Luke sat next to Amanda, while Colleen patted Shrive on the head. "Remember the last time you did this; I'm not helping you this time." Colleen sat down next to her friend. "It took five hours to get that mess under control."

Shrive stared forward, an angry scowl on her face as she grumbled, "Not in the mood for this right now."

Colleen snorted.

Shrive looked at her. "Why are you here? I thought you liked to stay in the office."

Colleen nodded. "I do, only fieldwork is needed once in a while." She paused for a moment before saying, "That's if I could get *into* the office."

Amanda asked, "When did they close the admin building?"

Colleen shook her head in frustration. "No, the other office. I'm locked out of the Great Hall and Sanctuary." Her demeanor showing her obvious disappointment.

Amanda turned to Luke and asked him to explain. He told them that all nonessential staff were temporarily banned from the Great Hall and only allowed limited access to the Sanctuary. He said that only hunters, unaccompanied, are permitted to enter when called.

Colleen picked up on that, saying, "It had to be one of you," pointing to Selese and Amanda.

Selese joked, "Or both."

Amanda rolled her eyes. "Not helping, Selese."

Luke continued telling them that there was restricted travel through the Shadowed Hall and that more guards are posted throughout the Forge. His news put Amanda at ease, at least somewhat, but she knew they weren't telling Luke everything. Amanda was sure Dr. Brentwood ordered them to keep Luke in the dark.

As the night went on, they talked. Shrive had learned what she could about the icons. But for some reason, the icon of Spirit always seemed to be forgotten. Amanda noticed Selese become uncomfortable when the Spirit icon was mentioned. *Does she know something about the Spirit icon?* Selese must have felt Amanda staring and looked toward her. When Amanda mouthed the words, "You know, where it is, don't you?" Amanda gave a nod in affirmation seeing the rage grow behind Selese's eyes. In Amanda's mind Selese just confirmed she was withholding information. That was something Amanda could understand, and thought, *Selese either knows or is protecting who or what the icon was.*

Amanda took a napkin and started to sketch the symbol she saw with Tyler and showed it to Luke. She purposely didn't finish it, as per Shrive's warning earlier.

"That's an activation symbol. It's used to pull power from the Circle to enhance an element. Where did you see it?" Luke asked.

Amanda said, "I saw Tyler using it with those glasses he has."

Luke sighed heavily. "You memorized it from just a glance?" he asked, making Amanda nod.

"I have a good memory for images."

"Well, I'm glad you didn't finish it. You don't have an element to link to." He took the napkin from her and drew another symbol. He then finished the element she had drawn, and the napkin started to fade.

"What happened to it?" Amanda asked.

Luke shook his hand as if holding something. "Nothing, it's still here, just invisible." He handed her the napkin. Amanda could feel the paper, but not see it. She looked to Luke to explain further, but he slowly took the napkin from her hand, letting his hand linger for a few seconds, making Selese chuckle. Luke placed the napkin into the glass in front of him and it reappeared.

"Dissolve the element, the spell is done," Luke said as he looked back toward Amanda.

"You are showing them our best tricks, Luke." The words surprised even Selese, who jumped before she realized who it was behind her. She turned to see Cayden smiling at her.

"Shrive, I'm going to need your claws over here," she said, turning in her seat. "You know it's not nice to sneak up on a lady."

Shrive gave a laugh. "Then you certainly don't need my claws."

Everyone started to laugh, even Selese.

They ordered food and Amanda asked, "All right, if things can become invisible, what's to stop you from using that to, say, sneak into the showers?"

Luke smiled, "Who says it can't?"

Amanda hit him as she smiled. "So, you've never turned yourself invisible with this?"

Luke shook his head. "Nope. I couldn't if I wanted to."

When Amanda asked why, all Luke said was, "Because I made that one. Most elements can't be used on the person creating it unless designed to."

"Wait, what are you talking about?" Colleen asked. "I thought all scroll witches could use elements."

Luke nodded. "They can, but if you make it yourself, to be used by you on yourself, it has to be extremely specific, and I mean *very* specific."

Cayden confirmed his statement, making Colleen ask why. Luke's response, "So it can't be used against you."

Amanda nodded. "Makes sense." She paused. "Okay, so we have three icons missing. Two still to be found. And a bad guy to search for." Amanda looked around at everyone. She turned to Luke after hearing his phone alerting him.

Amanda looked annoyed. "Lose it or turn it off. You're not bailing on me again." She could hear Cayden's phone alert as well.

Luke looked forward and pulled his phone before his face. "It's part of my job." He gave no emotion as he read the alert.

But when Amanda asked, "You have you go?" he lowered his head and nodded.

"Yeah, sorry."

"Promise me that if this gets too dangerous, you'll step away from this," Luke said as he stood, before leaning down and kissing Amanda. He then joined Cayden standing next to Selese. They watched the two hunters walk away. Shrive joked, "If you two want to go tackle them, we'll vouch for you that they deserved it."

Moments later, they all started laughing.

They called it a night around closing time. Amanda headed back to her apartment and checked in on Gabriella. She was happy to find that her friend had a rush illustration order come in and that she was okay. Although, Gabriella never said who it was for. Amanda now felt better for not bringing her along to the meeting and decided to get some sleep.

* * *

The next day, Amanda didn't have any classes. As per the secretary, her one professor was out, but Amanda thought she had seen him while out for a run. So she decided to get to the gym early and get in some additional exercise.

Amanda was throwing jab after jab at the punching bag. Selese stood by watching her and said, "Remind me not to piss you off."

Amanda grunted, "Gotta keep in shape. Never know what you may come up against."

A woman next to her overheard her and said, "Yeah, it's dangerous out there. Criminals everywhere."

Amanda nodded and returned to punching as Selese said, "Not what you meant, but hey, she's right anyway."

Selese reminded her that somebody took the Pertu icon, and only the Tarnus was left. Selese continued to look to Amanda for what they should do.

"Why are you asking me?" Amanda asked.

Selese stepped back with her hand's up,. "Because you've been against things like this before, and whether you know it or not, we all look up to you."

Selese leaned in, quietly saying, "Even some in the Circle, from what I hear." Selese again stepped back. "Come on, Amanda, you're smart, you have resources and information. Whether you know it or not, you're pretty damn lucky."

Amanda looked at her, confused, making Selese roll her eyes. "Oh, come on." She watched Selese motion like she was holding a small chain with a ring on it before saying, "Not to mention that cute, tall, dark-haired, brown-eyed man of yours."

Amanda looked quizzically toward her. "What?"

Selese huffed, "You can deny it as much as you want, but we already know you and Luke are together." Selese looked at Amanda. "Let's work on the problem at hand, shall we?"

Amanda shook her head and laughed.

Selese smiled, "He is cute; you two look good together. But come on, girl, there's something we're all missing. This is your thing. What are we not seeing?"

Amanda smiled and started hitting and kicking the punching bag again. After a few minutes, she let out a growl of frustration and punched the bag with both hands only to turn away from it, panting from the exertion. She could see Selese standing by as she remarked, "Seriously, remind me not to piss you off. That bag didn't stand a chance."

Selese noticed a serious stare come over Amanda's face as her friend muttered, "The symbol."

"What?" Selese asked.

"When the air icon was stolen, or attempted to be stolen, there were three people, right?" Amanda asked.

Selese confirmed her statement.

Amanda looked to the ceiling taking a breath, "The symbol causes misfortune. How come only two of them were injured? They were close to each other." She paused. "Luke said that they kept logs of known elements. What if the third person there was immune to the symbol?"

Selese perked up. "I see where you're going with this."

Amanda looked at her. "Maybe if we find who made the symbol, we'll find out who's behind the thefts."

Amanda headed to get changed as she muttered, "And who the hell is Vikander?"

Selese asked, "Who?"

"Tyler mentioned him when I ran into him the other day. We should probably look into him as well," Amanda said.

"Now you're thinking," Selese said just before the ground shook under their feet. They could see outside that people were stumbling all the way to the dorms.

"Was that an earthquake?" Amanda asked.

Selese shook her head. "I think that was something else."

There are no words of hope that cannot strengthen resolve. No words of favor that cannot bring a smile to another. It is when we forget these two simple facts that the world grows dim.

- Seth Roanoke Elven bard

Chapter Twenty-Four
The Trouble with Shadow-Walking

A glass jar shattered loudly against the wall, sending shards everywhere. A man wearing a cloak had only a moment to avoid being hit by it. A stream of unintelligible obscenities followed the loud crash. The only words coherent were, "You incompetent idiot, now they'll be on guard! You were supposed to get in and out without them knowing."

Across the room, Paul Vikander continued to criticize Jarrad but as the old mage leaned on the table from the exertion of his tirade, the man spoke. "I have never failed the Broken Feather."

Paul looked at him. "Until now. That's twice you've failed to return with my prize. I need results, not excuses!"

The man knew of the wraith mage and his temper yet continued to make excuses for not returning with the *Effigy of Tarnus*. "As it stands, the Forge was too well-guarded. It would take an army to retrieve the icon. But I did leave a present for them."

The man and Vikander continued to argue, the younger man saying, "I was not aware that the old shaft was closed. It was not in the information you provided."

Vikander looked at Jarrad. "Am I to assume that the great thief, Jarrad Ruscha, is ill-prepared for the task I've set?"

The man pulled his shoulders back as a hint of anger entered his eyes.

The old mage smiled, "I see, you still have pride in your profession; that's good." The old man looked toward the woman in the cage. He was transferring the essence from the fire icon. Vikander gave a heavy sigh. "Perhaps it is I who should accept some patience." He walked toward the thief. As he neared, the mage could see part of a scroll element on his hand.

With disappointment, he said, "You were ordered to use the scroll watch that we made. The symbols you wear can be traced too easily."

Jarrad replied, "It takes longer to cast, and it's not as effective. Besides, that new guy you have, he is always looking at that wrist display he created."

The angry mage reached out to strike but stopped. Vikander could see Jarrad never flinched. Centering himself, the old mage nodded. "He may become a liability. But for now, he is essential. When the time comes, I will deal with him." He stepped back; his hands now covered her face. When he removed them, he said, "You have served the Feather well. This is merely a setback. We will have our place soon enough."

Vikander placed his hand on the hunter's shoulder. "Jarrad, you are one of the best thieves I've known. I only know of one better, and she is not on our side. Go. I'll contact you with further instructions."

* * *

On-campus, Amanda and Selese were searching for an answer to the unexplained earthquake. They were also hoping to tell the hunters they may have found a way to find whoever was behind the thefts.

"We'll tell them everything we know, agreed?" Amanda said before Selese tried to shadow-walk. However, instead of them disappearing into the darkness and appearing in the Shadowed Hall, Selese found herself dizzy, and Amanda had to prevent her from falling to the ground.

"What's wrong?" Amanda asked.

Selese took a moment to answer. "Felt like I hit a stone wall. Let me try again."

As she did, the same thing happened, and Amanda again had to grab onto her. When pressed, Selese gave the same response, adding, "Something is blocking me from entering."

As Amanda helped Selese to her feet, they heard someone yelling their names, only to see Colleen running toward them. "Did you feel that? What happened?"

"Yeah, what was it?" Selese asked.

Colleen looked at them, wondering, hoping they had an answer. Colleen didn't know what was going on but could see Selese holding onto Amanda as if she were injured. When she told Colleen she had just tried to shadow-walk and couldn't. Colleen didn't believe her and pulled up her hood. But as Colleen entered the shadow of the tree, Selese was there to grab her as she immediately fell backward.

"She can't shadow-walk either," she told Amanda. "This is something bad."

Colleen recovered quickly. "Maybe they locked down the Shadowed Hall." She looked to Selese. "But, you don't need the Shadowed Hall."

Selese shook her head. "I wasn't trying for there the second time. I was trying for Cale's office."

Amanda looked at Selese. "What does she mean, you don't need the Shadowed Hall?"

Selese threw her head back in annoyance. "Darkling's don't need it. It's ah, it's, um, complicated."

"Then why can't either of you shadow-walk?" Amanda asked, but neither of them knew.

When Amanda's phone rang, she could see it was Shrive and answered. On the phone, Amanda heard her friend yelling, almost in a panic. "Someone tried to break into the Forge! The whole place is on lockdown! I'm stuck here!" Amanda asked what happened. All Shrive knew was that every door was sealed. "I can't shadow-walk out of here. They are not letting anyone near the Shadowed Hall either. Can you ask Selese if she can come down?"

Amanda told her that they tried, and something was blocking her as well. When Shrive asked her to say to the professor that she would be late, Amanda told her classes were already canceled. While all of this was happening, Amanda realized she was the only one who knew what was going on, so she turned on the speakerphone.

"You all right? Any injuries?" Amanda asked.

Colleen looked concerned. "What happened?"

Shrive told them again, "Someone tried breaking into the Forge."

A moment later, they heard a phone hitting the ground and then silence.

Amanda and the others called out to their friend, but there was no response. Selese and Colleen tried several times to get into the

Sanctuary, even trying the regular entrance. They were surprised to find it locked. They spent most of the night searching for another way into the Sanctuary when finally, exhausted, they headed back to Amanda's place. It was around 1:00 a.m. as the wearily they entered, not of the seeing the symbol glowing on the tab of paper over the door. As the door closed it fell from the wall and tuned to dust before it hit the ground.

Colleen locked the door as Selese flopped down on to the small sofa, before groaning. "My heads feel like that punching bag you were hitting earlier." Colleen turned worried about Selese. But didn't understand what Selese was talking about. Amanda found it amusing but explained they had been at the gym earlier.

Amanda sat nearly exhausted in the chair facing the television. Colleen was able to sit after Selese moved back on the small sofa. They both heard the loud annoyed sigh that Amanda gave, it was the perfect statement of the last few hours. The room filled with silence as Amanda thought. *Who tried breaking into the Forge? Was the statue still safe there?* She turned to ask if they were all right but was surprised to see them both now fast asleep.

Must have taken a lot out of them trying to shadow-walk so many times. Amanda thought but as she tried thinking of another way to get into the Sanctuary her eyes fell heavy.

It was just after 6:00 a.m. when the door to Amanda's apartment creaked slowly open. As it closed, what looked like a shimmering figure walked toward the three now unconscious in the room. The intruder held up his hand to watch it solidify and again reappear.

Useless, there must be a protection spell on this place. Jarrad thought as he removed his hood, becoming visible. He looked toward Amanda and could see the fairy ring glowing beneath her shirt. He turned his attention toward Selese. He despised Vikander for considering her a better thief than himself. The element he used would keep them under for some time, so he decided to take his time killing them all. He looked over Selese as she slept. *You were predictable. It was easy to track you down. Nothing personal, my dear, I'm just not fond of competition.* Jarrad thought before he pulled out a small blade. As he moved closer, the dim light of the morning made the poison glisten on the edge of the weapon. He was interrupted hearing several loud bangs on the door of the apartment.

"Mandy, you up yet? I've got great news." He didn't recognize the woman's voice.

However, as the woman continued to try the door, Jarrad knew he had to act fast. If it were a hunter looking for Amanda and the others, he would have a fight on his hands. Instead, he hurriedly moved to unlock the door. He pressed himself against the wall and waited for the person to enter. Jarrad kept the blade ready to strike as soon as the person was far enough inside the room. But as the knob turned, the door flew open with enough force it pinned him against the corner. Jarrad felt the poisoned blade he held slice into his arm. His eyes watched as a fair-haired woman rush past. But as his vision started to blur, he reached into his sleeve to pull out a vial containing an antidote.

"Mandy, you awake?" Gabriella asked as she shook her friend. Amanda Shifted, but didn't wake. Gabriella still hadn't noticed the man hidden behind the door. She turned to see the others sleeping, "Must have been some party, too bad I missed it." Gabriella huffed, "It was nice seeing Cindy again, though." She looked back to Amanda, "My Cousin loves those stories too." Gabriella moved closer, "I didn't tell her they were real, I kept things a secret."

Jarrad fought to stay conscious as he pulled off the protective cap and injected the antidote above the injury. The thief's hands trembled as he scrolled through the watch to find the element Vikander provided that would allow him to shadow-walk while the others could not. His vision started to clear, but for now, killing his competition would have to wait. As Jarrad faded into the shadows, Gabriella heard the door creak behind her, making her turn.

"Should probably close the door, don't want some creep just walking in here," Gabriella mumbled as she bounded over to close the door. She turned back to her friends with a smile. "I know what all of you need, I'm making you some coffee and breakfast." She headed into the small kitchen. "ooh, she's got a waffle maker. I love waffles," Gabriella said as she rummaged through Amanda's kitchen.

* * *

Amanda woke to the smell of coffee and waffles. She stiffly pulled herself out of the chair. Her shoulder and neck were in an unconformable position, and Amanda struggled to move.

Gabriella was in the kitchen, cooking breakfast, and smiled as she turned to see her friend. "Oh, good, you're up. I made waffles and coffee," Gabriella said as she pulled one from the iron.

"Gabs, how did you get in my apartment?" Amanda asked as she stretched.

"Through the door. You should lock it, you know."

Amanda turned to look at the door. "Thought it was; Colleen said she locked it."

Gabriella shook her head. "Nope, I turned the knob and came in. You guys must have had a fun party last night." She leaned in. "I also heard there was an earthquake yesterday."

Amanda was confused. "Wait, where were you yesterday?"

Gabriella smiled, "I went to see my cousin, remember? She's only a few hours away." She handed Amanda a cup of coffee and a waffle. "So, tell me what happened."

Amanda took the waffle and stared at the coffee. "I'm going to need more than this to give you that information."

Gabriella looked at her before picking up a cup of tea and handing it to her, "Sorry, gave you mine."

Over the next few hours, she told Gabriella everything they knew and how neither Selese nor Colleen could shadow-walk into the Sanctuary. Gabriella then said, "Oh my gosh, what about the fairies? Are they all right?"

Amanda didn't know; none of them did. But as Amanda checked her phone, she said, "Nothing about classes being canceled; I wonder if they fixed everything."

* * *

It was ten o'clock when she headed to class. She arrived to find the door locked and everyone standing around waiting for the professor, his assistant finally coming to tell them that they canceled all classes for today.

Amanda and Selese were heading back and could see someone waiting outside the apartments. It was Shrive, who seemed even less chipper than usual.

Selese walked up. "What happened? You all right?"

Selese's question was greeted with a hug, and until then, Selese didn't realize how strong Shrive really was. Her mouth uttered a quiet, "You're crushing me."

Amanda joined them. "This can't be good."

Shrive looked at them. "They brought me in for questioning, wanted to know why I was helping you and Selese. I was in the holding room when the whole place shook. I was stuck in there for hours."

Amanda could see how upset she was and found out that it took several hunters to get the holding room doors open, and that no one could shadow-walk. Something was preventing it. She turned to Selese. "When I heard that you couldn't shadow-walk, I knew something bad had happened."

Selese hugged her back, saying, "Wait, were you in trouble because of us?"

Shrive shook her head. "No, Lord Cale wanted to know if you mentioned any other entry points, and he was asking me to work with you and Amanda on finding others."

Selese smiled in victory. "See? They need our help!" Shrive didn't seem so happy about it and pushed her away.

"Wow, someone tried breaking into the Forge?" Gabriella asked.

Selese joked, "Even I wouldn't take on a challenge like that." She paused, looking up as if thinking. "Well, maybe if it was worth my while."

Shrive became angry. "This isn't a joke, Selese; they almost got in. If it wasn't for the hunters in the area, I think they would have succeeded."

When Amanda said it was good, they were in the area and no one was hurt, Shrive became reserved, making Amanda ask, "No one was hurt, right?"

Shrive looked up as a tear fell down her cheek. She held up three fingers. "Killed by poisoned blades."

Amanda reached out to hug Shrive this time. The woman half-heartedly tried to push her away. Selese looked saddened and could see people staring as they walked by. She sternly glared at them, and when someone asked if everything was all right, she replied, "It's not good, but she'll be all right," and politely motioned for the woman to keep walking. They all sat on the small stone wall of the raised garden.

As Amanda released Shrive, a sudden panic filled her. "Luke?"

Shrive wiped the tears from her eyes. "He's fine; so's Cayden. But he may have seen one of the people who tried to break in."

Selese sat forward. "If they know what they look like, a simple finding spell will work."

Shrive shook her head. She informed them that they only had a glimpse of the scroll element on his arm when he reached toward the vent shaft. And that it wasn't enough to use a finding spell since it was a common symbol.

As they spoke, Shrive said, "Luke told the elders that he saw a flash of something, like glass, before he saw the symbol. Like a watch."

Amanda sat back and thought. Selese continued to console Shrive but then looked across and could see Amanda staring into space.

"You got something?" Selese asked.

Amanda nodded. "What if it was a watch, or something like one, with a larger screen?"

They looked at her, not knowing what she was talking about, and she described the watch Tyler wore.

"You mean they are making element watches?" Shrive asked.

Amanda shrugged her shoulders. "Maybe."

Selese seemed to think about it a bit. "It may not be as effective, but it could work." This made Amanda look at her for clarification. Selese smiled, "I know a couple of scroll witches. Okay? The best way to use certain ones is to write it on yourself where it's easy, but not show if you want to keep it secret."

Amanda smiled, "Luke has one on his shoulder, and another here," she pointed down her side. "He told me it was for . . ." She paused, seeing the expression of sudden wide-eyed interest from everyone around her.

When Selese said, "Go on, please, tell us more," Amanda blushed.

"No, think I'll stop there," making them all laugh.

Seeing the world as it is now, full of fascination and magic. It's disheartening to see so many who do not cherish what wonders exist.

- Linda Henderson-Wilt

Chapter Twenty-Five
It Takes a Thief

It was about two o'clock when the four of them had enough waiting around. Gabriella had another call from her unknown employer for another rush job and left to work on the project. Her friend's sudden departure made her wonder who the client was. When Amanda asked, Gabriella would only say, "I'll tell you later."

Selese had tried to shadow-walk several times and rubbed her temples from the pain it was causing. Something had happened in the Great Hall and the Sanctuary that no longer allowed them to enter.

"Maybe if you try the lower levels?" Shrive suggested. Selese shook her head, telling her it was like banging her head into the wall. Amanda could see the frustration in her face and understood. She couldn't shadow-walk, at least not yet, and that was something she was starting to look forward to.

Amanda went to the window. She could tell it was beautiful outside and opened it to smell the late autumn air. She pulled out her phone, deciding to check and see if there was an update from the school. She chuckled, seeing a notice that there had been plumbing damage from the earthquake, and it would be early next week before classes would resume. Amanda found it odd when she checked to see if they had any assignments, finding nothing.

"No homework, no class. This is something severe," Amanda said as she leaned on the sill.

She heard Shrive and Selese arguing and closed her eyes. She thought about what had happened. She pulled up her phone to look through to see if any messages had come in. A moment passed before she had a concerned look on her face and turned, still staring at her phone.

Shrive turned toward Amanda, wondering what was going on. Selese followed suit before asking, "What is it?"

Amanda shook her phone. "You called me yesterday." She looked at Shrive, who nodded. Amanda shook her phone before looking back to them. "You called yesterday. But if things weren't working, I wouldn't have gotten your call."

Selese sighed, "Yes, we know she did. Come on, come on, what else do you have? I can see the wheels turning over there."

Amanda smiled. She decided to try a different number. She dialed Luke's phone, but someone other than her love answered. She looked at the other two and smiled. "Phones are working."

Selese huffed, "So the phones are working, what that prove?" her impatience becoming annoying to Shrive, and she told Selese to shut up.

Amanda sat in the chair. "You were able to call yesterday, and today someone picked up Luke's phone." She paused as she thought. "That means the phones are working. But, why would they not answer us?"

Amanda thought for a moment before saying, "You said they wanted our help finding a way in, right?"

Shrive nodded.

Amanda smiled, "They know no one can shadow-walk in. I think they want us to break in."

Selese squealed with delight. "Break into the Great Hall, Oh, my, oh my." Shrive stared at the plastered look of joy on Selese's face as she took a breath before saying. "I want to do it." Amanda could swear Selese was drooling.

Amanda laughed, "Selese, you can't just shadow-walk in. This is going to require a thief's mindset."

Selese smiled, "I'm thinking. Give me a minute."

Amanda waited, and Selese gave several options, but they were not viable when they thought about them. Shrive was able to counter all her suggestions given the recent security upgrades.

"You aren't making this easy, you know," Selese griped.

"Focus, Selese. What other ways can you think to get in?" Amanda asked.

Selese threw her hands up in frustration. "I'd need a week to figure out how else to get in. If only I had some building plans."

Amanda sighed, "Do they have any in the museum library?"

Selese shook her head. "No, the only place that might have anything on the Great Hall and the Sanctuary is probably in my mother's . . . .uh, Dr. Brentwood's office."

Amanda chuckled, seeing Selese hesitate when it came to admitting that she did think of Claire Brentwood as her mother. But as suddenly as she started, Amanda's eyes went wide with an idea.

"Brentwood's office. That's it!" Amanda yelled, startling Selese.

Amanda asked if it was possible to shadow-walk anywhere else, reminding them that they had only been trying to enter the

Sanctuary or the Great Hall. Within seconds, Selese ran toward the shadow of the wall before appearing in the alcove outside.

"I can shadow-walk! What's your idea?" Selese yelled before appearing back in Amanda's apartment.

Amanda asked about the portal Dr. Brentwood used to get to the Great Hall from her office.

"It may be secure, but I think I can get in." Selese paused. "I've escaped from there enough times."

Amanda continued to tell everyone about her plan. They were to get into the office, open the bookcase lock, and walk in. Selese thought for a moment. "The combination's probably been changed. If it was, there's no way in unless we can break the lock."

Selese took a breath. "Let me see if I can get in." She walked toward the shadow, and her friends heard a string of expletives echoing from the corner as Selese came around it again, holding her head. "Nope. Room's protected."

Amanda thought for a moment. "What about just outside her office?"

This time Selese grabbed onto Shrive and Amanda. She was tired of doing this alone.

As they entered the shadows, they found themselves outside Dr. Brentwood's office, with Shrive smiling at the startled expression on Colleen's face as she jumped back.

"How are you able to shadow-walk?" She grabbed onto Selese's arm. "No one can. How are you still able?"

Selese grabbed some of her dark hair, holding it before Colleen. "Part darkling, remember?" She turned to Amanda. "It's definitely something in the Shadowed Hall; getting here was easy."

Amanda nodded in agreement as they tried the door to the doctor's office. Colleen shook her head. "It's locked, and you can't shadow-walk in." She pointed to the symbol above the doorway.

"I can't believe she sealed the door?" Selese was upset.

Shrive agreed, saying, "If it's sealed, we can't get in."

Amanda said, "When in doubt," before she took a step back and kicked the door as hard as she could. The heavy wooden door opened slightly. Seeing this, Amanda kicked it again. It moved even more. After two more hits, the door finally opened. Amanda stood, rubbing her knee from the impacts. She looked up at Colleen. "If you can't open a door with magic, brute force usually works."

They entered Brentwood's office and tried the combination on the bookcase. Colleen huffed in frustration, as the combination she knew no longer allowed her access.

Amanda scanned the bookcase and along the sides. "Selese, how are you at cracking magic locks?"

Selese smiled, "Good." She looked at the wall of books before her. "But I don't think we'll have enough time."

Shrive looked at the shelves, seeing them climbing to the ceiling and all along the wall. Amanda continued to examine the room and noticed a stone pillar in the center joined at the top in an arch. "Wait, that's not part of the building, is it?" she asked, pointing to the stone archway.

Selese told her it was the portal entrance before telling her, "We need to get through the door to use it."

Shrive seemed uneasy at the two of them conspiring to break into the portal.

Then Selese said, "Let me try something." Selese spoke the spell she used to become intangible and placed her hand through some of the books. Suddenly, she felt a painful shock and pulled her hand out, rubbing it as if in pain. "Nope, she thought of that too."

When Colleen asked her to explain, Selese told her that all you need to do is move the lock. Most were not magical, since connecting it to the magic on the other side may be difficult. She turned to Amanda. "Well, that hurt. Any other ideas?"

Amanda looked at the stone arch behind the bookshelf. It seemed to extend out from the wall. Everyone watched, thinking it was humorous, as Amanda held her hands up to measure the pillar's width on the side before asking Selese to try something.

Amanda instructed Selese to try the side bookcase next to the pillar and see if she could put her hand up to the wall, and if she would try putting her hand through the stone. "Maybe only the bookcase is protected. Who's crazy enough to go through the portal support itself?" Amanda joked.

Selese cast her spell and walked into the bookcase. She was able to move toward the pillar and pushed her hand ahead. She pulled it back quickly and moved through the front of the bookcase, giving a labored exhale as she exited. "Phew, had to hold my breath. But I could feel the air on the other side."

Amanda looked up at the pillar. "I think as long as we stay inside the pillar, we'll be fine."

Her words made Colleen say, "This is not a good idea."

Shrive looked unsure. "Uh, you can go first, Amanda."

Selese chuckled and held her hands up to measure the pillar before holding them next to Shrive with a mischievous smile before saying, "Might be a tight fit."

Shrive raised her hand and extended her claws. "What?" The room chilled from the anger in her voice.

Selese laughed it off. "You're both fine. Let's go."

Selese grabbed Amanda's hand. They both held their breath as Selese guided her through the pillar wall. They felt the breeze as the cool air of the tunnel wafted over them. Selese said some words, using a spell to light the area they were in, but Amanda turned on the light on her phone first and scanned the room. Selese looked around, then to the pillar. "Do I have to get cat-girl?"

Amanda nodded. and Selese smiled before taking a breath and disappearing into the stone pillar. It was almost a minute before Selese returned with Shrive in tow. Amanda heard Shrive exhale and gasp for air before hearing, "I don't want to do that again. I hate being intangible."

Amanda responded, "It wasn't that bad. It was like walking through water."

Shrive shook her head. "No, it's not easy. I hate that darklings are the only ones who can do it."

Amanda stared at her for clarification, but Selese, suddenly angry, interrupted her. "What, you think I'd leave you in there?"

Shrive shook her head, yelling back, "I hate being intangible! I've never liked it!"

Amanda looked to Selese. "Wait, what did she mean only darklings can do it?"

Selese gritted her teeth. "Yeah, only darklings can do intangible spells. We can stay like that as long as we need to. And that goes for whatever we are holding at the time."

Amanda raised her brow. "What happens if you let go?"

Selese looked sheepishly toward the ground. "Um, they stop being intangible."

Amanda looked at Shrive before holding her hands to her face. "You let me suggest this and didn't tell me?"

Selese rubbed the back of her neck apologetically, "Well, you never asked."

Amanda leaned her head back, groaning with annoyance, before looking down the dark tunnel toward the small light at the end. "C'mon, let's go." But as she walked, she tripped on something and turned the light to see what it was before pointing it forward, telling the others to watch their step. Shrive instead told her to watch her step just as Amanda tripped on another stone.

"How are you two not tripping? I can't see a thing, even with the light!" Amanda huffed.

Shrive pointed to herself. "Cats can see in the dark."

Selese did the same. "So can darklings."

Chapter Twenty-Six
Amanda's got a Plan

The walk through the portal seemed longer this time. Amanda, Shrive, and Selese sighed with relief as overhead became the familiar vast, ornate ceiling of the Great Hall. They were greeted with a flurry of hunters surrounding them as they appeared from the darkness. They all stood ready to fight before Luke yelled, "Everyone, stop! They were invited; they're not here to attack." Luke took a breath, seeing the others confused. "At least, I hope they're not."

Luke stood before Amanda with a smile. She returned the gesture, telling him that they would have had a fight if the hunters had started one. Luke nodded then looked over his shoulder, making the others disperse.

Amanda walked beside Luke as they entered the council chamber. It wasn't long before she explained how they accessed the portal. By this time, Cayden had arrived; he had been standing guard outside Lord Cale's office while Dr. Brentwood was there. When Selese asked where Lord Cale was, she gave a concerned smile when Cayden told her, "He's with Dr Brentwood."

Amanda asked about the symbol Luke had seen. He replied, "It was a teleport symbol, I think, but it's pretty common. There's no way for us to trace it easily."

Amanda asked where it was on his arm, and Luke rolled up his sleeve, showing her. "Usually, it's by the wrist. You want it close to make sure it's easy to activate."

"But why was it back so far?" Amanda asked, and thought for a moment. "You told them you saw a reflection, right?"

Luke nodded.

Amanda asked for some paper and grabbed a pen from the table. Within seconds she started sketching something with a long, flat screen and a wristband. As she was adding details, Luke said, "That's it! Where did you see that?"

"Tyler had one. I saw it on him.," Amanda replied.

Cayden spoke up. "It couldn't have been Fenris; he's too tall. This guy was short, around five foot one."

Selese chimed in, "Then there are more of them around." She inspected Amanda's sketch. "It may not be enough for a finding spell."

"Then we'll go with our original plan. We'll find the maker of the element," Amanda said, making Selese agree.

When the council asked what they had in mind, Amanda explained, "There were three people in the museum in Ohio." She paused. "Okay, five, counting Ron and the guard."

One of the council startled her, asking how she knew others were there. She spent the next few minutes telling them about everything that happened, even confirming Shrive never saw Ron in the shadows. Her story bringing several glares of disapproval focused on Shrive before Amanda defended her. "It's not her fault; he has one of these protecting him." She pulled up the chain from around her neck, showing the wooden ring she wore. Amanda could hear in the murmur, "Oh great, another FOF."

Amanda took control of the room. "Look, I have an idea how to find the person connected to these thefts. But I need access to the scroll repository. Whoever made the symbol may have been there."

When the council asked what proof she had, she replied, "There were three people, yet the element's power injured only two. Why wasn't the third harmed?" She paused. "I believe that was the element's maker."

"The whole place is locked down. They'll never let you in the repository. At least not alone," Luke told her.

Amanda replied, "Maybe an escort, then? If there are similar elements, I can figure it out. I know exactly what the symbol looks like, I can identify it."

Selese looked around the room as Amanda tried convincing the council of her plan. Selese mentioned to Cayden that she wanted to check in on her parents. He thought it was a good idea, but when they turned to leave, several council members glared at them intently.

Selese paused, then turned toward the council. "I'm going to check on my parents."

Belerose was becoming tired of listening to Amanda and huffed at Selese's remark. "The thief is not going anywhere," and motioned for her to be detained.

That action angered Selese and she walked up to him. She stared down at Belerose and with a cold, determined voice said, "If people you cared about were in danger, do you think a few guards would stop you?"

The old council member stared back at her with a confident smile. He reeled back when Selese leaned down, placing her hands on the arms of the chair. Her actions made the once sure council member cower. Selese gave a whispered growl, "Go ahead; stop me," before standing, her eyes fixed on his. Everyone watched as he waved the hunters to stand down.

As Selese walked away, the tension was broken when another member said they should vote on Amanda's plan. Amanda rolled her eyes as they argued, but they decided, eventually, to allow her to try.

Accompanied by Luke, Amanda jumped right in and they began their search. But as they did, another person entered the room. The short man stopped at the door when he saw Luke. Jarrad remained on guard. He could see them engrossed in searching for something. The assassin didn't want to alert them to his presence. He turned to leave when he heard Amanda say, "I think I found it." She closed her eyes and focused. "I'm sure this is it. The maker was Dennon Fierst."

"Dennon Fierst? He's the best hunter there is. You looking to copy his work?" Jarrad said, startling them. Trying to appear innocent, he handed Amanda a book from the table. He moved closer and as he pulled his hand back, Luke noticed a flicker of light from his wrist.

"You're Jarrad Rousch, right?" Luke said as he walked around the table. Jarrad could feel the suspicion in Luke's eyes as Luke walked up behind Amanda. Jarrad turned to leave.

"Could you show me your left arm for a moment?" Luke asked.

Jarrad stopped and as he turned to look back, pulling two knives from his cloak. He released them with the full force of his spin as he turned. Amanda's fairy ring deflected one; the other pierced Luke's side.

Luke stumbled as the injury of the blade burned in his side. He knocked several books off the table as he tried to hold himself up.

Amanda watched as blood dripped to the floor and she yelled for help as Jarrad disappeared into the hallway.

Amanda tried to stop the bleeding, even tearing pages from one of the books. She tried using them as a bandage before again yelling for help. Down the hall Cale had sent Cayden back to the main meeting hall. He had hoped to have an update on the security sweep. He could hear Amanda yelling and the urgency in her voice was not unnoticed by Cale or Selese in the office.

"Now what's that girl gotten into?" Selese wondered.

Unfortunately, Cale knew the sound of a desperate cry for help; he had heard them too many times before and as he rushed from the room, ordered Selese to watch over her mother.

Lord Cale nearly collided with Jarrad, the assassin drawing another poison blade, which Cale skillfully evaded. The blade sticking firmly in the wall behind him. Cale watched as the man headed toward the office. He was about to pursue him when a loud yell of a very angry Selese and the sound of a body slamming against stone filled the hallway. She wrapped the assassin with the rope and cloth of a tapestry. She also continued to kick and beat him as she did. But her efforts were thwarted as he slowly drifted through the floor.

Selese clawed at the ground, trying to grab him. Cale watched as her hands turned intangible to reach for the escaping criminal. He was torn from the pride he felt hearing Amanda again cry out for help.

Back in the repository, Amanda was still trying to save Luke. She yelled at him to wake up. She knew he had a spell for healing but as she felt the blood soak through the pages, she tossed them aside. She continued to staunch his wound and never noticed the ghostly mist from the documents forming in a circle behind her. She turned, startled, hearing the apparition say, "I do not like blood offerings, young mistress; I should punish you for attempting to bind me."

Amanda yelled, "Who the hell are you?" before turning back to help Luke.

The apparition was cross, but noticed the young man bleeding on the floor and the torn pages she had used on his wound.

"Ah, I am mistaken. You did not summon me as I deduced. My apologies, mistress. What is your desire?"

Amanda turned to look at the apparition. "What? What do you mean? Can you heal him?"

The spirit laughed, "Heal? Surely you jest, mistress."

Cale stood in the doorway. "Is he all right?" It took a moment for him to notice the spirit behind Amanda.

Amanda shook her head. "No, he's bleeding badly. We have to help him!"

Cale tried to enter the room, but was stopped by a wall of magic.

"You may not enter, hunter; this is my circle and my exchange," the spirit growled.

"You have to let him help!" Amanda pleaded.

"No, mistress, I do not. I was summoned in error and may do as I choose."

Amanda again yelled, "Luke, wake up! You have to heal yourself!"

Cale could see the young man's face discolored. The senior hunter muttered, "He's out cold."

From earlier, Cale had seen what the poisoned blades had done to others, and now his student was in danger of suffering the same fate.

The spirit overheard Cale's thoughts. "Yes, he is, hunter, and the poison that runs through him will take its toll soon. Such a non-chaotic way to die." The spirit looked disappointed.

"You're a spirit of Chaos?" Cale blurted out, remembering that thoughts were as good as words for a chaos spirit.

The spirit smiled and gave a nod.

"Amanda, do not make a deal with this, thing," Cale warned.

Amanda yelled, "Then how do I get rid of her?"

The spirit became angered. "Rid of me? How dare you." She used her power, firing lightning toward Amanda, and watched as it was deflected. Amanda stood, grabbing a chair and threw it toward the spirit. The apparition merely smiled.

"Mistress, such chaos from someone so young." The spirit beamed with happiness. "I will help your"—the spirit raised her eyebrow in the form of a romantic accusation—"friend?"

"What do you want?" Amanda asked.

"No! Do not make a deal with this spirit, Amanda!" Cale again warned.

The spirit stared at Lord Cale at the edge of the circle before saying, "You have no power beyond my veil, hunter."

Amanda again asked what the spirit wanted. The chaotic spirit could see Amanda ready to fight but instead slowly moved toward her, and with a simple wave of her hand, images of Amanda's life appeared and disappeared. As they flashed and grew in number, the spirit seemed elated.

"Such glorious chaos." The spirit turned her eyes back to Amanda. "You are drawn to magic, mistress, but have none of your own. And magic, it seems, is drawn to you."

The chaotic spirit turned to Cale. "She has the stench of order and the creatures that enforce it, like you, hunter. But she also bears the sweet fragrance of the demons and chaos that she has encountered."

Amanda stood her ground as the spirit moved even closer and she heard Cale again yell, "Do not make a deal with this spirit, Amanda!"

The spirit gently touched Amanda's face. "Oh, hunter, you are of such limited imagination. This mistress has faced more chaos in a day than you have in years of service." The spirit paused, giving a rejoicing smile. "She even tried to stop me. And the look on her face as she did, oh, such strength, such muster!" The spirit placed her hands on the sides of Amanda's face. "You have had many adventures, haven't you? You have faced things that few others have seen." The glee was evident in the spirit's praise.

"That's just every day; so what?" Amanda responded.

"Ha, ha, ha-ha!" the spirit laughed. "Such embracing of chaos, such strength! Oh, mistress, I see so much adventure still to come for you." The spirit moved Amanda aside and used her powers to lift Luke from the floor.

"What are you doing?" Amanda tried to stop her, her efforts only making the spirit laugh.

The spirit continued her work. "I am doing as you asked; I am healing your friend."

Both Amanda and Cale watched as Luke's body faded and solidified, as if time were running in reverse, each image overlaid on his body as the spirit healed him. Luke opened his eyes and started fighting to get free, but the spirit did not release him right away.

"I didn't make a deal with you. None of us did," Amanda said.

The spirit moved away from Luke and pushed Amanda toward him. "No one has made a bargain. But you have yet to understand why I have acted as such."

Cale blurted out, "You've just made a spirit of chaos heal someone. How?"

Amanda looked puzzled toward Cale as Luke stood to defend her against the apparition. When Amanda asked why the spirit healed Luke, the spirit smiled at her tenacity. The chaotic entity waved her hand before Amanda, and again pictures of her life showed before her.

"You surround yourself with chaos, mistress. I cannot take from someone who willingly allows chaos to fall wherever they step. It would be an injustice to my powers," the spirit said as she stepped back, crossing the circle where she was born. Her corporeal form began to fade, as did her magic wall, allowing Cale to reach the two. Before the spirit faded entirely, they all heard, "Do not trust those who are of the Circle, but trust the Circle itself, mistress."

There is no better thief than me. And, if there were, well, that is the reason I became an assassin.

- Jarrad Rousch

Chapter Twenty-Seven
Raven Hunters Regret

Luke was sitting in bed in the infirmary. Alicee used her magic one last time to make sure there was no trace of the poison left from the blade. Luke told her he felt fine. The others attributed his quick recovery to what the chaotic spirit had done to heal him.

Amanda waited nearby as Alicee used her magic to put Luke back on the bed as he tried to leave. He looked over to Amanda, saying, "A little help here."

Amanda said, "Nope, you're on your own. Even I know better than to go against a fairy when she is trying to heal you."

Cale arrived and heard Amanda chide the young hunter. Amanda glanced over to see him with Belerose in tow. As Cale approached, he was met with a very cross fairy blocking his way. She overheard Cale tell her that it was necessary. Alicee cautiously allowed the senior hunter to approach her patient.

"Are you two sure it was Dennon Fierst who made that element?" Belerose asked. Cale did not look happy as he confirmed their findings. Dennon was the same level as himself, and along with Belerose, all were masters, and all knew more than most about the icons.

"It's difficult to believe Dennon is part of the Broken Feather," Cale muttered.

His statement brought Belerose to say, "You were rumored to be part of them as well, Lord Cale."

Cale nodded; he had heard those rumors and stopped denying them. That rumor came from a choice he made. While still in training, he allowed another hunter belonging to the Feather to escape. Alex Foster had been a hunter for two months; Cale had trained with him before he met Claire. His allowing of a member of the Feather to escape earned him no favor with the Circle. It was a mistake that had provided its own ending when they found Foster petrified just outside campus. The disgraced hunter plotted revenge on the Circle, and he had been collecting Medusa flies. That night, there had been a storm, and Foster dropped the container, breaking the glass. To evade the rain, the flies attacked the nearest living being. Once they started to burrow into his flesh, they quickly turned him to stone.

Some time went by, and the floating fairy healer freed Luke. Cale had left with Belerose to continue to secure the Forge. Cale knew Jarrad had escaped, and since Dennon was involved, they had to act fast. He thanked Amanda, reminding them that they had to secure the walls of the portal they used to get in.

Amanda stayed with Luke before they headed back to Brentwood's office. Luke seemed despondent that someone he had trusted and learned from betrayed them all. Luke looked at his arm. The tattoos seemed to be of a simple design. But as he passed his hand over them, the symbols beneath revealed what they indeed were: elements.

"I thought those were tattoos," Amanda noted.

Luke smiled, "Yeah, they're not real. Having tattoos sort of messes up being able to use elements." He stopped walking as he looked at a particular one. The elements had been given to him by his mentor, Dennon, and Luke started to wish that he had never accepted them.

* * *

When they arrived at Brentwood's office, Selese faced them with an angry, determined look. Amanda put her hands up. "We surrender. Take us to your leader."

It took a moment before Selese started laughing. She looked at Luke. "Feeling better?"

Dr. Claire came from behind her desk and hugged the young man before turning to Amanda. She sighed before shaking her head. "Cale told us what happened. You really are full of surprises, Amanda."

Amanda wasn't sure what she was going on about, but finally understood as Dr. Claire continued. "You have a gift, young lady. You seem to be able to befriend even the most chaotic of beings." Dr. Brentwood shook her head and again. Selese felt a bit out of place, seeing this side of her mother.

Dr. Claire returned behind her desk; she seemed to be thinking about something, "Cale told us that the spirit said that magic is drawn to you and you to it." She looked to Amanda, who confirmed the statement.

Amanda watched as the doctor briefly looked at the palm of her hand, then shook her head as if answering a question in her mind before she sat. Amanda was about to ask What she was seeing when she noticed Luke staring at the symbols on his arm. She became concerned and turned to ask him if he was all right. Her momentary distraction causing her to not see the glowing ring that appeared on the doctor's palm.

Luke shook his head, muttering, "Can't trust anything he taught me." When Amanda asked who, Luke responded, "Fierst." She watched as Luke placed his hand on his arm, covering one of the symbols and speaking a few magic words, and the mark was gone. He continued to do the same to the other elements.

"What're you doing?" Amanda asked.

Luke stopped. "I'm removing them. I received these from Dennon for my accomplishments. I started my training with him before Lord Cale took over."

"Why? They could be useful," Amanda protested.

Luke looked at her. "Even if they are, I couldn't use them against him, remember?"

Amanda was confused by what she was hearing, but Selese understood and said, "I get it."

Selese looked withdrawn as she stared back at Luke. "He's removing something he received from someone he trusted. I get it."

When Amanda asked, Selese only replied, "I trusted someone who promised to keep me safe." Amanda could see the memory of old pain she felt as Selese looked to the ground. Amanda put her arm over her friend and waved Luke over, and she hugged them both. Dr. Claire smiled, seeing her hanging onto the two of them and a tear filled her eye. Amanda spied Claire smiling at them and asked why she was smiling.

Dr. Brentwood told her, "That chaotic spirit was right. But magic isn't drawn to you. Everyone, including myself, takes a liking to you. Even I trust you."

The doctor looked at her palm briefly and again shook her head. She looked back up at Amanda. "The magic isn't drawn to you, Amanda; like them, it trusts you."

Amanda asked what she meant. Dr. Claire's reply was, "You may not have magic, but you certainly have spirit. That's why it's drawn to you."

* * *

Cale and the other hunters worked to fortify the Forge. They used additional elements and set traps and alarms. Cale was busy moving rocks to close off the connecting hallways, making them loop back so people weren't trapped. In his mind, he was running back all the times Dennon had told him that he had found nothing. But in reality, he was hiding the simple fact that he was working as part of the Broken Feather.

Cayden was working with the other hunters as they fortified the remaining hallway.

While the other hunters continued to add spells and elements to the walls and floor, Cale ordered some to start patrolling the Sanctuary and Great Hall. He told Cayden to inform the Circle that things were on schedule and that they may need additional support to protect the remaining icon.

Cayden stopped by to update Dr. Brentwood before returning to speaking with the others. All agreed that additional security was needed until Dennon was found. The hunters were running short on people, so other creatures stepped in, including several fairies.

Cayden assigned additional help as best as he could. Lord Cale was counting on them, but Cayden was starting to second-guess himself. Since he and Luke were the only hunters close to apprehending those who tried to break into the Forge, his indecisiveness didn't go unnoticed.

"Dr. Brentwood, may I have a word?" Belerose asked.

Claire turned her head, nodding as she continued to focus on the arguing of the others regarding the problem of not being able to shadow-walk.

"Dr. Brentwood, you should be in the safety of your office. Who knows who else is working with Dennon?" Belerose said.

Dr. Brentwood took a calming breath. "I am aware of that, but I am needed here." She turned to him, "The Forge isn't our only problem at the moment."

The old warrior nodded. He understood that things were dire. He mentioned the difficulty that Cayden was having in assigning the new security and offered his services, telling her that he would have to forgo the meeting because as she had put it, "The Forge isn't the only problem."

A simple smile of relief graced her face as she said, "Thank you."

She looked him in the eyes. "Most of them are too young to have this responsibility. Not to mention that we have never faced such a task before, that I'm aware of."

Belerose nodded. "I have served fifty years as a hunter. I have never seen anything so formidable." He sat straight and took a breath. "I will help Cayden. Forgive me, but I cannot leave you with these politicians."

Dr. Brentwood smiled, "You're right, Belerose. Perhaps it would be better if I were to go someplace more secure."

* * *

Jarrad panted, stumbling as he entered Vikander's lab. He had shadow-walked several times after leaving the Sanctuary. Neglecting to tell them both about his encounter at the Amanda's apartment. He informed his master as Dennon stood nearby. Vikander became furious, and ordered the three of them to head to the Forge and retrieve the icon before it was too secure for them to try. Dennon pulled the hood of his cloak up and looked sternly toward Tyler. "No screw-ups. If we come back without the icon, I know of two more subjects that could be used for experiments."

Jarrad threw his shoulders back. "We won't fail this time." Tyler, however, remained silent.

Dennon grabbed Tyler, lifting him off the floor. "Do you understand?"

Tyler nodded nervously as Dennon dropped him. They all tapped the scroll watches they wore and headed to the museum.

They appeared in the basement, the same place Selese had taken Amanda. Dennon held his hand to the wall and they all watched it shimmer. The senior hunter motioned for the other two to head in, and he quickly followed behind. They arrived just outside the Forge and weren't seen by anyone. Dennon was charged to secure the ventilation shaft, and he had done just that but allowed himself a key in case they needed to use it later.

"The Broken Feather has been pushed to the darkness for far too long, my young allies. Today we will take a step further to securing our place as leaders of this world."

Wind is wind, the air and breeze, and all abound. Sylph and kin, move the leaves, when no one's around.

- Bresica of the Sylphs

Chapter Twenty-Eight
The Forge

Dr. Claire returned to her office just as Selese said, "We should go help secure the Forge." The doctor immediately told them that they would probably be in the way. Selese didn't think her father had any issues with securing the area. Dr. Claire knew Selese was feeling left out from the fun of having to think like a thief. Luke and Amanda agreed that maybe they could help, but Belerose scoffed at them.

"This office is one of the safest places right now, and I need a minimum of two hunters on guard here. We cannot spare more than we have," Belerose said before looking at Selese. "However, she may have a point."

The old warrior now stood, confronting Selese. He stood almost seven feet tall. She had to look up to look him in the eyes. "Perhaps they could go, Luke can remain, and when I have another to take his place, I'll send him down as well."

The young hunter looked concerned as Amanda and Selese agreed. Selese headed out, followed by Amanda, who stopped as she was passing Luke. She tapped his nose gently with her finger. "Don't be late. Don't want you getting there and taking credit after we did all the work," Amanda said as she gently kissed him and followed after Selese.

Luke turned to see Belerose with his brow furrowed before the old warrior looked toward Dr. Brentwood. The warrior then filled the room with a bellowing laugh as he slapped his hand down one the young hunter's shoulder with enough force to almost collapse him to the ground.

"You have a handful there, my young friend. I wish you luck."

* * *

Dennon and the other two stood facing a full squad of hunters outside the Forge. Instead of attacking, Dennon, being a seasoned hunter, ordered them to wait. He listened to the orders Cale gave and held back until the last moment to strike. When he saw his chance, all three walked from the shadows.

Although the hunters were still in the process of casting spells to fortify the Forge, they quickly stood ready. As he heard Lord Cale order him to surrender, Dennon smiled, "I no longer serve the Circle. You will give way to the Broken Feather."

Lord Cale ordered the hunters to attack. As they rushed forward, Dennon motioned for his acolytes to stay where they were. Dennon held up his open hand and grabbed his wrist, covering the locator element as he spoke a few words. Most of the hunters before them disappeared. Dennon looked at those remaining with a smile. "Jarrad, you know what to do."

The short man grinned as he launched several blades toward the remaining hunters. Dennon turned to Tyler. "Use that box of yours to get the cursed door open."

Back in the repository, Lord Cale and several dozen hunters appeared. Confused, they looked around to see if this was an illusion. They quickly discovered most hunters, including those on patrol, were now standing in or just outside the repository.

"He teleported us?" Cale deduced.

Cale fought his way out of the room and headed toward Dr. Claire's office. He saw Belerose standing watch as dozens of hunters now headed back toward the Forge. He informed his wife and Belerose what had happened before asking where Selese was. His heart sank when Claire said, "She's headed to the Forge to meet you."

Withing seconds, Luke was out the door as Cale followed. When they came to a group of hunters standing in the hall, Cale knew something was wrong. Ordering the others to move aside so he could inspect the issue, he saw a hunter pounding and using elements against a veil wall.

"He put up a veil; we can't get through," one of the hunters told him. Luke remained stuck behind the group as they worked to remove the obstacle. He made his way forward, and as he put his hand on the veil, it passed through. In a rush, Luke pushed his way past the other hunters. He turned to see them staring in astonishment from the other side of the veil.

Cale spoke, "We'll find a way in. Go. Stop them if you can."

Luke nodded and ran toward the Forge.

* * *

Selese hurried along the wall and was smiling as she turned the corner. She suddenly stopped, quickly backing up to hide behind the corner. When Amanda arrived, Selese motioned for her to be quiet, whispering, "No one's here."

When Amanda asked if she was sure, Selese carefully looked around the corner. She took a breath. "Looks like four hunters on the ground; I think they may be . . . dead." She paused. "And the Forge door is open."

They both looked down the hall but heard no one coming. "Something must have happened. Maybe we could try and stop them?" They both agreed that if things were dire, they would head back to try and get the others. The carefully walked toward the open door and looked inside. Amanda was in awe as the small room revealed a vast space inside. She could see the forges glowing a warm orange and the heat pipes that ran all throughout campus. They didn't see anyone right away and decided to see if maybe they were too late.

They entered the room silently but kept to the forge's outercourse, hiding along the tall arches that held the stone above at bay. Amanda felt her foot hit something. She looked down, whispering, "Golf clubs?"

Selese joked, "Maybe they're cursed."

Amanda tried not to laugh as she replied, "The way my father complains about them, I think all golf clubs are cursed." Selese covered her mouth, trying not to laugh out loud.

Amanda grabbed one of the clubs and held it, ready to strike. They could hear Dennon yelling for Tyler to hurry up. Selese nodded, and both went to take a closer look. As they moved through the causeway, they came across Tyler and Dennon working on the secured icon. Amanda swiveled her head. "Remember. There were three last time."

The two made their way closer, and Selese could see the man she had stopped earlier leaning against one of the arches while Tyler worked to open the case. Selese leaned over to Amanda and whispered, "I'll take the one with the knives. You get those two."

Amanda was upset. "Why do I get two?"

Selese huffed, "I don't think Tyler can fight, so technically, you have one."

Amanda sneered, "This is not a good plan."

Selese winked. "I know." Then both set their sights on their targets.

Selese moved behind Jarrad and reached around the arch. She pulled him back, slamming his head against the stone. The assassin fell to the ground, unconscious.

Hearing the man fall, Dennon looked toward where Jarrad had been standing. Before he could do anything, the hunter felt the sharp pain of a golf club fracture his shoulder as it hit.

Tyler had just opened the case and turned to see Fierst fall to the ground and Amanda standing behind him. In a panic, Tyler slammed his hand onto his scroll watch and fired lightning toward her. Amanda's fairy ring immediately dealt with the attack and she rushed him, taking a swing at him with the club. She missed as she felt her foot snagged. She was stunned for a moment before she looked back to see Dennon holding her ankle. He growled in pain before casting a spell. Amanda felt herself lift from the floor and the wind rushing past as she headed for the wall. Bracing for the impact she rolled into a ball, protecting her head and neck. When she felt the stone against her side, the wind was knocked out of her. Amazingly, she still held onto the golf club.

Selese rushed to help Amanda just as Jarrad was recovering and she heard Dennon growl, "Kill them both."

Jarrad pulled a blade from his holder but fell as several blows landed on him from behind. The assassin felt the world turn gray as he again fell to the ground. Luke finished with Jarrad and rushed Fierst, who was stunned by the anger of the young man's attack.

Tyler watched as Fierst looked at his scroll watch and tapped it. The room filled with a bright flash and Dennon jumped to his feet, ordering Tyler to follow. The flash blinded everyone but Selese recovered to see the two rushing toward the door, their prize in hand. She started to run and watched as Tyler began to pull the door closed.

"We'll be stuck in here if that closes!" Luke yelled.

Amanda threw the golf club and it landed just at the door. Selese ran as fast as she could but had an idea. She instead headed for the shadows and ported herself outside. Selese appeared in the darkness near the door and watched as Dennon and Tyler fought to close it, the club Amanda had thrown jamming it open. Dennon took that as a sign to leave. He was surprised to again feel pain in his shoulder as Selese used both hands to pound down on it. The old hunter kept his wits about him and produced a small box, throwing it at her.

The box hit Selese with enough force to send her backward and as she hit the wall, roots and branches grew from the box. Selese tried becoming intangible but was unable to escape.

Seeing her confusion, Dennon boasted, "That's ironwood, girl; you can't phase through it." He approached, but kept his distance. "You have turned on me for the last time, thief." He then produced another small box and opened it. "A gift from our mutual friend."

Selese's heart skipped, seeing the pyramite staring at her. Dennon gave it a straightforward command. "Bring me all the gold."

Selese screamed loud enough to vibrate the Forge door as Amanda and Luke tried to open it. Selese's eyes pierced the darkness as the small creature dug away at the ironwood covering her chest; when she felt the impacts of its claws against the metal chest plate, she again screamed for someone to help.

Amanda and Luke finally moved the door open and she grabbed the bent golf club from the floor. Luke and she could see Tyler and Dennon rushing down the hallway. They heard Selese scream again and Amanda headed to help her. Luke was going to chase after them but heard Amanda say, "It's going to kill her!" He chose to help Selese, allowing Dennon and Tyler to escape.

Amanda could see the small creature tearing at Selese's armor and she pulled back the club. The little creature, sensing danger, turned to look, only to have its face crushed by the blow of the club. The creature's blood splattered the wood covering Selese, who was still struggling to escape.

"Get me out of this!" Selese demanded.

Amanda tore at the bark while Luke chipped at it using the knife he took from Jarrad. When Amanda asked why she couldn't just become intangible, she heard Luke say, "It's ironwood, she can't."

Amanda freed one of Selese's arm and she pushed them both away. She placed her hand over her heart and felt the chest plate still intact, but scratched. Tears of joy started to flow from her eyes.

They all looked up as a sound of thunderous footsteps rose behind them and they could see a rush of hunters appear from the darkness. Luke yelled to them, pointing toward the hallway. "They went down there!"

Lord Cale could see Selese pressed against the wall and the glimmer of the golden chest plate he had made for her. "Selese?"

Selese started to cry, not in fear but anger as Cale asked if she was all right, making her growl back, "No, I'm not all right. They got away."

Cale touched her face caringly, causing her scowl of anger to become a subdued smile. "The armor worked." She laughed nervously as she fought back tears. "But I think it needs some repair."

Cale pulled at the ironwood holding her and ordered the remaining hunters to help get her free. Amanda stepped back as she and Luke watched them work to release their friend. They both turned to stare down the darkened hall the Broken Feather had left through.

* * *

Tyler stumbled as his feet touched the stone floor of the Shadowed Hall in Vikander's lab. Dennon followed behind, falling only to roll onto his injured shoulder. His groan of pain alerted Vikander to their return.

The old man hurried toward them. When he reached Dennon, he turned him on his back. However, it was not to view his injuries. Vikander threw his hands up with a declaration of, "You don't have it. Useless!" He turned to see Tyler standing, the young man's eyes staring, processing what he had just witnessed. The old mage knew the look of disgust and shame from many he had faced. He rushed over, grabbing Tyler's arm.

"Where is it?" Tyler remained staring into nothingness as the old man shook him.

Vikander could see the boy's eyes searching for redemption. The old mage's heart warmed by the torment the boy was now facing. He was about to put Tyler out of his misery when the recruit held up the *Effigy of Tarnus*.

The old man reached for the icon, and just as his hands were about to encompass the item he had sought for so many years, Tyler released his grip. Vikander scrambled to catch it but was not able to grasp the statue before it impacted with the floor. There was an echoing of shattered stone, like pottery falling from a window.

Within seconds, the Shadowed Hall filled with a bluster of energies. Wind swirled and buffeted all around them, its fierceness etching the very stone pillars that held the shadows they traveled in. Just as soon as it came, the air was again still.

Vikander watched the essence of the icon retreat to within the very hall he had built. His heart turned hard as he used his powers to encase Tyler in stone and dirt.

The anger of the old mage was evident as he held Tyler above the floor. The young man screamed as the stone started to crush him. His cries were muffled in the echoes as Vikander looked on. The wraith mage knew of many ways to kill or enslave a man.

"I have been working toward this for twenty years. And you have destroyed it in less than the time it takes to take a breath!"

The wraith mage constricted the stone and dirt tighter. Vikander noticed a glint from the scroll watch on Tyler's wrist and the anger on his face changed to a sinister smile.

"No, I won't kill you. You have proven clever, and that is useful to me. I may need that to retrieve the essence." Vikander lowered Tyler to the floor. As the stone fell away, Tyler gasped for breath. Vikander grabbed onto the young man's arm and tapped the watch he wore.

Tyler regained himself, and his eyes again searched for an understanding of what he had just experienced. Vikander grabbed Tyler's face, turning it to look directly into his eyes. The wraith mage's face became as still and unmoving as the stone that all geomages use. As the old man held up the watch Tyler so coveted, he scrolled through the symbols.

"You had shown promise, my boy, but failed me. However, I still need your talents." Vikander tapped a symbol as it displayed on the screen. "I just don't need the rest of you."

Dennon's vision cleared as he sat up. The old hunter's eyes witnessed as the mage pulled at Tyler's hand. He could see the image of shifting dark energy and flesh pulled from the young man's arm. Dennon watched the phenomenon cascade up Tyler's body, the sound of his screams making the old hunter close his eyes in commiseration.

Magic and life are intertwined, we strive to serve both.

- Raven Hunter's creed.

Chapter Twenty-Nine
Decisions to Make

Three days had passed, and the Great Hall was still a flurry of activity. The Raven Hunters were sent to search for Tyler. The young man was nowhere to be found until he walked into his apartment, seeming no worse for wear. He was terrified when the hunters stood in his doorway and restrained him.

Selese searched for the element preventing the Shadowed Hall's use and had watched as they brought Tyler in through the Great Hall. She could see the fear in his every movement and listened to his continuous pleading and denial of the situation. She swore she even heard him repeating, "This is a dream, just a bad dream," over and over. But as she looked at him, she sensed an emptiness. To her, it was something odd, like something familiar was missing.

Lord Cale and Dr. Brentwood continued to interview Tyler. Both felt sorry for his reaction to all the magical beings he had just encountered. They were both familiar with the effects of memory altering, but their experience with Tyler and his reactions was something they hadn't encountered. Dr. Brentwood looked to her husband, saying, "Even the others can't read his thoughts. It's like they no longer exist." Cale agreed, then had to decide what to do with the young man.

Tyler turned to see a fairy flying around him. He flinched as if the tiny magic being was going to cause harm. The fairy floated before the boy and smiled. She looked into his eyes. Cale could see the confusion Alicee showed and asked what she saw.

"Like melted snow, and dust that's gone. He does not know, surely something's wrong," Alicee rhymed.

"Physically, the boy seems fine," Dr. Claire said. They had all made sure of that, even healing his wounds from being apprehended.

Shrive stayed in the shadows. She felt sorry seeing Tyler sitting restrained in the chair. She had promised to claw the glasses from his face when she met him again, but seeing him like this, Shrive could only feel pity for him. As she approached, the light illuminated her face. Tyler looked over to see her and a simple, relieved smile appeared before turning to one of fear.

"Are you with them?" Tyler meekly asked, terrified.

Shrive felt her chest tighten as she slowly nodded her head. Looking to comfort him as Tyler tried to release himself to escape, Shrive placed her hand down on the table. She looked at the crystals they used to evaluate him and noticed something. When she touched the detector, it didn't glow. *What happened to him? Why can't they read his memory or the energy inside him? she thought.* She had known before from Amanda that Tyler was part darkling from the glasses. But now when she touched the detector crystal it showed no reaction. She hurriedly informed Lord Cale, and within minutes, they had brought Tyler down to the large detector. As they forced his hand onto the plate, they started the machine. Dr. Brentwood seemed to be searching for a response.

"Please show something, anything," Shrive heard the doctor pleading in a whisper.

Cale watched her reaction with concern. He could see the tears forming in her eyes when the machine showed nothing. He watched as his wife's eyes closed as she leaned her head back. Her words, whispered with sadness.

"He's human."

Cale could see her fighting to control her emotions as he asked, "And, what else?"

Dr. Brentwood turned to fully reveal the tears now falling down her face.

"Just human. Whoever did this, tore the boy apart."

Cale comforted Claire after their discovery that Tyler was now split. His human part was back on campus, but the other, the one that contained magic, was someplace else. He knew it was probably enslaved by whoever did this to him. However, Tyler wasn't their only concern.

As Cale went to the Great Hall looking for an update on the progress of the repairs, he hoped to hear better news.

Several hours passed before Selese found the small stone, a pebble that contained the element preventing anyone from shadow-walking. When she discovered it, her eyes fixed on the symbol. Her heart started to flood with anger, as she sensed something familiar in the magic it held. Selese showed the stone to Cale, who inspected it.

"We should put it on file take it to the repository," Cale said as he handed it back to her.

Selese was about to hand the stone to one of the numerous scroll witches around them when she began to feel a rage growing in her chest. As Selese stared at the rock, it's familiar energy shimmering all around it, her actions making Cale take notice of her attention and he was about to ask her what she could see. He stopped when he noticed a small tear falling from her enraged stare. Her father placed his hand on her shoulder.

Selese continued to examine the stone, her voice cracking as she said, "He made this."

When Cale asked her who she was talking about, Selese's eyes turned vacantly toward her father. *Why is this so familiar. I've felt this energy before.* Her head started to sway as she searched her memories, within moments her breathing hastened, *No, he's dead. Aiden killed him. No! he can't be alive.* Suddenly her eyes reflected the memory of the pain she hid behind them. Cale reached out to her but was pushed back as Selese's eyes now seethed with rage. Her father could only watch as her hand holding the stone shook angrily. Within moments the stone glowed, becoming molten in her palm. Cale quickly shielded the scroll witch beside her as the stone exploded to nothing but vapor, its explosive demise echoing through the Great Hall. Selese growled with an unmoving certainty, saying, "Jeffrey Britlan is still alive."

* * *

The next morning, Selese arrived at Amanda's apartment to find her just coming back from a morning run. She smiled, seeing Gabriella had decided to join her. She was surprised to hear that Gabriella had told Amanda; Linda was the one who had asked for the illustrations. She listened to Amanda gripe, "they sold out on me." But Amanda wasn't angry. She understood that her friends needed work done as well. And she could think of no one else better to fill in than her best friend, Gabs.

After the events of yesterday, Selese was happy to be able to shadow-walk from the Sanctuary. She needed to be among her friends. Selese told them both that Tyler had been found and that he didn't consciously remember a thing about the last few months, with the exception of classes.

"That's great, is he okay?" Gabriella asked.

Selese told her he seemed to be, but she mentioned that something was missing. When Amanda said that maybe Dennon had erased his memory, Selese shook her head. She disagreed, telling her it was much more than that.

"He remembers school and that he had made some money, but doesn't remember where he worked or who was paying him. And all records for any financial information have gone missing," Selese told them.

"But nothing else?" Amanda asked.

Selese shook her head. She seemed to be holding back a concern. Amanda asked what she was thinking about, and her friend's response was something she hadn't expected.

"I think they removed his magic," Selese replied.

Gabriella was gulping down a glass of water and started to choke before saying, "What?"

Amanda nodded, and her face showed a pensive stare. She then tilted her head toward Gabriella. Selese noticed, and asked Amanda if had seen this before.

Amanda nodded, responding, "Unfortunately."

There was silence before Gabriella said, "We should go see him. Make sure he's okay."

Amanda agreed. It was also a chance for her to see for herself what Tyler was like since he returned.

* * *

It was a few days before Amanda and Selese caught up with Tyler. Like her, Tyler still had classes. And Amanda was thankful that it was only a few more weeks. She had been working on her schoolwork since the rush for the end of the semester had started. Her other assignments, mostly the paid ones, had to be put on hold.

They found Tyler in the museum, finishing up on his semester project. Amanda was sketching him when Selese walked up.

"Thought you were done the projects for class?" Selese asked.

Amanda nodded, "Just drawing him." She held the picture up to show Selese. "I wanted to compare it to the previous one I did.

Selese laughed, "You could just take a picture. It'd be easier."

Amanda put her pencil down. "It looks like him. I mean, it's him, but not him." She paused. "Does that make any sense?"

Selese nodded. "Yeah, it doesn't seem like he's all there. That's what I get."

Amanda tapped Selese's arm as she stood and they walked over to speak with Tyler. They found him somewhat happy. He was working on his sketches for the computer project, but even Amanda could see something was lacking in the drawings.

When they spoke with him, he seemed normal, nothing out of the ordinary. Amanda noticed he kept looking toward Selese and his eyes seemed to be looking to remember something. When Selese asked if he was all right, Tyler hesitated before responding.

"It's weird. I look at her"—he pointed to Amanda—"and I know she's my friend." Tyler tilted his head. "But when I look at you, I feel like I've lost something."

Selese felt panic grow in her chest before Tyler chuckled, "That's really weird, isn't it? I mean, you seem nice."

Selese did her best to smile and they said their goodbyes. As Amanda and she were walking out of the building, Selese sighed. Amanda asked if she was all right. Selese's response was not one she was prepared for. "He seems to be doing good, for someone who has had something ripped out of them."

* * *

Dr. Claire returned to her office in the administration building. She needed to get out of the Great Hall. The ending of the semester was just around the corner, and she had a ton of paperwork to finish. Colleen had brought coffee to her and stood watching her take a sip. Dr. Brentwood took notice and said, "You can go home. I'll be fine."

Colleen shook her head. "Lord Cale told me to stay nearby."

Claire smiled, "I'll deal with Lord Cale. Besides, there hasn't been any attack or theft since we almost stopped them from stealing the icon."

Colleen again disagreed and told Dr. Brentwood that she was staying as long as she was there. The doctor begrudgingly allowed her to stay while she finished the pile of papers on her desk.

* * *

It was late when Claire returned home; she found her husband fast asleep. She looked at the clock and chortled, "I didn't realize it was that much paperwork."

She undressed and slid under the covers. Her eyes grew heavy, and she quickly fell into a deep sleep.

Dr. Brentwood found herself in a room. As she moved, the world seemed to slow; she felt no air across her skin. She'd had experiences like this before. This was a vision from the Circle itself. She turned to see Tyler standing in his room, facing his window, his arm extended as if desperately reaching for something. She rushed over to look and could see the vacant stare in his wide eyes. His mouth moving without words. She did her best to try and understand.

He was repeating, "Darkness lost, upon the scroll, harken cost, make me whole."

"Oh my, he can sense the darkling side he lost." The doctor felt for him. She had only seen this twice before during her tenure, and had hoped to never again. She turned to look out the window to see the earth itself, moving like waves. She had been inside visions before—the Key of the Spirit provided intense insight—and she knew how to work within them. Claire walked effortlessly through the wall and floated toward the ground. Her feet made a shuff-shuff sound as she landed. She scanned the landscape to see the buildings gone and nothing but an empty horizon surrounding her.

Claire's senses were startled as a tempest engulfed the world around; the air clouded and it became difficult to see. She held her hands to her forehead and concentrated—something she sometimes had to do to decipher what the Circle was trying to communicate. As the world started to clear, she could make out five figures surrounding her. Three were cold and lifeless, bound in chains, the other two she fought to recognize. When she approached, she saw a figure, a woman with long hair blown by the wind. When she grew nearer, she recognized the reflection of herself within the ringed mirror.

"Spirit," she whispered.

She approached the other and could make out the outline through the howling torrent surrounding it. It was the battle between a man and snake made of stone and mud.

"Earth." Claire suddenly felt the wind and earth again tear at her and she covered her eyes to protect herself.

"Claire, wake up!" Cale yelled as his wife buffeted the bed from her movements. She seemed to be fighting back some terrible attack. He put his arms around her and held her still. Within moments, Claire opened her eyes, yelling for him to let her go.

"I'm all right. I'm all right," she repeated.

Claire turned to see Cale looking worried and grabbed hold of him, her heart still racing from the vision. Cale held her till she calmed. When he asked what she had seen, all she said was, "It was a vision from the Circle."

Cale sighed in relief. "What did it show you?"

As Claire sat on the edge of the bed, she took a moment before telling him about Tyler searching for the darkness he lost. She hesitantly said to him that it showed her the pillars and suspected that this wasn't over. She then turned toward him, and Cale noticed the smile she gave. When he asked why she was smiling, she told him, "This may not be over, but I believe we have time to stop them."

When Cale asked why, Claire responded, "Tarnus was released. Those who were looking for the power, don't have it."

* * *

The next day Dr. Brentwood returned to her office. The end of the semester had finally arrived. She watched the video screens on her desk, and she felt a bit of loss as she watched students leaving for the summer. She knew that many would return, but still, a slight sadness filled her heart as she typed on her keyboard to finish updating the files she now had on Tyler. The Circle had much more information, but she needed to make sure he would be able to return to school after what he had been through.

She glanced over to the window, and could see Amanda outside the apartments, Clair watched as Selese and Shrive helped her pack her car. Since things had calmed down after the loss of the *Effigy of Tarnus*, neither Amanda nor Gabriella decided to stay for the summer. The doctor already knew that they would be returning in the Fall.

The doctor looked at her palm as she had done so many times before. But as the glowing ring appeared, she shook her head.

"No, she is too young. We will find another." The doctor muttered. "

"Dr. Brentwood, are you all tight?"

The doctor snapped her eyes in the direction of her assistant now standing before her desk. Dr. Brentwood nodded, "Yes, my dear. I was just thinking out loud."

Colleen smiled, handing her a small drive, "I have the files you requested. Although Lord Cale asked why you needed them."

The doctor responded in a playful tone, "I will deal with Lord Cale, later."

Colleen smiled as she left to return to her duties.

The doctor held the drive tightly in her hand as she stared out the window. She could see Amanda hug Selese and Shrive before she stepped into her car. Although, the icon was lost. Amanda, and Selese, had been of great help with the thefts; they both risked their lives to save everyone. That was something the doctor could not take lightly.

Dr. Brentwood sat and plugged the drive into her computer. She opened her email and started typing.

The letter was very formal, and she included a copy of the files. But, something in her knew she had to make this more personal. She again looked at her hand, and a glowing ring appeared on her palm. Whatever it told her; the doctor nodded in agreement.

She looked at the screen before typing Ron's email and addressed the email to both him and Linda. "Please review the files I am sending. I await your decision at your earliest opportunity."

The doctor turned to look out the window to see Amanda driving away. As Clair pressed her hand against the glass, she felt her palm warm and again turned it over to look at it. She could see the ring that appeared glowing brightly. The doctor smiled as she muttered, "Amanda, my dear, it seems the decision to join us has been made for you."

Other Books in This Series

What happens when an out of work ghost hunter saves a young girl injured in the forest? Something magical, what else? Enjoy the adventures that brought Amanda, Ron and Linda together in the original story.

A
Fairy's
Light

What is a good deed worth? Well, maybe you should ask a fairy, what could go wrong?

ABOUT THE AUTHOR

Stephen has experience in technology, engineering, and sales spanning over 30 years. He has been writing science fiction and fantasy for far longer—his work primarily for role-playing and short stories personally, using his knowledge and imagination within his life. He is always known to have a story to tell and usually sprinkled with a hint of adventure. Stephen decided to present his stories for all to see. And through his character's eyes, you find that life can be an adventure and it's always better with a bit of magic.